BLOOD ATONEMENT

MICHAEL WOJCIECHOWSKI

Black Rose Writing | Texas

ISBN: 978-1-68513-020-6
PUBLISHED BY BLACK ROSE WRITING
www.blackrosewriting.com

Printed in the United States of America
Suggested Retail Price (SRP) $20.95

Blood Atonement is printed in Book Antiqua

*As a planet-friendly publisher, Black Rose Writing does its best to eliminate unnecessary waste to reduce paper usage and energy costs, while never compromising the reading experience. As a result, the final word count vs. page count may not meet common expectations.

BLOOD ATONEMENT

PART I

CHAPTER 1

He appears on the horizon like a ghost. His gait is steady, determined, but he has no destination. No purpose. Just an idea and general location. Each new step takes him farther from a life he must escape. Each new step brings him closer to a life he does not care to live nor to exit. Now that he has fled, he only feels indifference. He will die when he is meant to, and until then he will live because there is nothing else to do. His name is Porter.

He brandishes a dusty hat. It sits low, shielding the world from him and him from the world. He wears dungarees faded from dirt and use and a green buttoned shirt bleached by the sun. The shirt he took off a man who had taken a wound and died soon after. Porter watched him die, heard his death rattle. He could not decide if he pitied or envied the dead man. Porter's boots are more worn than his clothes. The leather soft and cracking. These too he stole from a dead man. His knapsack hangs over his shoulder. One of the few things he did not take from the dead. His mom made it for him when he was a child. It pains him to imagine when he dies, someone like him will take his knapsack and claim it as his own. Such is the way of the world. Ownership does not exist for the dead. Inside the sack are books, some dried food, and bullets. His gun is tucked inside the front of his pants.

Quinn stands on her porch and spots Porter half a mile up the road. An hour earlier she had woken from a stiff bed and wondered how she would accomplish the day's chores. Her morning prayer contained all the usual rhetoric, save for one footnote: someone to help dig her father's grave. It has not rained in a month, and the earth is as hard as a saddle. Quinn's spade would be as useless as her arthritic back. She squints at the lone traveler and sips her coffee.

Porter does not slow his pace or even look in Quinn's direction upon his approach, but he knows she is there. Knows she has seen him. Quinn waits in vain for a friendly salutation. Porter chews on his lower lip and keeps his hand near his gun while he passes.

"You got someplace you need to be?" Quinn asks. Porter looks up and stops. Stares at Quinn and surveys the area for hidden men. War does that to a person. Makes a man distrust everyone and everything. Quinn smiles, showing the traveler she means no harm. "I said you got someplace you need to be?" Quinn asks again.

"What do you want?" Porter asks, feeling the steel of his gun pressing against his stomach.

"A hand," Quinn says. "I need help digging a grave."

Porter eyes Quinn. Is this a threat against him or an honest inquiry?

"Whose grave?"

"My father's," Quinn says. Porter does not appear satisfied with the answer.

"He died two days ago," Quinn explains, sensing Porter's uneasiness. "He's upstairs on the bed. The heat is getting to him. Starting to stink up the house."

Porter remains silent. Quinn spies the large oak in the distance. Somehow, twenty years ago, her father had dug a grave under the tree for Quinn's mother. His dying request was to be placed next to her. Twenty years ago, roots and buried rocks damn near broke her father's back digging the grave. Quinn aches just imagining what the task would do to her.

"You can stay the night," Quinn says. "You could take a warm bath and leave on a full stomach first thing in the morning."

Porter's insides turn at the promise of food. "You got a shovel?"

They arrive at the massive oak. A make-shift crucifix plunged into the dry earth. Porter notes the name—Mary—carved into the splintered wood.

"My mother," Quinn explains. "Died twenty years ago." Quinn bends and takes a rock from the ground, studies it, and then tosses the stone into some nearby brush. "The ground here is like stone, but it's where my dad wants to lie in rest."

Porter drops his bag and takes the spade. He plunges the blade into the ground and lifts the dirt and sets it aside. He repeats the action, each time pulling more dirt from the small chasm developing before Quinn's eyes. Within minutes Porter has a hole eighteen inches deep. Sweat runs down his forehead to the tip of his nose where it hangs until another bead pushes it from the tip and into the hole, staining the earth with his efforts. Quinn observes with an awed curiosity before excusing herself. She ambles towards her shed. Inside is her father's coffin. She must finish it before Porter finishes digging the grave.

Quinn returns an hour later. The dulled spade rests against the tree and Porter sits at the edge of the grave with his feet dangling and a book in his lap.

"You can read?" Quinn asks.

Porter nods without looking up.

"What book is that?"

Porter closes the book and stands. He walks to his bag and drops the book into it without answering.

"I read *The Bible* every night," Quinn offers. Porter gives no reaction to Quinn's admission. Quinn assumes Porter's silence reveals he is not familiar with *The Bible* and its teachings, for who would not want to find commonality in The Good Book?

Quinn stands at the grave's edge and stares into the gulf. "That is some hole," she marvels. To the side of the grave is a cache of rocks and discarded tree roots. Porter's exertions are impressive. The coffin will fit easily with four feet of earth packed on top. How Porter penetrated the ironclad earth with so much ease is a miracle, Quinn believes. "It would have taken me four days to dig a hole that deep," Quinn says. "You were an answer to my prayers."

Porter wipes his nose on his sleeve and looks over the barren land. This is a godforsaken place, but Porter finds comfort in it. He appreciates anything unsoiled by the whims of men.

"Let's go get my father," Quinn says.

•   •   •   •   •

The musty scent of death permeates the bedroom. Quinn's father lies on the bed. Hollow, lifeless eyes stare at the ceiling. His arms crisscross his chest. A wooden crucifix rests atop his hands. Quinn walks to her father's side and kisses his cold forehead. She mouths a prayer and then stands straight, her eyes wet.

The war taught Porter the most cumbersome and difficult object to handle is a dead body. Quinn suggests they carry the body down with Porter at the feet and Quinn at the shoulders. Porter knows the more sensible method would be to hoist the dead body onto his shoulder and carry it like a sack of flour.

"I'll do it myself," he says.

Porter steps past Quinn. He takes the crucifix and passes it to Quinn. Quinn takes the symbol and kisses it and drops it into her pocket. Porter sits the body upright, turns it away from the bed, raises an arm, and ducks under the corpse and lifts it onto his shoulder in one fluid motion. He exits the bedroom with Quinn in tow. Outside Porter places the body inside the coffin with the same ease with which he had lifted it. He and Quinn position the casket's lid, and Porter takes Quinn's hammer and drives in the nails.

Using a length of rope, together they lower the coffin into the grave. Porter retrieves the shovel and fills the hole. Quinn watches the coffin disappear under the soil. Porter completes the job in ten minutes.

"Would you mind if I said a prayer?" Quinn asks.

Porter shrugs and starts for the barn, but Quinn calls after him and asks if he would not mind staying. "After all, you dug the hole," Quinn says, as if Porter's service requires him to witness the eulogy.

Porter considers objecting, to tell Quinn he never met her father, so what does it matter if he hears her prayer? But he says nothing. He faces the grave and bows his head. Quinn closes her eyes.

"Lord, today I give you the body of my father. He was a good man. Hardhearted at times and hardheaded at others, but he did the best he knew how." Quinn pauses. Porter watches her. He cannot decide if her struggle stems from grief or because she did not rehearse her broken tribute. She bites her lower lip and continues: "My father taught me how to shoe a horse, till a field, and read The Good Book. He was your faithful servant and vessel. Tell him to keep a place next to the fire for when I see him again. And tell him to treat mom better in heaven than he did down here. Thank you, Lord. Amen."

Quinn lifts her head and opens her eyes. She looks at Porter. Something in the distance fixes his gaze. Quinn deems it strange he did not say 'amen.'

CHAPTER 2

Porter gnaws on a dry corn biscuit. He chases each bite with a mouthful of water to help soften the texture. It scratches his throat when he swallows, and his eyes water from the effort. The bacon is not much better. It has the texture of a saddle and a taste to match. The food is not good, but it is sustenance, so it will suffice.

"Had I known this morning I would break bread with a lonesome traveler, I would have made a peach pie," Quinn says. "It wouldn't have been much better than the corn biscuits, but I would have made one, nonetheless. I have an acre of peach trees. I never know what to do with them. Seems sensible to put them in a pie, but I can't bake to save my life." Quinn slides deep into a memory and laughs. "Damn near cost me my marriage."

Porter winces as he swallows another portion of biscuit. He can feel his stomach filling with the dense bread. The food is a welcomed struggle. He cannot remember the last time he did not go to bed hungry.

"So, where are you from?" Quinn asks. Porter gives Quinn a suspicious look, considers the question, and leaves it unanswered.

"I was born in Mississippi, but I remember little of it," Quinn says. "Father was from Boston. Started his church there and then moved south with his flock. Needed to find a place free from frigid winters. Stayed in Mississippi for seven years before coming out here. This is where God told him he needed to go." Quinn chews her bacon. After a moment, she vacates the task and spits the meat onto her plate.

"Mississippi was hard for my father," she continues. "Too many false preachers and charlatans deceiving decent folks. When he came to Oklahoma, he brought with him over two hundred followers." Quinn lifts her eyebrows, expecting Porter to acknowledge and appreciate her father's achievement. Porter remains stoic and unmoved.

"Pretty impressive, isn't it?" Quinn asks.

Porter shrugs.

"That's quite a following," Quinn says.

"Two hundred you say?" Porter asks.

"That's right."

"Why didn't any of those followers help dig his grave?" Porter asks.

Quinn ponders Porter's question. Two hundred followed her father to this dusty wasteland, but if Quinn considers all those who abandoned her father, well, that would double the number. She smiles to mask her sadness.

"That's a fair question," she says. "Some have fallen away, but most have joined with my brother. As my father got older, he...his faculties started to fail him. It was hard to watch such a great man with so sharp a mind become reduced to a shell of what he once was. My brother, James, was embarrassed by him in the end. Wouldn't even listen to my father preach. And yet, he got the church and our father's congregation. Yeah, James got the flock, and I got my father. Or whatever was left of him." Quinn drops her fork and kneads the callouses lining her palms. "I don't mean to sound bitter about it. It's just...well, you wouldn't understand."

Quinn wipes her eyes and shakes her head. "Family can be a burden," she says. "You got any family?"

Porter ignores the question. Eats.

"I'm sure you do. Everyone has family somewhere. My brother and I, we get along well enough, but I'd be lying if I said it didn't hurt when he took over the church." Quinn pauses and looks at her silent guest, gives Porter a kind appraisal. She cannot decipher anything about him. He is expressionless.

"What's your religious affiliation, if you don't mind my asking?" Quinn asks.

Porter's eyes remain fixed on his plate. A single piece of bacon remains. He does not want it. His jaw aches, but he is not yet full, and he knows he should not waste the meat.

"I can respect your silence," Quinn says. "One's faith is sacred." Quinn waits a beat, allowing Porter a moment to interject. He does not.

"Not much of a conversationalist, are you?" Quinn asks, and she senses Porter feels no inclination to answer. "I reckon with your age you must have been fighting. Are you a deserter?"

Porter stiffens at the accusation. Anticipates where this interrogation may lead.

"Look, you're a guest in my house," Quinn says. "You dug my father's grave, and now we're breaking bread. I don't care if you're running—"

"Running insinuates I'm escaping something," Porter says.

Quinn ponders this. "Perhaps, but there ain't no shame if you're running for the right cause. Is that the case? Were you fighting in the war?" Quinn offers enough time for an answer, but none comes. "You're young enough, and you came from the east. So, if you're not fighting, you must be running. Again, I'm not insulting you if you're running. Sometimes it takes just as much courage to leave something as it does to stay."

Porter tosses the last bacon remnant into his mouth and chews until it softens enough to swallow.

"I'll respect your silence when it comes to matters of war," Quinn says. "It's an atrocity that needs no explanation. But tell me, why head west?"

Porter sits straight, rigid, and unflinching.

"Come on, son," Quinn prods. "Indulge me. I ain't lookin' to tell anybody. Besides, ain't nobody here but me."

Porter remains silent, and Quinn forsakes the task, certain she cannot convince Porter to speak. Quinn makes to stand when Porter opens his mouth. When he speaks, Quinn masks her surprise. She settles back into her chair.

"There are no states west," Porter says.

"No states?"

"Just territories," Porter explains.

"A territory is better than a state?" Quinn asks.

"Yes."

"Why?"

"No government regulation."

"What does that matter?"

"A man doesn't have to fight some other man's foolish ideals," Porter explains.

"So, you were in the war?" Quinn asks, but Porter does not answer. "Is that how you view the war? Fighting someone else's ideals?"

"Is there any other way to view it?"

Quinn narrows her eyes at the question. "I guess in some respects you're right. Which side were you on?"

"The wrong side," Porter answers without pause.

"I wasn't aware there were right and wrong sides in war."

"There is in this one."

"And which side is the right side?"

"The one that treats humans as humans."

Quinn nods. "I am inclined to agree with you. A lot of colored folk came with my father. He taught me to look to one's soul before casting judgment on their skin color. So, you're an abolitionist?"

"I'm nothing."

"How did you get out from the fighting?"

"I left," Porter says, his admission not much louder than a whisper.

"Just as I suspected—a runaway," Quinn says. "War is a terrible thing, especially when it's fought in your own backyard. I don't begrudge you for deserting. The Confederacy don't need your help to lose the war. They can do it on their own. They may come lookin' for you, though."

"They won't come this far west."

"They may if they get desperate enough. Were you wounded?"

Porter nods.

Quinn places a consoling hand over Porter's. Porter flinches at her touch and pulls his hand away. Quinn smiles, unoffended by the gesture.

"God saved you," Quinn says, and Porter laughs. He did not mean to, but he could not help it.

"I say something funny?" Quinn asks.

"God had nothing to do with it."

"Now that's where you are wrong, son," Quinn says, her voice sharp. "You're sitting at my table because God spared you."

"I'm sitting at your table because I left the war of my own free will."

"Free will granted to you by God."

"God had nothing to do with it."

"You've already said that."

"And I'll keep saying it."

"Why?"

"Because it's the truth."

"What a moronic thing to say," Quinn says, smiling. "My daughter taught me that word: 'moronic.' It means…not too smart." Quinn basks in her superior knowledge. Porter picks at his teeth, uninterested in exchanging opinions on God.

"So, how far west are you lookin' to go?" Quinn asks.

"To the ocean."

"And what will you do once you get to the ocean?"

Porter shrugs.

"Seems you haven't thought this through."

"Just want to get as far away from the war as I can."

Quinn nods. "Well, it's good to have a plan," she says. She gathers her plate and stands. She holds out her hand for Porter's empty dish. He hands it over and nods, wordlessly offering his appreciation.

"I didn't ask earlier because I doubted I would get an answer, but tell me, son, what is your name?"

Porter bristles at the question.

"Boy, you sure are jumpy," Quinn says. "It's an innocent question. Just like to know who I'm talking to."

"Porter," Porter says.

Quinn smiles. "Pleasure to meet you, Porter. Name's Quinn."

CHAPTER 3

Porter stands over the bed naked at the waist. His stomach and shoulder show old bullet wounds healed and scarred. His body is lean, sinewy. Cruel and alert from living a life where enemies outnumber allies. He takes his shirt from the chair in the corner and puts it on. Spilled onto the bed are the contents of his knapsack: a worn copy of *Frankenstein*, some bullets, a gun, and food. Someone knocks. Porter turns, and Quinn stands in the doorway. She gives Porter a brief overview before her eyes settle on the gun. Porter steps in front, blocking Quinn's view.

"You sleep all right?" Quinn asks. Porter gives a slight nod. "I don't know how pressed you are to head out, but, well…I…I spent the better part of the past year looking after my dad." Quinn looks everywhere but at Porter trying to find how to ask what needs asking. "As a result, I paid little attention to the farm." Quinn appears sad, forlorn, as if her father's death were her fault, and now she needs Porter to absolve her.

"Anyway," Quinn continues, "if you'd like, you could stay here a bit longer and help me get things in order. It's a lot of work for one person."

A fly drifts through the air, lands on Porter's shoulder. It appears to have captured Porter's attention more than Quinn's offer.

"Look, son, I'm damn near sixty," Quinn says with more resolve. "Stay a month. Oklahoma is only a territory. Home Guard won't be huntin' you out here. You can sleep in a bed and eat hot meals. That's gotta be more tempting than whatever you have waiting for you out west. I've heard tales of the ocean. It stinks, and it's salty. Stay for a month."

Porter's eyes are inscrutable. After a beat, he nods.

"Great," Quinn says. "Coffee's on. Get your fill and then meet me by the barn."

Quinn exits the house, and Porter slips into the kitchen and pours himself a cup of coffee. He stares out a kitchen window at the plains ahead. Nothing but the horizon and barren land. Quinn asked for a month. Porter knows she will need him longer.

He finishes his coffee and starts for the front door. He comes upon a bedroom. The door is cracked open. Porter noted the room yesterday. It was sealed shut. Quinn must have gone into the room this morning. Through the crack, Porter spots a shelf saddled with books. He enters the bedroom.

The room is small, simple. A made bed, a small dresser, and the bookshelf. On the bed is a small stuffed rabbit—a child's toy.

Porter walks to the books and reads the different titles: *Pride and Prejudice, Jane Eyre, Oliver Twist, The Iliad, The Odyssey,* Shakespeare, Milton. Porter knows the books, either by reputation or because he has read them. His accounting stops on a particular book: *The Book of Mormon.* He pulls the book from the shelf, examines it.

"What are you doing in here?"

Porter turns and finds Quinn in the doorway, standing erect, hands on hips. A healthy outline of sweat already stains her shirt. Porter returns the book. Quinn steps into the room, squints, and reads the title.

"Do you know that book?" Quinn asks.

Porter does not answer.

"Don't waste your time with it," Quinn orders. "You want to read the true word of God, read *The Bible*."

Porter glances at the shelf, taking stock again of the various titles. He wonders how many he could read in a month.

Quinn's eyes shift from the bookshelf to the stuffed rabbit on the bed. She tightens. Reflecting on a past life. Revisiting demons she has yet to conquer.

"Come on," she says. "I'll show you the farm."

▪   ▪   ▪   ▪   ▪

Quinn and Porter stand on the fringes of a watermelon patch overgrown with weeds. Had Quinn not revealed earlier what stood before them, Porter never would have guessed the barren field once produced watermelons. Porter shields the sun with his hand and explores the terrain. The land is as desolate as his life's purpose, he muses, appreciating the simile.

"Like I said, lotta work for one person," Quinn says.

Porter kneels and pulls a weed, tests the soil. It is dry but better than he expected.

"There a horse in your barn?" Porter asks.

"Only by definition. More mule than horse. Not sure how much work we could get out of him." Quinn spits. The wetness dries immediately. "Used to have a cow. Used to have several, as a matter of fact. Had to slaughter the last one last winter. Used to have chickens, too. Used to have a lot of things," Quinn adds as an afterthought. She kicks at a dirt clod. It breaks into dust.

Porter stands and again takes in the vast expanse of land. It is formidable. Yes, he is certain a month will not suffice. He cannot decide what he sees when he explores Quinn's dusty land: job security for the unforeseeable future or a life sentence pulling weeds and praying to a nonexistent God for rain. Porter has spent his life avoiding anything he cannot walk away from—the war included. Quinn is old and alone. Her land could keep Porter working for years.

"I had a son, too," Quinn says, continuing her accounting of things lost. "It was his bed you slept in last night. He went and fought. He didn't have to, but he thought it was the noble thing to do. Foolish child died in the first month. I didn't say anything about him last night because, well…I just didn't. So, like you, I'm not a fan of war."

Quinn pauses, anticipates Porter may have something to offer. He does not, so she continues: "When my father got sick, I couldn't keep things going the way I should. I have a brother, too. I mentioned him last night. He lives about twenty miles west of here. He sent food every month. Done out of pity and guilt." Quinn shields her eyes, looks past Porter. "He took over the church from our father. Rather, he took the church *from* my father. What remained of it, anyway. Now that father's gone, I doubt my brother's going to continue to extend his Christian charity." Quinn's eyes burn. "I need this land to provide for me, Porter."

Quinn exhales with a great flourish. Wishes Porter would say something, acknowledge her grief. Porter is uninterested in Quinn's history, but he listens and lets Quinn speak unencumbered. Porter's mom taught him to listen when a woman spoke.

"I had a husband too," Quinn adds, purging herself of her memories. "Died seven years ago. Came out here to till the ground and keeled over dead. I blamed the Oklahoma heat, but his mama blamed me. Said God cursed us for subscribing to my father's heathen ways."

Porter wants to retreat to the barn and test the horse. It promises to be a hot day, and the sooner he can start his labors, the better.

"For heaven's sake, Porter," Quinn says. "I just opened my soul to you. Ain't you got nothing to say to any of that?"

Porter has nothing to say about Quinn's misfortunes. Life is a series of misfortunes, so he does not see the value in paying special attention to Quinn's. He reads in Quinn's demeanor she requires some kind of reaction. Porter deliberates a bit, scavenging for anything Quinn said that is worth further inquiry.

"Your boy went to war?" Porter asks.

"That's what I said."

"And he didn't have to?"

"Nope."

"So why'd you let him?"

"It is what he wanted."

Porter bites his tongue, debating whether to voice the thoughts imprisoning his mind. He frowns and swallows, silencing what he wished to say. His mother also taught him to stay silent on matters concerning mothers and children.

"Rose, my eldest daughter, lives with my brother," Quinn says. Porter sinks in his boots, anticipating more confessions rising from the horizon. The sun teases him with the prospect of work.

"She wanted to be closer to the congregation," Quinn says. "At least that's what she told me. Truth is she's hoping to find a husband. Nothing out here but weeds and sorrow. She helps with the children, too. My brother has six of them. His wife got sick last winter, so my brother needed an extra hand." Quinn pauses. Sighs. "My other daughter—Sammy—she…she…" but Quinn leaves the thought suspended. Porter stares at the barn wishing he could escape, but he knows Quinn has more to say.

"Sammy is fourteen," Quinn resumes. "She left a few months back. I…I don't know if I'll ever see her again."

Porter waits for Quinn to continue, but it appears she may have finally exhausted herself. Her melancholy has stripped her will and no more admissions are forthcoming. Porter takes a tentative step toward the barn, ready to halt if Quinn speaks. She remains silent, and Porter takes another step away from her and toward the barn. Quinn remains trapped in her own thoughts, in her own unforgiving past. Porter hastens his step and is halfway to the barn before Quinn lifts her gaze and notes Porter's absence.

CHAPTER 4

Quinn sits on her porch. An empty dinner plate on her lap. She watches Porter in the distance, plowing a field, working the horse she presumed did not have any work left in it. It has been a good day with a lot accomplished. More accomplished than spoken— just how Porter prefers it. A week ago Quinn guessed it would take at least a year to restore the farm to working order. With Porter's help, she supposes that timeframe could be cut in half, assuming she can convince Porter to stay. She only asked him to help for a month but trusts she can compel him to extend his tenure. He does not appear to have family, a lover, or anything else worth pursuing. Warm food and books seem to entice him above anything else. Quinn has plenty of both.

An hour later Porter ascends the porch stairs. The sun sets behind him, peaking through clouds that promise rain. Porter is filthy. The sign of a man working to survive. Quinn had fallen asleep on the porch but wakes upon Porter's arrival. Porter spies Quinn's empty dinner plate. Licks his lips.

"Food's inside," Quinn tells him. Porter enters the house, wiping his feet on the doormat as he goes. These simple niceties have not gone unnoticed. To Quinn's detriment, Porter does not say much, but outside his reluctance to converse, she cannot deny he is well-mannered.

Porter prefers to eat outside, and he also prefers to eat alone. Tonight, like all nights, Quinn will only grant him one of his preferences. In a moment, he will return to the porch with his dinner and Quinn will still be there. She will burden the night with chatter while Porter scrapes his plate clean. They have done this same ritual for the past ten nights. Porter eating and Quinn talking—mostly about God. Porter listens and reserves judgment. It is a fair exchange. Quinn can pontificate, and Porter gets to sleep in a feather bed with a full stomach. Each rises the next day content with how they finished the previous one. It is a simple life, and one Porter does not wish to escape soon.

A moment later, Porter takes his familiar seat, his dinner plate overloaded with foodstuff. Quinn marvels at the helpings but does not protest Porter's appetite. She would need similar rations if she worked half as hard as him. Quinn has taken to cooking larger portions. She wants to make it harder on Porter to leave if he ever decides to follow his life west. Porter senses her tactics but does not voice them. He appreciates Quinn's generosity. Porter has gone to bed full every night for a week. A first in his lifetime.

Lightening flickers in the distance, illuminating the vast land. A low thunder follows the flash.

"Rain oughta help the crops," Quinn says, issuing her customary weather analysis. Quinn does not know it, but Porter had begun counting the moment he sat down guessing how long it would take Quinn to break the night's silence. Porter speculated forty-five seconds. Quinn spoke at fourteen.

"I noticed you took Shakespeare from the bedroom," Quinn says. The bedroom, Porter suspects, belongs to Quinn's daughter even though this assumption has yet to be confirmed. "I tried reading him once," Quinn says, "at my daughter's insistence. Couldn't though. Didn't understand what I was reading. Bunch of words strung together with little coherence."

Porter takes up a chicken leg and pulls the meat from the bone with sharp teeth. His lips welcome the grease and fat from the meat.

"I hope you're reading Shakespeare because you've lost interest in that other book," Quinn says. 'That other book' is *The Book of Mormon*. Porter had sneaked into the daughter's bedroom three nights ago and had taken it, along with *Don Quixote.*

"I don't need to tell you, since you've already taken the liberty, but help yourself to any of those books in there. You can read 'em, you just can't keep 'em. Lord knows I'll never read any of 'em."

Porter begins a new silent count, ticking off the numbers until Quinn mentions *The Bible*.

"That's my daughter's room—Rose. She would read anything she could get her hands on. Not me, though. *The Bible*. That's the only book I need."

Seven seconds. Porter smirks at Quinn's predictability.

"You ever read *The Bible*, Porter?" Quinn asks.

Porter licks his fingers and takes up another chicken leg.

"You ought to read that before wasting your time with that Mormon book." Quinn's voice has an unfamiliar edge to it. The longer Porter remains silent, the ornerier Quinn becomes. Porter has learned to space his remarks in accordance with Quinn's disposition.

"I'll return it," Porter says.

"Hell, you can keep it," Quinn exclaims. "That's the only book you can keep. Better yet, burn it. If you're looking for God, you'll find Him in *The Bible*. My father read us *The Bible* every night."

Porter yawns. It was not intentional, but he could not help it. Quinn balks at the unintended slight.

"Am I boring you?" Quinn asks, her voice sharp and accusatory.

Porter does not answer while he tries to suppress another yawn.

"I guess I should not complain if I am," Quinn says. "You work harder than any man I've ever seen. I shouldn't begrudge your weariness. Here I am trying to engage in pleasant conversation and you're fighting off the lure of sleep."

"Sorry," Porter says.

"Can you humor me with conversation?" Quinn teases. "I know that's a tall order for you."

"I can on one condition," Porter says.

"Name it."

"Are you capable of talking about something other than *The Bible*?" Porter asks.

Quinn looks at Porter with a discerning eye. This is the most he has ever said. Was this comment made in jest, or was he voicing a genuine inquiry? Porter's inscrutable face does not reveal which.

"Just sayin' you ought to try reading it," Quinn says. "You seem inclined to read everything else so why not the word of God? You might find something in it. I sure have."

"I've read *The Bible*," Porter reveals.

Quinn lifts an incredulous eyebrow. "Oh, yeah? What's your favorite passage?"

"'Transgression is at work where people talk too much, but anyone who holds his tongue is prudent,'" Porter recites without hesitation.

Quinn smirks. "Is that directed to me?"

Porter says nothing, but Quinn detects the slightest grin developing on Porter's face.

"What has you so curious about Mormons?" Quinn asks, but she knows Porter will not answer without Quinn's usual prodding, so she adds: "Come on, son. What danger is there in indulging me in a spiritual conversation?"

"Curiosity," Porter murmurs.

"You have a curiosity for cults, do you?"

"I have a curiosity of human nature."

"It's a garbage book. Someone should burn it."

"Why don't *you* burn it?"

Quinn sighs and looks over her fields. "I promised Rose I would leave her room exactly as she left it in case she ever comes back home. I can't, in good conscience, get rid of it, but if a stranger were to take it without my knowing, well then, I would be free of blame, wouldn't I?"

Quinn massages the back of her neck, loosening muscles that have grown tight from her recent toils.

"My other daughter, Samantha, she fell under the spell of a Mormon who passed through here last year. He had a stack of those Mormon books. Offering one to anyone who would take it. That's how it came to be in my home. I knew little about Mormons at the time. Just knew their leader, Mr. Smith, ran for president and lost. Later, they put him in jail and some Free Masons gunned him down. Killed him and made him a martyr."

Quinn pauses long enough for Porter to confirm or question her claims. It does not surprise her when he chooses indifference.

"Anyway, this rich Mormon from Arkansas showed up here last fall with three of his wives. It was raining for Noah when they knocked on our door asking if they could bed down for the night. The women were shivering and hungry. One of them was damn near my age while another was not much older than my Sammy. She was pregnant. I tried turning them away, but my father would not let me. He thought it the Christian thing to let them stay. Rain didn't stop for seven days. The day it did, I walked into Sammy's room, and she's lying naked with the man. Two other wives sat in the corner of the room watching like it was the most normal thing in the world. He told me he had baptized my daughter Mormon, and then God commanded he take her as his wife." Quinn looks to the sky and expels a painful laugh. Fights the invading tears. "'His wife,' the man said. Sammy was a month past her fourteenth birthday."

Another ribbon of lightning flashes in the distance. It captures Quinn and Porter's attention. Quinn is grateful for the distraction. She needs the reprieve to bridle her budding rage.

"I was so consumed with my father's health I didn't notice the man courting my daughter. I was livid when I found them together, so I did what any sensible parent would and kicked him out, to the chagrin of my daughter. He returned the next night, and Sammy ran off with him. Left a note saying she was going with him and his other wives to Utah to help build Zion. She told me she never wanted to see me again. That my father's church was of the devil, if you can fathom such nonsense."

A thunderclap shakes the porch, and the rain starts. It paddles the roof and kisses the dry soil.

"I wanted to go after her. I did, actually. Got as far as Santa Fe, but I had to turn back. My father needed me. Rose, my other daughter, was upset with how I handled things. Said I drove Sammy away. Come winter she packed up and went and stayed with my brother. She hasn't been back since."

Porter can smell the rain. It reminds him of something distant and almost forgotten. He believes this moment could be perfect if Quinn would stop talking.

"The point to all this is, don't get fooled by the witchcraft in that book," Quinn commands. "Not a word of it is true."

Porter knows he should let this declaration go unchallenged. He feels nothing for Mormons nor any other faith, but he has a sudden desire to engage with Quinn. Perhaps it is because Quinn will not let the night pass undisturbed. Perhaps it is because Quinn reminds Porter of his own mother—wise and stubborn and incorrigible.

"I didn't know a person could look for truth and God at the same time," Porter sneers.

Quinn straightens, taken aback with Porter's sudden desire to speak. "Excuse me?"

"You said nothing in the Mormon book is true."

"That's right."

"So I'll repeat my assertion: I didn't know a person could look for God and truth at the same time."

"Well, that's where you're wrong, Porter. *The Bible* is true. It's God's book. You'll find both in it."

"So you've said…several times."

Quinn screws her face up to Porter. "Don't pander to me, son. If you got something to say, say it."

"It's all just fiction," Porter says.

"Say again."

"You have *The Bible* for your God, just as the Greeks and Romans have books for theirs."

Quinn digests this but does not see the connection. She says as much.

"None of them are true, just as that Mormon book isn't true either," Porter explains. "They're just stories disguised as prophesies to brainwash the foolish."

"Well, that is a harsh thing to say," Quinn exclaims. "And ignorant!"

Porter watches the rain.

"Then why read it?" Quinn asks. "If you don't believe in any of it, why spend the time reading it?"

Porter shrugs. "I enjoy fiction."

"Ain't no fiction in *The Bible*," Quinn declares.

"Large parts of the world would disagree with you."

"Godless parts!" Quinn cries. "This here is God's country."

"Now you sound like a Mormon," Porter teases. "And a Muslim and a Hindu."

"How so?"

"You're claiming parts of the world are holier than others."

"Some parts are!"

"So you say."

"Are you telling me Christians and Hindus and Muslims…we're all the same?"

"If I find a distinction, I'll let you know."

"Well, son, you are a marvel! Here you sit on my porch, breaking bread, and talking all sorts of nonsense. Saying *The Holy Bible* is the same as that Godless nonsense the Mormons read."

"All religious texts are just stories of Gods and monsters," Porter says.

Quinn guffaws. "You are a loose talker, Porter. I hope God doesn't judge you too harshly for the things you're saying."

Porter cannot believe how much he has already said. His intuition tells him to bite his tongue and watch the rain, but something keeps him engaged. He cannot help himself.

"Look at what God has taken from you," Porter says. "It seems you believe in him more than he believes in you."

"Watch your tongue, son," Quinn snaps. "That's blasphemous. God is in all things. A dust ant don't move from here to there without God knowin' about it."

Porter scoffs and shakes his head.

"Say your peace, son," Quinn instructs.

"You told me to watch my tongue."

"Well, now I'm telling you to turn it loose. Say what you must!"

"Look out at that rain," Porter says. "What's causing it?"

"God!" Quinn exclaims.

"That isn't God," Porter says, nodding to the rain.

"What is it then?"

"It's weather patterns," Porter explains. "God's just a character in books. He ain't any more real than...Hamlet or Othello. The only difference is he has a larger following."

Quinn whistles a cautious tune and chuckles at Porter's absurd analysis. "You could not be more wrong, young man."

Porter fingers a hangnail. He brings his finger to his lips and tears the nail free with his teeth. He spits the shard onto the porch.

"When I was wounded, other men were in the hospital," Porter explains, finding himself thrust into a memory he wishes he could forget. "Men who lost arms and legs. They couldn't get themselves to a bathroom without help. Couldn't eat a meal. They couldn't even tie their own shoes, and they'll spend the rest of their lives dependent on other people. They have bodies stripped of the things that made them who they were. You want to torture a man, you take his dignity. You take his limbs. Let him live but make him a prisoner inside his own mind."

Quinn cannot find fault in this argument. "I suspect you've seen a lot of ugly things coming from where you've come from."

"I have," Porter says.

"No disrespect, but I do not find the common thread to what we were discussing."

Every muscle in Porter's neck and jaw is clenched and taut. "If you're telling me that God has a hand in all things, well then, he had a hand in the things I've seen, and if that's true, then God isn't worth the paper his stories are written on."

"I wonder how you can say such things without fear of reprisal."

"I cannot fear what I do not believe in."

"I should set you out on the road for spouting such nonsense," Quinn says, but her tone tells Porter she does not mean this. "God is merciful," Quinn says. "If He took the limbs of those men, He did so to teach them a lesson."

"Yeah?"

"That's right. God is mysterious, and His knowledge far exceeds our own."

"What lessons have you learned from what he's taken from you?"

"Quite a lot," Quinn says. "Humility. Patience."

"You don't need God to learn those things."

"How else would I have learned them?"

"By living. You needn't give God so much credit."

"You're walking a very fine line, son. I hope you're speaking in jest, but I'm compelled to remind you—blasphemy is a sin worthy of death."

Porter picks at a piece of chicken lodged between his teeth. He regrets humoring Quinn with conversation tonight. Talking about God with the religious gets a person nowhere in a hurry.

"Well, if I'm not struck dead in the morning for my blasphemy," Porter says, "I'll get to work on that watermelon patch."

"Blasphemy *is* a sin, Porter, but it may not be 'till the next life that you'll have to pay for it. That and the rest of your sins."

"I've paid for plenty of sins, but it's always been man's will that's made me suffer."

"Men are instruments of God," Quinn says.

"That's absurd."

Quinn laughs so hard tears form on the edges of her eyes. A full minute passes before she can speak again. "Tell me then, what do you suppose is waiting for you after you die?"

"Nothing," Porter says.

"Nothing?"

"No."

"That's bleak."

"Such is life."

"Nothing?" Quinn repeats, choking on the incredulous assumption.

"Yes," Porter says. "Then my suffering can end."

"Suffering?" Quinn says. "You're suffering?"

"Aren't we all?"

"If you're suffering, why not just end it now? Take that gun from your sack, walk out into that pasture, and pull the trigger?"

Porter shrugs.

"It's because you know there may be something else, something more than this life has to offer. Something beyond it."

"No, that's not it."

"No? What's keeping you alive?"

"Dumb luck," Porter says. "Same as anyone."

"Dumb luck? That's what's keeping you alive now?" Quinn asks without expecting an answer. "Well, does anything inspire you? Anything keep you hopeful?"

"Sure."

"Let's hear it."

"A good book and a better cup of coffee," Porter says. The thought of reading a good book with a strong coffee forces his eyes closed so he can better envision the fantasy. On the fringes of his vision, he hears the rain hitting the metal sheeting on the barn. The hypnotic rhythm drifts him to memories long forgotten.

"The setting sun," he whispers. "The way a woman smells in the morning."

"You got yourself a woman?" Quinn asks. Porter tightens and opens his eyes. "Is she out West?" Quinn asks. "Is she why you left the war?"

"You're missing the point," Porter says.

"What is your point?"

"There are still some things man's corruption has not yet stolen."

"So that's what you're living for then?" Quinn asks. "A woman? Coffee and the setting sun?"

"Those reasons are as good as any," Porter says. He takes his empty plate and stands. This conversation has exhausted itself.

"I will say this much about God," Quinn interjects before Porter can escape the night. "I've been trying to loosen your tongue for over a week to no avail. It wasn't until God intervened that it worked. This is the most I've ever heard you talk, son." Quinn smiles, basking in Porter's defeat. Porter concedes the point and enters the house.

"Goodnight, Porter," Quinn calls after him. The front door slaps shut, and Quinn looks to the heavens and ponders on her daughters. A moment later her eyes glisten, and she cannot help but wonder if some hidden logic lives in Porter's corrupt wisdom. She pushes the thought from her mind as quickly as it had entered. God is in all things. Quinn knows this. To question that axiom now would be to question fifty years of a life devoted to that one, universal truth.

CHAPTER 5

Quinn and Porter work the ranch. As is his custom, Porter does not speak much. Monosyllabic grunts or simple gestures are all that greet Quinn's attempts at conversation.

Porter never seems to fatigue. His endurance has inspired Quinn's. The work is good for them both. It is a much-needed distraction from the things they have lost. The things they want to forget.

A lone man on horseback appears in the distance. Sensing the rider, Porter stands straight and lifts his hat. Quinn stands too, wondering what could cause Porter to stop working. She follows Porter's gaze to the distant rider. Quinn squints and shields the sun with her arm. It is her brother—James. She does not know why her brother has come, but she wishes he had not. Quinn drops her tool and retrieves the canteen from the tilled soil. She takes a long pull and holds it out to Porter. He ignores it; the rider holds his attention. Quinn caps the canteen and drops it to the ground. She places her hands on her hips and waits.

Porter kept his gun in the bedroom this morning. He second-guessed his decision the moment he stepped outside the house. He could not remember the last time he navigated the world without the cold metal pressed to his body. Seeing the rider now, instinct forces Porter to reach for his gun, and he curses himself for his folly. He has become comfortable on the ranch. Too comfortable. Comfort gets men killed.

The rider approaches. Porter looks to Quinn, hoping to find recognition drawn on her face. She looks curious and concerned. Quinn senses Porter's consternation and shakes her head.

"It's not Home Guard," Quinn explains. "It's just my brother. James."

Within minutes, James arrives. He pulls his horse to a stop and looks down at his sister, expecting a proper greeting that never comes. Quinn stares at James, waiting for him to explain his visit.

"Quinn," James says by acknowledgement.

"James," Quinn says.

James looks at Porter. "Who's this?"

"He's standing right there," Quinn says. "Ask him yourself."

"What's your name, son?" James asks.

Porter stares at James, tightening his grip on the spade.

Quinn smiles. "He don't talk much," she explains.

"What's he doing here?" James asks.

"Helping," Quinn explains. "Best help I've ever had."

"He got a name?"

"All men got a name."

"What's his?"

"You can ask him."

"I already did."

"Well, it's his business whether he wants to share it," Quinn says.

James sits back in his saddle, but the movement is cautious and unnatural. James is not a rider. Porter glances at his hands and suspects James is not a laborer either. Porter concludes not much about James is worth admiring.

"How's Rosie?" Quinn asks.

"She's…well," James answers, but Quinn knows he does not mean what he says.

"What is it?" Quinn asks.

James's eyes shift to Porter, studies him for a beat, and then returns to his sister. "Can we talk inside?"

■   ■   ■   ■

Quinn sits at the kitchen table. James stands, taking in the house, noting the changes since his last visit. A new hollowness permeates the house. Its soul left with his dead father. Now his childhood home is a sarcophagus, void of all life. James shudders and sits down across from his sister.

"I'm sorry about Dad," James says. His words, offered from a custom to appease, hold no merit.

Quinn taps the table with her finger. She hates her brother right now. Hates herself too, but if asked to explain why, she would come away empty.

"He was a…good man," James says. His comment lacks sincerity and serves only to fill the uncomfortable silence.

"You should have been here," Quinn says.

James frowns. "It's hard for me to get away."

"The shepherd can't leave his flock?" Quinn asks with derision.

"Don't start, Quinn—"

"Not even for your own father."

"*The Bible* tells us, 'Let all bitterness and wrath and anger and clamor and slander be put away from you, along with all malice.'"

Quinn scoffs. "'Honor thy father and thy mother.' It's a commandment!"

James anticipated the conversation would take this detour. He shakes his head. "Is this about Dad or us, Quinn?"

"They were *his* followers, James."

"The people needed a leader."

"They had one—Dad!"

"Dad went crazy. He stripped himself naked the last time he gave a sermon because he felt the devil was trying to—"

"I know what happened, James. I was there."

James stands from the table and paces to the living room. A splintered crucifix hangs on the far wall. James remembers the cross from his childhood. He hated the rusticated, archaic appearance of it. One could not handle the jagged, unpolished wood without becoming riddled with splinters. When he asked his father why he would not replace it with a more ornate one, his father proclaimed: "When they nailed Jesus to the cross, do you suppose the Romans planed the wood? I'm sure splinters were the least of their concerns."

James scrutinizes the crucifix. It seems to represent a different era. One that has passed, thank God. He bows his head in reverence and returns to the kitchen.

"Father fell from grace, Quinn," James says.

"He got old," Quinn says. "And I was the next in line."

James goes to his sister's side and places a hand on her shoulder.

"The pulpit is no place for a woman," he says.

"Where is that written?" Quinn asks. "*The Bible* does not speak of it."

"The Bible also does not mention nor chronicle the ministries of any female prophets, Quinn. You must accept your place."

Quinn removes her brother's hand from her shoulder. She gets to her feet and steps away from her brother. Her eyes sharp and unforgiving.

"You men disgust me," Quinn says. "You believe God parcels out certain privileges at birth based on sex. It was men who nailed Jesus to the cross. It was men who waged the war that took my son's life. Maybe men need to sit down so the women can restore some normalcy to the world."

James is tired. Quinn has spouted these exhausted musings her entire life. In the past, their father always intercepted these ridiculous tangents. He would sit Quinn down and cite scriptures to better justify gender roles and expectations. Later, when Rose exhibited similar rebellions as her mother, once again Quinn's father used *The Bible* to explain why men held dominion over their female counterparts. Quinn and Rose could argue the shortcomings of men but not God. He was beyond reproach.

"Quinn, you're not a spiritual leader," James says. "Your tongue gets tied if you're speaking to a crowd larger than five. God did not choose you, Quinn. He chose me. You have a kind heart, sister, but you lack the language and charisma needed to spread God's message."

James's assertion stings, but Quinn does not dispute it. If God chooses His prophets on the merits of their tongue, James is a worthy representative.

"Why are you here, James?" Quinn asks.

James exhales and leans forward. "Samantha's been writing Rose. She's trying to convince her to come to Utah."

Quinn laughs. "What? And become a Mormon?"

"Yes," James answers with complete seriousness.

"Rose knows better," Quinn says, but even as she says this, she is not sure she believes it.

"I'm not so sure," James says. "Sam's telling her there are men in her congregation. Men looking for wives."

Quinn raises a disbelieving eyebrow. "Wives? Plural? Rosie would never…she would not want to share her husband."

"She's getting older, Quinn."

"She's twenty-three."

"That is past marrying age. I took Claire and Benjamin took you before your twentieth birthdays. Dad married mom when she was only seventeen. Twenty-three is not young regarding marriage, Quinn," James pauses. His retelling of their history forces his sister silent. He contemplates how best to say what needs to be said next. "Besides, Rose is…well, you know her reputation is…somewhat…tarnished."

"Don't you say it, James!" Quinn snaps.

"I must say what needs to be said."

"Not in my house, and you know it's a lie!"

"She's unclean, Quinn."

"Goddamn you, James!"

"Quinn, I am not passing judgment."

"Like hell you aren't."

"The town—"

"The town does not know the truth."

"Neither do you."

"I know what Rose tells me, and she has no reason to lie."

"She has every reason," James says. "Her reputation is at stake."

"James—"

"Men don't want to enter a defiled bed."

"Shut your lying mouth!"

"*The Bible* says—"

"*The Bible* says liars will spend eternity with Lucifer," Quinn hisses. "She did not lay in that man's bed. He lied about it and then lit off with another girl, taking Rose's reputation with him."

"Is that Rose's version of events?"

"Yes!"

"And you believe her?"

"Of course I believe her. She's my daughter."

James exhales a heavy sigh. His audible grumblings have grown more pronounced over the years.

"Did you come here just to remind me of Rose's past indiscretions?" Quinn asks.

"So you admit that—"

"I admit she loved someone not worth loving."

"Quinn—"

"How can you speak ill of her? She's helping Claire with the children. She has shown you nothing but love and kindness."

James did not come here to disparage his niece's name. He loves Rose, regardless of her past iniquities. He cannot, however, pretend the evidence against his niece does not carry some merit.

"I cannot fault a mother's compassion for her own offspring, but regardless of what happened, her name is blackened. She won't find a suitable mate in my congregation. The people have reached their own conclusions. Besides, Rose is embarrassed that she is still unwed when her younger sister is already married and expecting a child."

"Child?" Quinn says, lifting her gaze to meet her brother's.

James nods.

"She's barely fourteen," Quinn says.

"It's common for those people. Brigham Young is expanding his fold. He's raising an army for Zion."

Quinn sinks into a nearby chair. "She's fallen under the spell of a charlatan," she whispers.

"Samantha wants Rose to come to Utah," James says. "Rose can help Samantha with the child and marry a fellow member, possibly even her husband."

"Rose wants to marry Sam's husband?" Quinn asks. She is incredulous.

"She's twenty-three, Quinn. Her options are...lacking."

Quinn stands and paces the room. "What is the world coming to?"

"He's a rich man," James says. "Sam's convinced Rose the life she could have in Utah is better than the one she has here. The people in Salt Lake, they don't know about Rose's past...transgressions."

Quinn turns a sharp eye to her brother. James lifts his hands in solemn deference.

"She wants to go, Quinn," James says. "She is not my daughter, so I have no authority to tell her she cannot."

"I thought she was helping with your children," Quinn says. "I thought Claire needed the help."

"She did. Claire and I are both grateful for Rose's help. Our children are thankful, too. But Claire is getting better, the boys are getting older, and Rose wants her own life now."

"So what? Am I supposed to go and save her?" Quinn asks. "Bring her back here where it's just me and barren fields? She won't go in for that."

"Rose would never admit it, and she'd kill me if she heard me say it, but she misses you. She needs you, Quinn."

"She knows she is always welcome back."

"Pride keeps her from returning. She left, and she wants to be chased. Go get her. It breaks her heart to picture you here alone now that Dad's gone."

James's words reach Quinn. She wipes her eyes. "It breaks my heart, too," Quinn says, choking on the admission.

"We can't let her join up with that group, sister," James says.

Quinn nods agreement. "She know you came here?"

"She thinks I went into town."

Quinn walks to a window. Spies Porter in the fields walking behind Quinn's stubborn horse. "Keep her two more days. I'll be there by the end of the week."

"Thank you, Quinn."

James stands, waits for Quinn to acknowledge his departure, but Quinn stays drawn to the window. James starts for the door.

"Dad's buried under the oak," Quinn says. "You should pay your respects before you leave."

James nods, embarrassed that he had not thought to visit his father's resting place when he first arrived. He opens his mouth to say something more, thinks better of it, and steps outside the house.

That night Quinn abandons the porch giving Porter a night free from talk of *The Bible*. Porter takes the chance to read long into the night, burning a candle down to a nub while the cicadas sing at the blackness. Porter is content, maybe even happy in his solitude. He closes his eyes and dreams of owning his own land, of sitting on his own porch away from politicians and wars. He could live in a world disentangled from the corrupted whims of men. The fantasy almost makes him smile.

The screen door bangs shut, forcing Porter to escape his fantasy. He opens his eyes and finds Quinn standing on the porch. Her presence, disturbing Porter's idyllic, solitary moment, irks Porter. He wonders why she is not asleep at this late hour.

Quinn paces the porch. She wants Porter to ask what is troubling her, yet she knows Porter will not grant her request. If Quinn wants to talk, the task, as always, falls to her to force the conversation.

She takes the chair next to Porter. Sinks deep into it like a man drowning under the weight of his regrets.

"It appears my daughter is thinking of heading into the Utah territory," Quinn says. "My brother tells me she may even become a sister wife. She's looking to marry my other daughter's husband."

Quinn pauses, giving ample time for Porter to interject his own thoughts. Porter ruminates on the information, but he does not think it worth making a comment.

"I gotta go try and talk her out of it," Quinn says. Porter hopes this means he can tend the ranch alone, but this hope does not last long. He knows the request that is coming before Quinn has even voiced it.

"I want you to come," Quinn says.

Porter runs his finger along the side rail of his rocking chair. The wood is rough, coarse. A splinter buries itself into Porter's thumb. He wants Quinn to retract her invitation. Her daughter's decisions do not concern him. Porter avoids meddling in the religious affairs of men. The entire enterprise is absurd.

"Will you come with me?" Quinn asks.

Porter knows Quinn's question is not a question but a demand. Porter must agree to this now, so he can keep working the ranch later. What he does not understand is why Quinn wants him to go with her.

"Why do you want me to go?" Porter asks.

Quinn rubs her eyes and gets to her feet. "I want you to bring your gun. If I can't convince her not to marry her sister's husband, I want you to shoot her."

Quinn enters the house before Porter can ask any more questions. Once inside she pauses, wondering if she must explain to Porter that she made her last comment in jest. But she does not return to the porch. The longer she dwells on it, the more she is not sure if she was joking.

CHAPTER 6

Quinn rides her horse at a clip that puts little strain on the stubborn animal. Porter walks beside them. Quinn promised they would take turns walking, but every time she asks Porter if he wants to ride, he does not respond.

The two-story colonial house comes into view just before dusk. Quinn spots a young woman—Rose—outside hanging clothes on a line. Quinn halts her horse and watches her daughter work. The sight of her daughter leaves Quinn breathless and consumed with sorrow. Even with the distance between them, she can sense her daughter's defeated countenance as she performs the rudimentary mundane house chores James has assigned to her.

As a child, Rose railed against domestication. She had opinions and theories early in life. Literature will do that to a girl.

Rose learned to read from *The Bible.* She spent her childhood with Quinn, huddled at the kitchen table, pouring over the holy text. Quinn felt the fundamental exercise was mundane, but Rose never seemed to tire of it. Each new passage inspired more questions, piqued a deeper curiosity. She loved learning. Often, Quinn had to defer Rose's questions to the men of the house. Her husband, Benjamin, was better versed in the scriptures, and when he could not provide answers to one of Rose's many inquiries, they consulted Quinn's father. He was the expert, a true biblical scholar. A self-proclaimed disciple of God called to help usher in the rapture. A question did not exist for which he did not know the answer. He delighted in Rose's thirst for spiritual knowledge and later in life scorned Samantha, the younger sister, for not inheriting the same traits.

A week after Rose's twelfth birthday, a fellow church member, Mr. Halliday, fell from his roof and broke his back. He never walked again, and after his accident his wife returned to Mississippi. She believed her husband's paralysis was proof that Rose's grandfather was no man of God. Several of his promised prophesies had not come to pass, and it became obvious that her preacher was not a vessel called to assist in the Second Coming.

Broken and alone, Mr. Halliday needed assistance. The church's remaining devotees divided the responsibility of caring for the injured member. Rose's grandfather assigned her to deliver dinner to Mr. Halliday every Wednesday—a responsibility she accepted with silent animosity. On her first Wednesday, she entered Mr. Halliday's home unannounced, stationed herself bedside, and spooned flavorless soup into the cripple's mouth. She could not leave soon enough. When she rose to say goodbye, she spotted a book on the opposite side of Mr. Halliday's bed. She crossed to the book and picked it up. *Macbeth* by William Shakespeare.

"Can I borrow this?" she asked. Mr. Halliday gleamed.

Rose returned home and spent the night reading the tangled language to her brother and sister. No one understood a word of it. Rose went to her parents for guidance, but the words made even less sense to them. Rose's grandpa was no help either. He would not even look at the text.

"All literature is a waste of time," he growled. "Read *The Bible*!"

Rose had read *The Bible*. She wanted something more. Although she could not decipher Shakespeare's cryptic text, she believed he spoke of things fundamental and worth pursuing. She returned to Mr. Halliday's home the next day.

"Do you understand Shakespeare?" she asked.

"Yes," Mr. Halliday answered.

"Will you teach me?"

His eyes glimmered. "I'd love to."

Rose sat down and opened the doomed play. She remained at Mr. Halliday's bedside for the next four hours drinking in The Bard's prose. She particularly related to the theme that women, especially Lady Macbeth, could be just as assertive as men. This was a concept Rose subscribed to, but never voiced for fear of a sharp reprimand from her grandfather. When Rose realized the sun had set over an hour ago, she thanked Mr. Halliday for his insights, and then stood to leave.

"Before you go," Mr. Halliday said, "peek into the bedroom on the left."

Rose went into the hall and entered the bedroom. Inside was a bookshelf littered with books.

"Choose which one you want to read next," Mr. Halliday instructed from the other room. Rose pulled *Gulliver's Travels* from the shelf.

Soon, Rose was visiting Mr. Halliday every evening. He taught her Shakespeare, Faust, Milton, Swift, Voltaire and others. She returned home each night with new knowledge and understandings. She bounced around the house, often in Quinn's wake, explaining newly acquired analogies and themes. Quinn and Benjamin supported their daughter's inquisitive nature. Rose's grandfather did not.

After reading Mary Wollstonecraft, Rose stopped being silent regarding a woman's assumed role as a homemaker. She believed women, especially herself, had more to offer the world than obedience to men. Her grandfather had heard enough. He sat her down and cracked opened *The Bible*. They revisited countless scriptures that "proved" a woman's duty was to God first and her husband second.

"Your lot in life is to find a husband," Rose's grandfather explained. "Any aspiration beyond that is an affront to God."

Rose turned to her parents for support. They lowered their heads, deferring to her grandfather's wisdom.

Rose continued visiting Mr. Halliday, but she no longer returned home eager to share with her parents or siblings what she had learned from Mr. Halliday. Her defiance to the outdated notion that she had no more to offer the world than appeasement to a future husband died when Mr. Halliday did.

She had just turned sixteen and found a package on Mr. Halliday's table one afternoon. Attached was a note that read: "Rose, you'll appreciate this. G. Halliday."

Rose tore open the package. Inside was a new novel—*The Scarlet Letter* by Nathaniel Hawthorne. Rose rushed into the bedroom. She greeted Mr. Halliday with a hug, took her bedside chair, and began reading. Five pages into the novel, Mr. Halliday began snoring. Mr. Halliday used to stay awake for hours while Rose read. Their discussions were enough to keep him engaged well into the night. It was obvious his condition was deteriorating. Now he could not outlast the setting sun. Rose slid out from the house, her new book in hand, and returned home.

That night, Rose and her sister became sick. Rashes covered their bodies. They were feverish and nauseous. Samantha vomited. Their bodies ached, and they remained bedridden for weeks. Then their fevers broke. A week later and Rose returned to Mr. Halliday's eager to resume reading *The Scarlet Letter.* She bounded inside and found him lying in his bed. He looked emaciated and somber. Rose approached and discovered he was dead. On his kitchen table was a note.

"The books are yours," it read. "G. Halliday."

To her grandfather's chagrin, Quinn and Benjamin helped Rose transport the burdensome books home. Rose mourned in her room for two days reading *The Scarlet Letter.* At the funeral, Rose's grandfather claimed a new sickness had invaded their community.

Something called the scarlet fever. The grandfather offered this proclamation behind a fiery glance at his granddaughter. The assertion did not go unnoticed: *The Scarlet Letter* caused the scarlet fever.

Three days later, while working in their watermelon patch, Rose's father keeled over and died. Again, Rose's grandfather claimed the red fever was responsible.

Rose had no way of discovering the truth. Yes, she and her sister had contracted scarlet fever, but the fever was not what killed Mr. Halliday. During Rose's monthlong hiatus, Mr. Halliday contracted pneumonia. He was already in a fragile state, and the pneumonia did him in. When his death was imminent, he penned the letter giving his books to Rose.

A simple heart attack took her father.

The Scarlet Letter did not lead to the scarlet fever, nor did Rose infect Mr. Halliday or her father with her illness. The deaths were just unfortunate coincidences. But a house rooted in faith ignores coincidences and instead chronicles all events to signs from above. Rose's grandfather made Rose believe that her reading caused her sickness, and when she did not abstain from reading, she infected others. She killed her friend and her father.

"God is teaching you a valuable lesson," Rose's grandfather explained. "You questioned your role. You questioned God. He took your father and Mr. Halliday to prove a point."

Rose dashed to her mother for comfort. She offered none. Having just lost her husband, Quinn's own grief racked her, so she could not assume her daughter's.

The grandfather's fear mongering worked. Rose never picked up *The Scarlet Letter* again, and any dissenting thoughts she had while reading, she locked in the recesses of her heart.

She tried, but she could not completely tear herself away from her books. When they sparked thoughts that did not align with her grandfather's teachings, she always fell to her knees and prayed for forgiveness. When she left for her uncle's ranch, she kept all but one of her books behind. Abandoning them was the only way to rid herself of their temptations.

Watching her daughter now, trained and submissive, pangs of regret sting Quinn's heart. Is it any wonder Rose is contemplating entering the Salt Lake Valley to find a husband and sentence herself to a life of domestication? Rose is just following the path her grandfather forced on her.

While these contemplative reflections arrest Quinn, Porter keeps walking, not wanting to stop just to start again. It has been a long day.

Children, six of them, play in the yard. They run about and act as children should. Quinn cannot help wondering if being surrounded with so much life assaults her daughter as a constant reminder of the things she does not have.

Rose pulls a wet shirt from the laundry basket and pins it to the line. She bends to retrieve another when she notices the two travelers. It does not take long to recognize her mother, but she cannot place the mysterious man who walks beside her.

Rose orders the children inside to wash for dinner. She finishes hanging the laundry and then follows the children inside the house.

The house is spacious. On the far wall hangs a large crucifix, polished and ominous. Its ornate appearance screams opulence. Underneath is a long oak table littered with various foodstuffs. James and his family sit at the table to supper. James assumes his customary position at the head. His wife, Claire, sits to the left. She is unappealing and plain. A devoted wife to a man of God. Sorrow laced with exhaustion lives deep beneath her eyes, but James has never called any attention to it, and Claire understands, being a Christian woman, it would be improper to voice her frustrations. Every day she questions her life choices, and every night she prays for forgiveness for feeling so unfulfilled. Her life is blessed, so she is often told, but she feels empty. If only she dared give volume to her despair, she could find twenty other women in her husband's congregation who suffer the same afflictions.

The children, along with Rose, fill out the rest of the dinner chairs. The children are well-mannered at supper time. James has driven the fear of God into them, and they do not act out or engage in childish antics customary for children their age. They sit with their hands in their laps, obedient, while their father blesses the food. Rose sits at the other end of the table. She appears distant and out of place, a bystander invading her uncle's family. She alone does not bow her head in prayer, but spies everyone with unexplained contempt while they showcase their devotion to God and James's solemn prayer.

Rose shifts her gaze to the door awaiting her mother's arrival. James finishes his prayer, and everyone recites a collective "amen." Claire lifts her head and gasps. All eyes follow hers to where Quinn stands in the doorway.

"Hello, Mother," Rose says.

CHAPTER 7

Porter prefers Quinn's home to James's. Fewer people and less noise. More privacy. More places to escape if he must decompress alone.

He finds a modicum of refuge on James's porch, but even now, while he sits outside, he cannot escape the conversation between Quinn and her daughter. Their voices carry, penetrating the wall that shields them from Porter. He takes up a book and tries to read. It is a struggle to focus.

"What are you doing here?" Rose asks.

"I came to see you," Quinn says.

"You've never come to see me."

"I have a ranch to tend."

"You could write."

"I have. I sent letters."

"Two letters," Rose says. "Two letters in a year."

"I figured you didn't want to hear from me."

"You're my mother."

"I'm sorry, Rosie," Quinn says, and Rose can sense she means it. "Grandpa got sick and the ranch…" Quinn trails off. "There's no excuse for my behavior."

"I'm sorry about Grandpa," Rose says, softening her tone.

"Is it true about Sammy?" Quinn asks. "Is she pregnant?"

"James told you?"

Quinn nods. "Is it true?"

"That's what she tells me."

"She tell you anything else?"

Rose displays a hurt smile. "I suspect you have these answers, Mother. I'm sure James told you everything."

"Please tell me you're not considering—"

"I am."

"You can't go to Utah, Rose. Those people…they…they're not real Christians."

"That's not true," Rose retorts. "They believe in Christ, Mother. They do."

"*The Bible* warns of false—"

"They believe in *The Bible*."

"No, they don't," Quinn says. "They read a different book."

"They read them both. They honor them both. It is possible to find truth in more than one book."

"Do you really want to share your husband with four other women? Not women—girls! One of which is your sister?"

"*The Bible* speaks of polygamy," Rose says.

Rose's defiance frustrates Quinn. She has an answer for everything. Why must God curse her with insolent daughters?

"It's not a real religion," Quinn says.

"Then what is it?"

"It's a cult!"

"It's not!"

"Their leader was murdered in a jail."

"Brother Smith is a martyr. Just like Christ!"

"He is nothing like Christ!" Quinn barks.

"He died for what he believed in."

"He was an adulterer and a con man."

"God chose him," Rose says. "Angels spoke to him. They told him he needed to restore—"

"Who's telling you these things, Rosie?"

"Sammy."

"Sammy has fallen under the spell of—"

"It's not just Sam, Mother. It's others. Hundreds are going to Utah. Brigham Young's flock is ten times that of Grandpa's or even James's. If their church weren't true, why would God lead so many astray?"

Quinn opens her mouth to voice her rebuttal, but a door behind her creaks open. Rose and Quinn turn at the sound. James stands in the doorway, Bible in hand. His reading glasses hang low on his nose. His eyes are intense, and he stares hard at Rose, angry with her assertions. Rose blanches under his gaze.

"I'm trying to write my sermon," James says. Quinn and Rose note the annoyance in his voice. Quinn mumbles an apology; Rose lowers her head in deference. "If this conversation must continue," James says, "perhaps you could take it outside?"

"Sorry," Quinn says. She looks at Rose, tired and defeated. "We'll finish this tomorrow."

Rose sighs and pushes past her mother. She debates going upstairs and into bed, but their argument has heightened her emotions. Sleep would be a failed endeavor. She changes course and exits the house through the front door. On the porch she stops to collect herself.

She looks to the heavens, beckoning guidance and pleading for patience. She closes her eyes and measures her breath to soften her rage. When she opens her eyes and turns back to the house, she finds Porter alone on the porch. Although he pays her no attention, his presence startles her. She shrieks, but Porter does not react. He has a book opened and is reading, indifferent to Rose. She appraises Porter, skeptical about him for reasons she cannot understand. She approaches him.

"Who are you?" she asks.

Porter ignores her.

"What book is that?" she asks and cranes her head and reads the title: *Moby Dick*. Recognition seizes her—the book is hers. She snatches it from Porter. "This is mine," she cries. "Why do you have it?"

Porter looks at Rose as if seeing her for the first time. His eyes bury deep into hers. She retreats a step.

"I've asked you three questions, and you have answered none of them," Rose says. "Are you mute? Or Perhaps you're just slow?" Rose waits for a response that does not come. "If you are slow, I don't see how you could read, let alone understand, a book of such literary merit," Rose sneers.

Porter stares at Rose for a lifetime. It is easy to find Quinn in her. Rose buckles under Porter's sharp glare. She turns away, and he averts his eyes and gazes into the night. Rose becomes indignant by his indifference.

"I'll ask again, and I demand an answer: Why do you have my book?"

Rose gives Porter ample time to answer, but he gives no indication that he plans to offer one. Rose is about to inquire a third time, when Porter, knowing she will not stop asking until she receives an answer, says: "Your mother said I could read it."

"Oh, did she? Well, it is not hers to give."

Rose turns the book over in her hands, unsure what to do with it now that she has it. When she reflects on it, she does not care that her mother lent the book to this stranger. She cannot explain her behavior. Her anger has nothing to do with books.

"What else of mine have you claimed for yourself?" Rose asks.

Porter stays silent.

"Why are you here?" Rose asks.

Porter looks out into the night.

"You are very rude," Rose says. "Do you know that? It wouldn't hurt you any to be civil." Rose gives Porter a minute to speak before starting for the house.

"I came with your mother," Porter says. He questions why he says this. Had he kept silent, Rose would have left him alone. That was what he wanted. Or at least, that is what he thought he wanted.

Rose pauses at the front door and turns to Porter. "That much is obvious," she says. "*Why* did you come with my mother?"

Porter picks at a callus lining his palm. "I'm supposed to shoot you if you decide to take up with the Mormons."

Rose gasps and examines Porter. "Is that meant to be a joke?"

Porter shrugs.

"What does it matter to you or my mother what religion I decide to 'take up' with?" Rose asks.

"It doesn't," Porter answers.

"It appears it does," Rose says. She moves to Porter and narrows her eyes. "What are you to my mother?"

Porter does not answer.

"Are you living with her on my grandfather's ranch?"

Porter does not answer.

"Where did you come from?"

Porter does not answer.

Frustrated, Rose slaps the book in her hands and stomps her foot. "Why won't you answer me?"

Porter sighs, inconvenienced. "I suspect if I answer you, it will lead to more questions, and then I can't enjoy the silence."

Rose scoffs. "That is a peculiar thing to say."

Porter pulls the callous from his palm and flicks the dead skin to the ground.

"I figured you came with my mother as an authority to talk me out of going to Utah. Is that why you are here?"

Porter stares into the night. Rose opens her mouth to ask another question when Porter shakes his head.

Rose studies Porter. His features are rigid. His eyes calculating. Wiry veins traverse his tan arms. She suspects he is a man of labor, not one prone to the intellectual insights found in literature.

"Do you know about Mormonism?" Rose asks. "Or about Salt Lake City?"

Porter yawns.

Rose inches closer to him and goes on in a gentler tone. "That's where my sister is. She wants me to join her church. Become a Mormon like her." Rose waits for Porter to react; he does not. She has never met a man who operated with so much indifference. This conversation serves no purpose.

She holds her book out to Porter. "Here. You can read it."

Porter takes the offered book and nods.

"I never would have suspected you as a reader," Rose says. "Just based on your appearance."

She does not know why she offers this slight. Perhaps it is because his disinterest strikes her and insulting him may showcase her own apathy. Perhaps it is something else.

Porter caresses the book cover and places the novel in his lap. Rose can sense he is grateful for the book.

"Do you want to know what I would take you for?" Rose asks. "Just based on your appearance and the impeccable conversation skills you possess?"

Porter remains inscrutable. Rose's indignation is near eruption.

"A savage," Rose says, answering her own question. "You look like a savage."

Rose designed her comment to hurt. Porter knows this, but he does not care. Her remark does not sting, but it awakens something in him. He does not begrudge people worshiping how they wish, but it is arduous to remain mute when he encounters a Christian acting ignorant of her pretend faith. Rose's ignominy is what forces Porter's tongue.

"Try not to hurt your arm while casting your stones," Porter says.

"I am not casting stones," Rose says.

"You called me a savage."

"Was that inaccurate?"

"Savagery is for the religious and the rich," Porter says. "I'm neither."

Rose's mouth drops open while she contemplates Porter's assertion. She feels it contains an insult somewhere, but she cannot decide what it is or to whom he directed it.

"That is a hard thing to say," she says because she does not know what else to say.

"No harder than labeling me without knowing me," Porter says.

"Then explain yourself," Rose says. "Tell me who you are. Tell me what you are."

Porter crosses his arms and leans back in his chair.

"Just as I suspected," Rose says. "You must be hiding or running from something." Rose waits for this analysis to warrant a response. It does not. "Or maybe you're running *from* someone," she says.

Porter still does not react. Getting him to speak has become a game for Rose. She hates his coldness. She wants to leave him, to reciprocate his rudeness, but something keeps her immobile. Keeps her prodding for an entry into Porter's stoic demeanor.

"Where are you sleeping?" Rose asks, hoping a change in subject will garner a better interaction. She does not expect an answer, so she adds: "You can at least reveal that much, can't you?"

"Out here, I guess," Porter says.

"The bugs will eat you alive," Rose says. She can sense, however, that Porter does not care about bugs. He does not care about anything, it seems, other than books. "You can sleep in my room," Rose says. "I can sleep with the children."

"That's not necessary," Porter says.

"I know it's not necessary, but it is proper. I don't want to give up my bed, believe me. My uncle and mother told me I must. It's the Christian thing to do."

"The Christian thing to do is offer a bed and complain about doing so?" Porter asks.

Porter's discernment silences Rose. She lowers her head from her realized hypocrisy. "Take the bed, please," she says, then, as an afterthought, adds: "The moon shines right through the window, and there's a good reading candle on the desk."

Porter mulls over this and thanks her. He is not one to disregard a good reading light.

"So that's how to entice you to speak?" Rose says. "Offer you a good reading spot? Well, perhaps we have that in common. I wonder how many of my other books you have stashed in your bundle. Did you bring others?" Rose waits for an answer she suspects will not come. "I'm not upset if you did. I'm just curious is all. Maybe we could discuss them seeing how you're such an astute conversationalist."

"Just this one," Porter says, "and your Mormon book."

He does not know why he added the second admission, for he knows it will lead to more questions. Perhaps, he admits, this is what he wants.

Rose peers through the screen door to ensure no one is within earshot before sitting in the chair next to Porter.

"Have you read it?" she whispers.

Most of it.

"What did you gather from it?"

Porter shrugs.

"Please," Rose says. "Give me an answer."

Porter rubs his cheek and thinks. "The prose is lacking, and the story is derivative."

"Derivative of what?"

"Of works that came before it."

"What works?"

"*The Bible* for one. *View of the Hebrews*. Hoffman's Golden Pot."

Rose frowns. "What are you saying?"

"What I've already said."

"You think Joseph Smith…copied it?"

"It reeks of plagiarism."

"My sister is certain *The Book of Mormon* is true," Rose says, raising her voice. "Do you?"

Porter laughs.

"What is so funny?" Rose asks.

"The learned man and the fool can find truth in anything if they're looking for it."

"Is that scripture?" Rose asks, and Porter shakes his head. Rose considers Porter's axiom. "Well, I suppose there is some truth to what you say," she concedes. "People have an inclination to subscribe to things they find most agreeable."

Porter rubs his chin but does not respond.

"Has my mother told you anything about me? Or my sister?"

"Nothing worth repeating," Porter says.

"Did she really tell you to shoot me if I join the Mormons?"

"I believe she said it in jest."

"What do you know about the Mormons and their plight?" Rose asks. Porter considers the question but decides it is not worth answering. "Please talk to me," Rose pleads. "I...I feel so...lost. Please tell me what you know."

"I know I wouldn't get involved with them," Porter answers.

"Why?" Rose asks. "My sister is so sure they are God's loyal followers. She feels it when she prays."

"That's reason enough not to get involved with them," Porter says.

"How so?"

"Be fearful of the certain."

Rose pulls her brows together in confusion. "I'm not sure what you mean."

"If you're certain, you don't give yourself any room to be wrong."

"Why would anyone want to be wrong?"

"To evolve."

Rose massages her temples. She is growing weary of Porter's crooked wisdom. "You speak so vaguely. I don't understand what you mean. Being wrong does not help one evolve."

"I disagree."

"Of course you do. Cite me one example."

"Galileo."

"Galileo wasn't wrong," Rose counters.

"I know he wasn't. But the church was, and they still won't admit their error. Their certainty won't allow it."

"Why not?"

"Because their followers may start to question certain truths…certain…certainties if science can prove God's messengers wrong."

Rose cannot be sure because of the night, but she believes Porter punctuated his point with a knowing smile. She sighs, exasperated with her inner struggle, and studies the night.

"I need to walk to the well," Rose says. "Will you join me?"

Porter considers the offer, believes it best to decline, then without warning, stands to accompany her. Rose, surprised with his sudden willingness, gets to her feet and leads the way. From a window, Quinn watches.

CHAPTER 8

The sound of chopping wood wakes the house. Rose slides out from bed and ambles downstairs. Quinn drinks her coffee and stares out the window. Rose sidles next to her mom and follows her eyes to the barn. Next to the barn sits a massive pile of logs. Porter stands at the base splitting them. He is a sight. Every swing of the ax splits the wood into two even portions. He does the task with little effort. He may as well be casting a fishing line.

Porter rose with the sun so he could read on the porch undisturbed before the day stole the morning. Like any man, Porter does not know how many more sunrises he has. He wants to experience each one before they run out.

After the sun climbed the horizon, Porter made his way to the wood pile and found the ax lodged into a knotted log. He freed the ax from the lumber and got to work.

Porter happened upon the vast wood stack the night before while walking to the well with Rose. He made a note of it. Work entices Porter. Gives him purpose. Provides him a physical release from the demons he cannot exercise. He has been splitting the logs for more than an hour.

"At the rate he's going, he'll have that pile split by noon," Quinn says. Rose watches Porter in a trance, hypnotized by his movements, by him. She bites her bottom lip and tugs at the knot on her sleeping gown.

"Keep your thoughts clean, dear," Quinn teases. Rose returns from her reverie, blushes, and turns away from the window.

"You want to take him some water?" Quinn asks.

Rose opens her mouth to answer, but her mother's knowing smile is intolerable. Rose pivots on her heel and sprints up the stairs. Quinn shakes her head, having forgotten the wild inclinations of youth.

An hour later, Quinn appears from behind the barn carrying a tin cup of water. Porter halts the chopping and flicks the sweat from his brow.

"James is much obliged for your efforts," Quinn says. She hands Porter the water. "He doesn't have much time for the chores. His sermons require most of his attention."

Porter downs the water. Some spills onto his chin, and he wipes it away. He hands the cup back to Quinn and returns to the logs.

"James says to split the pile in two," Quinn explains. "He says if you chop it, we can take half back with us. That's a square deal if you ask me."

Porter splits a log. He takes the two pieces and tosses each into two new piles.

"I noticed you were talking with Rose last night," Quinn says. She looks over both shoulders to ensure no one other than Porter can hear this conversation. "She say anything?"

Porter splits a log and glances at Quinn. "About what?" Porter asks.

"About going to Utah?"

Porter shrugs.

"What does that mean?" Quinn asks. "Use your words. You must know some with all those books you read."

Porter pauses, ponders how best to answer Quinn. "She hasn't said anything you haven't already discerned," Porter says.

"Do you think she'll leave?"

Porter shrugs.

"Do you think she should?"

Porter shrugs.

"What would you do if you were me?"

Porter shrugs.

"You're a pain in the ass, Porter." Quinn says.

Porter nods.

"And now you've got me swearing," Quinn says. She watches Porter a moment longer and then starts back toward the house.

.   .   .   .   .

The family sits at the dinner table, each member in their usual spot. Quinn sits on the far end next to Rose. Porter takes his dinner outside on the porch. He is thankful the table cannot accommodate an additional guest.

An hour earlier Rose delivered his meal plate. A generous amount, and Porter was grateful for it. He earned it. He spent the day splitting logs, finishing in one day what would have taken James a month.

"You're welcome to come inside and eat with the family," Rose suggested.

Porter, as Rose suspected, declined the offer. She returned to the table and spent the next hour stealing glances at the front door hoping Porter would walk through it. He remained outside. She was not surprised.

Once James excuses the children, Rose hastens to the porch to recover Porter's plate. He has scraped it clean, and now full and content, he studies the night. She wonders what he sees. Wonders what thoughts find their way into his head. She gives him his reprieve uninterrupted. She gathers his plate and reenters the house.

Fifteen minutes later she returns to the porch. "I need to fetch more water from the well," she says. She looks anywhere except at Porter. "Would you like to join me?"

Porter takes his time offering an answer. Rose questions if he heard her. He gets to his feet.

"Will you speak with me, or will you remain obstinate in your silence?"

"I will speak if the conversation requires it."

"Is that your attempt at a joke?" Rose asks, a smile creeping on her lips.

"Did it make you laugh?"

"It did not," she says.

"Then it wasn't a joke."

"Is *that* a joke?"

"Did you laugh?" Porter asks.

Rose suspects this is as close as Porter gets to playful banter. "I'll be out shortly," Rose says. "The night may be cool, so I want a shawl."

She enters the house and returns a moment later, a shawl wrapped around her shoulders, her hair tied into a loose bun. She is beaming, beautiful. Porter feels to tell her as much but does not. It is not his place nor his character to voice such observations.

The sun has set. The moon's light cuts their path. Rose spies Porter from the corner of her eye. Porter senses her constant appraisal because he is doing the same to her. The moon lights their darkened features.

"Are you married?" Rose asks.

Porter shakes his head and realizes the night may conceal his answer. "No," he says. He is glad she asked this. He wants her to know he is unaccounted for.

"Have you a woman waiting for you?" Rose asks. "Wherever it is you're from."

"No."

They walk in silence. Rose contemplates how best to ask what she wants answered most.

"Have you ever…been with a woman?" Rose asks.

The question hangs in the air. Porter knows Rose struggled summoning the courage to ask something so personal. He takes his time in answering, prolonging her suffering. He waits for her to look at him and then gives a slight nod.

Rose is aghast. It is the answer she expected but hoped would not come. "But you've never been married," she points out. "Fornication is a sin."

"According to whom?" Porter asks.

"God," Rose answers, appalled she must state the obvious.

"He tell you that?"

"Not me, no."

"Who did he tell?"

"His chosen. He speaks to them."

"He speaks to them and then they tell you?"

"Yes."

Porter feigns contemplation, but Rose knows he believes her answer is nonsense. "How do you know they're telling the truth?" Porter asks.

"Who?"

"The people God speaks to."

Rose stops. "Why would they lie?"

Porter stops. "Why wouldn't they?"

Porter's assertions bewilder Rose. "Because they need to do God's work. It would not benefit them to lie."

"Men have a storied history of lying for their benefit."

"Men are corrupt," Rose counters. "God's prophets are not."

"Prophets are men."

"Yes, but God chooses prophets."

"So that recuses them from the vices plaguing men?"

"Yes."

"*Prophets*?" Porter repeats. "Plural?"

"I suppose so."

"God speaks to more than one?"

"If He chooses."

"So how can you tell which one is telling the truth?"

"What do you mean?"

"Suppose God speaks to your uncle, but he also speaks to Brigham Young," Porter explains. "Your uncle tells his followers God's will as does Brigham Young, but their messages aren't the same. Which one is right?"

Rose has never considered this. She searches for an explanation. After a moment, she finds one. "That is where prayer comes in," Rose says. "One must pray for guidance."

"I'm sure your uncle's followers will receive guidance that differs from Brigham Young's. Can they both be right?"

Rose knits her eyebrows together in consternation. "I have never pondered these questions. Can God not speak to both?"

"If he exists, he can do whatever he wants."

"Well, then it's settled." Rose says. She begins walking again.

"Sure," Porter says, "unless the people he speaks to are proven liars."

Rose stops. Anger in her eyes. "My uncle is not a liar."

"I never said he was."

"Are you saying Brigham Young is?"

"I've never met the man."

"Then what are you saying?"

Porter stares ahead, lost in a memory. He walks. Rose follows.

"In the war I fought alongside a man named Elijah Abel," Porter says. "Best soldier I've ever known. Probably the best man, too. By all appearances, Elijah was black, but he told me that his father was white."

"I don't understand."

"His father was his mother's slave master. He raped Elijah's mother. Several times. One such time produced Elijah."

"Why are you telling me this?" Rose asks.

"He's what one would call 'mixed race,'" Porter explains.

"So?"

"So, Brigham Young promised that when a mixed-race baby is born, it will die on the spot. He proclaimed it is God's will to kill such offspring."

"That's absurd!" Rose exclaims. "Did he really say that?"

"It is written in his Journal of Discourses."

"How do you know this?"

"You're asking the wrong questions, Rose. It does not matter what *I* know. What matters is what *you* don't."

"I'm trying to learn."

"Consider what I just told you about Elijah and Brigham Young's promise."

"I'm not sure I'm following."

"You have a mind—use it."

"I do!"

"Then why do you deny such obvious truths?"

"I don't!"

"The world is crawling with men pretending to know God's will. Has it never occurred to you something other than divine intervention may drive them?"

"Are you now casting aspersions on my uncle's church?" Rose asks. "My grandfather's?"

"Theirs and others."

"You may want to keep a civil tongue. Blasphemy is a sin."

"You sound like your mother," Porter says.

"My mother is a good woman."

"I agree."

"Then why speak in such a disdainful manner about her?"

"If she is such a good woman, why not go home with her?"

Rose turns a discerning eye toward Porter. "So that *is* why you're here? You have come to convince me to return home."

"I work on your mother's ranch," Porter says. "She asked me to come, so I came."

"Just like that?" Rose asks.

Porter nods.

"How well does my mother know you?" Rose asks.

"Well enough."

"Is she aware of your…propensity for…debauchery?"

"It has never come up."

"Well, it would be wise to keep your sins concealed. Mother has a low tolerance for sinners."

Porter laughs.

"You find your transgressions funny?" Rose asks.

"You and I differ as to what constitutes a transgression."

"And what, in your erudite disposition, would you consider a transgression?" Rose sneers. Porter dismisses her mockery. He is enjoying their dialogue, even if Rose is using it to hurl insults. He cannot remember the last time he engaged in enjoyable conversation.

Rose asks her questions again: "Cite me one example of what constitutes a transgression."

"Passing judgment on others as to the definition of a transgression," Porter says.

His words are sharp, and they cut Rose deep. She is appalled and halts her walking. Porter continues although he slows his gait. Rose runs to catch up.

"You may be the rudest person I have ever met," Rose says.

"You have mistaken chivalry for rudeness."

Rose guffaws. "Are you mad?"

Porter stops and looks hard at Rose, the moon outlines his sharp, rugged features. "Since I've arrived at your uncle's house, you've intruded on my solidarity, passed judgment on me, cast aspersions, and accused me of stealing books that your mother lent me. My reaction to your rudeness has been quiet dignity. I listen when you speak, and I only offer my opinions when you press me for them. And contrary to why you think I'm here, I've not told you what you should do with your life while you've belittled mine."

Rose absorbs Porter's rebuttal. She steps away, hoping the brief escape can restore her composure. "I'm sorry," she whispers.

Porter goes to her. Stops less than a foot away. She has her back to him. He places a gentle hand on her shoulder, and she turns. His eyes have softened. Rose desires to hug him, if only to experience the touch of another person, but knows it is not proper. She brushes past him and catches the breath that he has stolen. A deep silence cuts into their journey.

"Can I ask a question without offending you?" she asks.

Porter nods.

"Was she…pretty? The woman you…were with."

"Which one?"

"The one you…bedded," Rose says, reddening.

"Which one?" Porter repeats.

"Which one?" Rose cries and covers her mouth. "There have been others?"

Porter nods.

"Well, you are a savage," Rose says. "How many?"

Porter shrugs. Rose cannot fathom how the seriousness of his sin appears to eclipse him.

"Too many to count?"

"All but one were whores," Porter says. His admission contains no embarrassment or contrition.

"Whores?" Rose repeats. The word stings her tongue. "You have just dashed any remorse I may have suffered for judging you. I would appreciate tonight that you do not sleep in my bed. You probably have some Babylon strumpet you keep hidden somewhere scheduled to arrive once everyone is asleep. I prefer my sheets remain unsullied."

Porter cannot help but smile.

Rose is indignant. "I amuse you?" she asks. "I can see the wheels turning in your head. Looking to convince me you're just being *chivalrous*, but I will not fall for it! And yes, I'm passing judgment.

It's hard not to when you learn of the man that makes love to whores."

"I said nothing about love," Porter says.

"Of course, you didn't. I'm sure love's a foreign concept to someone with such stringent morals."

Porter reaches for Rose and takes her by the elbow. His touch is stern, but not meant to hurt, and it does not. He pulls Rose toward him and releases his hold.

"You want to go to Utah to marry a man who already has four wives, and you question me about morality?"

"They're his wives," Rose says. "God commanded—"

"God has nothing to do with it," Porter interjects. "God is just a guise used to hide men's perversions. You talk of whores? Your sister's husband is a whore and so is any man who uses God as justification to bed multiple women. Not women—girls."

Rose flushes at Porter's harsh assessment. "You cannot make such claims," she says.

"I know that so long as there are men, they will use God as a pretext to commit transgressions."

"That is not true!" Rose cries. "You must stop saying such things!"

Porter laughs.

"What is so funny?" Rose asks. "Why are you always laughing at me?"

"'I know not what all may be coming, but be it what it will, I'll go to it laughing,'" Porter says. "*That* is scripture worth following."

Rose knows she has heard these words before, but she cannot place the maxim. She scoffs and turns up the path. They walk to rest of the way in silence. When they arrive at the well, Porter lowers the pail. Rose watches him, fascinated and frightened, but above all, drawn to him in ways she cannot understand. He pulls the pail from the well and starts back to the house.

"You said all but one were…women of ill repute," Rose says.

Porter stops. Faces Rose, confused.

"When I asked about your…nocturnal habits," Rose explains. "You said one wasn't a…whore." Rose still cannot say the word without embarrassing.

"That's right," Porter says.

"Who was she? The one different from the others."

Porter escapes to a memory. "She was reason enough to sleep with whores," he answers.

Rose wants to say more. Wants to inquire further. *How could a woman drive a man to seek other women*, she wonders. She does not ask her question. They return home without saying another word.

CHAPTER 9

James, as usual, wakes early to revise his sermon. The morning is when he can get the most work accomplished uninterrupted. He enjoys the mornings. They are tranquil and void of the madness that accompanies a house with too many children. He always prays before writing. He, like most men of faith, believes God hears and answers his prayers. Offers guidance and inspiration. In a world of countless people, James is convinced God reserves an hour each morning just for him. Egotism masking as divine direction.

He does not get far into his sermon before the echo of driving nails captures his attention. He removes his glasses and massages the bridge of his nose. The labor coming from outside is a distraction he did not anticipate and cannot tolerate. James lacks the introspection to question why God would permit something to intrude in their spiritual work.

He stands and walks to the window. The rising sun peaks into his den. A silhouette of a man—Porter—hunches on the roof of the shed fifty feet from the house. Porter lifts his hammer and drives nails into the splintered roof rafters, securing shingles. James had forgotten about the shingling job. He is not a craftsman, so it is convenient for him to neglect such tasks. He had asked church members months ago for help repairing the shed's roof. Some gave half-hearted offerings, but most strode out from the church house avoiding the reverend's pleading stare. They had their own duties to attend to. Although James will never admit it, Porter is a godsend, even if his efforts prove distracting and performed on the Sabbath. Porter has provided James with enough wood to get his family through the winter. The repaired roof will be another luxury. He cannot find fault in Porter's labors, just the time in which he performs them.

An hour later, after giving up the struggle to write anything worth reciting, James exits his den. He finds Quinn standing at the kitchen window sipping coffee. She watches Porter with a wry grin spread across her face. Watching the war deserter work has become her custom. She suspects Porter's efforts are distracting to James, yet she also understands the necessity for the chores to be completed. She enjoys the conundrum this presents for her brother. Therefore, she smiles while Porter endeavours.

James ambles beside his sister. "Where did you find him?" he asks.

"He was just walking past one morning," Quinn says. "I asked if he would help dig Father's grave."

"He a deserter?"

"I know nothing about him other than he reads everything he can get his hands on, and he's the hardest worker I've ever seen."

"Desertion is a crime."

"Only in the states," Quinn says, but she is not altogether certain if she is right. "Oklahoma is a territory."

James does not dispute the point. He does not know the law well enough to recite it.

"It's the sabbath," James says. "I don't approve of labor on the sabbath."

"You're free to tell him to stop," Quinn says and smirks. James frowns, fearful that if he presses the point, his shed may never get new shingles.

"Should I conclude since he has no compunction for working on the sabbath, that he is not a man of faith?"

"I think that is a safe assumption."

"Should I also assume he will not be accompanying you for Sunday services today?"

"That too is a safe assumption."

"It's a poor example for the kids."

Quinn turns to James. "What is?" she asks. "Skipping church or doing the tasks you've neglected?"

Quinn does not understand why she desires to defend Porter. Maybe it is not so much she is Porter's ally as she is James's adversary. Truth be known, Quinn had hoped Porter would join them for Sunday service.

James brushes past Quinn. As he does, Quinn spots Rose standing at the living room window, eyes fixed on Porter. She bites her lower lip and clutches her robe tight at the neck. Like her mother, watching Porter work has become her morning ritual.

"He'll be staying with me for a while," Quinn says. "Said he'd help me get the ranch back to working order."

Rose turns to her mother.

"Should that interest me?" she asks.

"Looks like it may," Quinn teases. "Seeing how you're staring out that window and gnawing on your lip."

"What are you implying, Mother?"

"You seem to like him."

Rose tightens her mouth. "Leave it to you to find a suitor who works on the sabbath and beds women of ill repute," Rose says.

"Women of ill repute?" Quinn repeats. "Child, what are you talking about?"

"Your ranch hand has loose morals," Rose says. "He told me last night he's…he's been with women."

Quinn looks out at Porter and fits this new piece of knowledge to the man she barely knows.

"I suspect from your tone those women did not include his wife?" Quinn asks.

"He's never been married."

Quinn absorbs this new information. "Well, I reckon that is a flaw in God's design. It seems any man who can plow a field or split a log has danced with the devil in some capacity."

"What are you saying?"

"You are probably too young to remember your Uncle Otis."

"Dad's brother?"

"That's right."

"What about him?"

"He chased every skirt and bottle of whiskey he could get his hands on. When the women and whiskey got stale, he gambled like the world was on fire. But he was also the hardest working man I'd ever seen before Porter. Otis got the brawn, and your father got the brains."

"I never knew you to be so accepting of such depravity," Rose says.

"It's not my place to judge, Rosie. Porter may have a storied history, but unless he brings his iniquities to my doorstep, I will not burden myself with them."

"It does not bother you to learn he's slept with whores?"

"Rosie, before our conversation this morning, the only other person I knew who associated with whores was Christ. If I cannot begrudge my savior, how am I supposed to resent a simple ranch hand?"

Quinn's wisdom silences Rose. She steals one last glance at Porter before ascending the stairs to change into her Sunday best.

■　　■　　■　　■　　■

When the family returns from church, Porter is gone. Over dinner James comments that Porter likely deserted them like he had deserted the war. No one seconds his assertion; no one dismisses it, either. Quinn knows the comment serves only to highlight James's own insecurities. Porter has spent the week doing the things James cannot. He wants Porter to desert. He believes Porter's flaws somehow mask his own.

Porter's absence saddens Rose. She does her best to hide it. Quinn wonders why Porter left without finishing the shed. It is unlike Porter to leave a job unfinished. After dinner, Quinn rides her brother's horse a mile in either direction looking for Porter. She does not find him.

The next morning Rose wakes with a start to the echo of hammering nails. She rushes down the stairs and draws back the curtains. Porter kneels on the shed finishing the job he abandoned the previous day. Rose smiles.

"You're happy to see him?" James asks.

She drops the curtains and steps away from the window. "Uncle, you frightened me."

James casts a judgmental stare to his niece, lets it linger for a painful beat, and then enters his den. Rose waits for the door to catch and then peeks behind the curtains again.

Porter works through the morning. Quinn brings him warm biscuits and iced tea for lunch. Porter takes the offering without saying a word. He downs the iced tea and hands the glass back to Quinn. She does not ask where he spent the night. Porter shoves an entire biscuit into his mouth and returns to the shed. Quinn returns to the house.

Porter sets the final shingle just before dusk. He surveys his work, pleased. In the nearby trough, he washes himself. He can smell food. Chicken, beans, cornbread, pie. His mouth waters. He hopes Rose will bring him a plate.

He retires to the porch with a book. The spread inside wafts through the wooden home and teases Porter. Rose exits the house carrying a massive plate. She hands over the heaping portions, and Porter nods his appreciation. Rose stands immobile for a moment, wanting to say something, but words escape her. She digs a toe into the porch's floorboards.

"We surmised you'd left us," Rose says, giving voice to what had troubled her all day.

This is not a question, so Porter does not offer a response. Had she asked, he would have told her he spent the night next to a creek under a large oak tree. He noted the spot about four miles outside James's home when he and Quinn had arrived the previous week. It is a pleasant spot. The grass under the tree is soft, and the creek water is cool. Porter stripped naked and washed himself in the water.

Porter made for the oak and the creek because he did not want to be present when everyone returned from church. He knows it is best to avoid Christians once they return from a service. They feel inspired and will try to convert anyone who will listen to their Christian philosophies.

The temptation to not return at all plagued Porter. He does not like James. He is a man devoted to God, and he uses his faith to recuse him of other obligations—like chopping wood or roofing a shed. Porter does not consider faith a good pretext to abscond life's responsibilities.

It is a mystery how much longer Quinn will stay with her brother. Porter trusts Quinn will never leave if it means Rose will stay. Not since the day Quinn arrived has she mentioned Salt Lake or the Mormons to Rose. She believes if she does not discuss the reasons that inspired her arrival, Rose will not act on any desire to leave for the Utah territory. Porter finds it all ridiculous—not speaking on the things that need addressing.

Quinn's inaction is why Porter considered sleeping under the oak and then starting for the ocean with the rising sun. His time at James's has expired. He woke before the sun so he could pass the preacher's house before anyone was awake. But he stopped. He knows why he stopped even if he will not admit it. Rose.

He paced outside the yard for several minutes before dropping his bundle and climbing onto the shed to finish the job. He had already worked up a sweat by the time the sun had risen. With every nail he drove, he tried convincing himself to forsake the shed and journey west to the ocean. He wishes more than anything he would have. His presence, he will learn later, only brings grief.

These thoughts inundate Porter while Rose hovers nearby, waiting for him to say anything. She wants an explanation for his absence but knows it is an entitlement she will not receive.

"I'm glad you're back," she says. "I'll come gather your plate later."

As promised, she returns an hour later. Porter has scraped the dinner plate clean and now sits reading a book. Rose carries her own book. She hands it to Porter.

"It's my favorite, so be careful with it," she says.

Porter closes his book and takes Rose's. He reads the title: *Wuthering Heights.*

"Have you read it?" Rose asks.

Porter shakes his head.

"Well, I hope you enjoy it." Rose says. She stands awkwardly, not sure what to do next. Porter fingers the book's spine and thumbs through the pages. His hands, so rough and raw, always turn tender when handling a book. Rose observes this and wonders how he would handle her if they ever touched. She pushes the thought from her mind and takes Porter's empty dinner plate.

"You are a romantic," Porter says.

Rose straightens. "Aren't all women?" she asks.

"Not whores," Porter says.

Rose is not sure if he offers this as a joke or an absolute. His stoic demeanor does not imply which.

"Are you looking to offend me?" she asks.

Porter glances at her; he does not answer, but his eyes are warm.

"I...want to apologize for my conduct when we walked to the well," Rose says. "Although I don't think my behavior warranted some of the things you said, nevertheless, it was unchristian of me to judge you the way I did. I am not your judge. God is."

Porter makes no reaction to this. Rose sits in the chair next to him. She glances at the door and the turns back to Porter.

"Can I ask you something?" Rose says. She knows Porter will not answer, so she poses her question without waiting for permission. "What is it like to…be with a woman?"

Porter scratches his chin, digging past the beard that has overtaken his face. "It fulfills a physical need," he says.

"What about love?" Rose asks.

"Love?"

"Yes."

"You mean like in your books?"

"Yes."

"I wouldn't know," Porter says.

Rose studies Porter. She detects something hidden in his expression. "You're lying. A woman always knows when a man is lying." Rose's boldness surprises her; she is even more surprised when Porter does not contest her analysis. "Who was she?" Rose asks.

Porter has no intention to answer.

"You're a deserter, aren't you?" Rose says. "When you left the fighting, why didn't you return to her?" Rose waits for an answer she knows is not coming. She fires off a series of questions. "Did she die? Did she leave you? Did you leave her?"

Porter remains unmoved by her inquiries. Rose perceives her cause is lost. She stands. "It's supposed to rain tonight," she says. "I'll be in with the children. You're welcome to my bed again." Rose takes Porter's empty plate and starts for the house.

"Rose," Porter says.

Rose stops and turns to Porter. He is holding his own book out toward her. She takes the novel and studies the cover: *Frankenstein*.

"That's my favorite," he says.

Rose understands the significance and intimacy of this gesture. She nods and enters the house. Porter stares after the door hoping she will return. She does not. Porter returns to his seat. He opens her book and reads.

CHAPTER 10

The children play outside. Running and making trouble the way children do. Porter stands at his bedroom window and watches. Envious and appreciative of their playfulness. Wishes he could reclaim his own childhood. Wishes for a lot of things.

If asked when grief and harsh realities replaced his childlike innocence, his answer would be immediate—the day he learned about his father. It was the same day his mother explained the bruises were not from clumsiness but from poor matrimonial judgment. Porter understood but pretended he did not. Listened while his mom described, through split lips and broken teeth, how his father had hit her.

"Why?" Porter had asked.

His mother shook her head and answered: "Because he can."

That was Porter's first lesson in a series highlighting how weak men will stop at nothing to feel strong.

The first time Porter watched his father strike his mother, he abandoned any remaining notion that life was harmless and unassuming. He began intervening in the assaults and often succeeded in transferring the father's rage from mother to son. The days that followed were always the same. Porter's father would recite *The Bible*, excusing his behavior while explaining his anger resulted from *their* actions. He was justified because The Holy Book made it so; they were at fault for the same reason.

Relief blanketed Porter when he killed his father. And although his mother never admitted it, relief swept through her too.

She was away at her sister's. Helping the local midwife deliver a child who would not enter the world alive. At home, Porter emptied the whiskey bottles and waited. The moon was high when his father stumbled home drunk. He reached for a bottle and brought it to his lips to ensure his inebriated state would last long into the night. When no spirits emerged, he cocked one eye over the neck and glared inside. It was too dark to see anything. He turned the bottle over, confused by its emptiness. Porter stood in the corner and watched. Waited for his foolish father to understand what Porter had done. His father stumbled and faced his son and asked what happened to the whiskey. Porter did not answer. His father asked again and received the same answer. He understood. The anger came quickly. Porter's father threw the empty bottle at his son. Porter ducked, and the bottle shattered against the wall. His father cursed him and advanced.

Porter ran outside, and his father followed. Porter baited him, swore at him, called him names, encouraged him to follow just a little farther, just past the trees to the creek. At the creek, Porter pretended to trip. His father increased his drunken step and reached for his son. Porter took hold of a tree branch he had stashed earlier. He turned on his father and struck him with all his force into his stomach. His father gasped and fell to his knees. Porter stepped behind him and swung the branch again, knocking his drunken dad in the back of the head. His father staggered and pitched face-forward to the ground. Porter laced his arms around his dad's shoulders and pulled him to the creek. His father muttered and spat blood, but his words were unclear. Porter jumped on his back and drove his father's head into the shallow water. He pressed all his weight onto his father until he gave up the ghost.

Porter made for home. He gathered all the empty whiskey bottles and returned to the corpse. He littered the area with the bottles. Once he finished, he walked home under a welcoming moon. He slept well that night.

Someone found his father the next day. No one questioned the accidental drowning. The town had lost many men to drunken stupidness. Some men just could not hold their liquor. Porter's mom did not cry at the funeral. She pulled her lips tight, clenched her jaw, and fought every urge to smile.

She and Porter had several good years after that. They often sat near the creek and read together, getting drunk on the silence, and lost in worlds outside their own.

Porter was bedside when his mother died. She coughed blood into dirty rags and when a neighbor asked if she wanted a priest, she shook her head and asked, what for? The neighbor, bewildered, said it was customary. Porter's mom laughed and told the neighbor to get out. Porter stroked her hair and told her he loved her.

The day she passed, tears flowed from her eyes, and she whispered "thank you" to her son. Porter looked down at her with inquiring eyes. *Thank you?* he thought. *For What?* Puzzlement then turned to understanding. This was the most they would ever speak of Porter's dad. His mother smiled and drew her last breath. Porter held her hand until the blood fled and the skin turned cold. He kissed her head and pulled the blanket to her chin and left the room.

In the next room, a girl waited. Porter entered the room and fell into the waiting girl's arms. She stroked his head and told him everything would be all right. He believed her.

The following month, the Conscription Act forced Porter into the war. He had no desire to fight, not out of cowardice but principle. He told the girl he would head west, to a land uninhabited by men ignorant enough to believe God preferred one color to another. He asked her to come with him. She shook her head. He could not convince her, but she promised to wait if Porter entered the war.

"What if I don't make it out alive?" he asked. She assured him he would. God was on their side, she claimed. He would protect Porter and all the righteous soldiers fighting for an ideology Porter did not support.

He entered, but she did not wait. The letter came soon after. The wound came soon after that. He never blamed her; all the blame was his.

■　　■　　■　　■

Quinn stands over Porter while he repairs a broken wagon wheel. Earlier Quinn had offered her assistance, but Porter shrugged her away, preferring to work alone. Now she hovers, watching Porter work, relishing in the knowledge that this is one more task he will complete because her brother cannot.

"I've noticed you and Rose talk often," Quinn says. This is an invitation to converse, but Porter keeps his attention fixed to the broken wagon wheel.

"She say anything about going to Utah?" Quinn asks.

"Nothing worth repeating," Porter says.

"She talk about her sister at all?"

"No."

"What about me?"

"No."

Quinn examines Porter, trying to decide if he is telling the truth. Porter, as always, appears indifferent and distant.

"Well, hell, Porter," Quinn says, "what do you two talk about every night?"

Porter stands, works the stiffness from his back. "Books," he says.

"Books?" Quinn repeats.

Children's laughter reaches Porter and Quinn. It captures their attention for a moment. Quinn watches the children chase each other about the yard. Recognizes her own daughter's innocence in James's offspring. Quinn recalls the days when Rose would trip and run to her to mend her scraped knees and bruised elbows. She would kiss them better and the crying would stop. Those days have passed. It is an ugly tragedy when a parent learns she can no longer protect her children from the pitfalls the world has in store for them.

"I don't want to lose her, Porter," Quinn says.

"Then don't," he says.

"How do you suppose I do that?" Quinn asks.

"Give her a reason to stay."

Quinn steps away from Porter. Paces. Debating whether to say what has been racking her brain. "It appears she may have taken a liking to you," Quinn says. "What if you were her reason to stay?"

Porter inhales.

"She needs a man," Quinn says. "A husband."

"I'm sure she'll find one," Porter exclaims.

"Trust me, son, you are not my ideal candidate."

"I am not a candidate."

"What are you then?"

"Just a drifter."

Quinn laments. "What do you want from this life, Porter?"

Porter focuses on the broken wheel.

"A mother wants what is best for her children," Quinn says. "I need to protect Rose." Quinn waits for Porter to respond to her remark, but he says nothing.

"Rose nearly had a husband before," Quinn says, reaching into the past. "Things didn't work out the way we had planned." Quinn pauses, rubs her neck. "I don't want to get into it."

"No one asked you to," Porter says.

"Your indifference confounds me," Quinn says as she takes a hammer and strikes the wagon axle. "You can't deny her beauty."

"I haven't."

"How are you not smitten?"

"Beauty is no reason to marry someone," Porter says.

Quinn laughs. "It is as good a reason as any."

"Not for me."

"Well, tell me then. What do you want in a wife, son?"

Porter works. Ignores the question.

"I see how you look at her," Quinn says.

"I look at her when she speaks," Porter says. "It would be rude not to."

"You don't cast eyes in my direction when I talk," Quinn mocks. "I think you fancy my daughter. Hell, Porter, this conversation proves it. The only time I can get you to say more than two words is when I speak of *The Bible* or my daughter. Anything else and you don't seem to have an opinion." Quinn spits into the dirt. "Just be straight with me, son. Do you feel anything for her?"

Porter remains silent.

"You obstinate fool," Quinn says.

Porter positions the wheel onto the axle. Hammers it a few more times and stands straight. "You don't even know me," he says.

"You can fix anything, till a field, and you're not Mormon," Quinn says. "That's good enough for me."

Porter shakes his head, incredulous.

"Don't you want a wife?" Quinn asks.

"No."

"Why?"

"I would not make a good husband."

"Why not?"

"Women tend to believe I have a hard time communicating."

Quinn cannot help but laugh, but she does not know if Porter is joking.

Porter sits on the porch looking out at the night. Rose sits in the chair next to him. A weak candle flickers on the small wooden table next to her. She leans toward the candle reading from *Frankenstein*. She finishes the book and closes it, stares into the night with a contemplative countenance.

"Who do you see as the monster?" Rose asks. "Victor or his creation?"

"Victor," Porter answers.

"I suspected that would be your answer," Rose says. "Why?"

"Victor is the creator. His creation repulses him, but he refuses to see his own flaws."

Rose considers this analysis. "So, in a sense, he's like God?"

"In the sense that God is a character in a book, sure."

"Victor created life," Rose says. "You don't see him as God?"

"I see him as an example of what not to be."

"So, you side with the monster?"

"Do I have to take a side?"

"Yes."

"The monster did nothing wrong."

"He's a murderer!" Rose cries.

"He only murders after suffering the indignities of man," Porter says. "He is a product of an environment Victor forced him to live in."

"Murdering for spite is not justified."

"For vengeance it is."

"I disagree."

"Of course you do."

"What does that mean?"

"Your sheltered life has not exposed you to the atrocities of man."

"My life has not been sheltered," Rose exclaims.

Porter will not contest her point. "The creature is what his creator made him."

"Creator?" Rose repeats, smiling. "You mean God?"

"I mean Victor."

"Victor represents God. The monster is Adam. Don't you recognize that?"

"I recognize the metaphor," Porter says.

"But you don't believe in God."

"I never said that."

"Do you?" Rose asks.

"Not in the traditional sense."

"What other sense is there?"

"I'm open to the possibility that something bigger than me, than us, exists."

"What do you call that?"

"An inquisitive nature."

Rose frowns at Porter's circular reasoning. She grapples with the truth that, aside from books, she and Porter have little in common. Even so, she cannot break the spell he has cast over her. He fascinates and frightens her. She wishes to crawl inside his head and reprogram the parts of him she cannot reconcile.

"What would you say if you could speak to your creator?" Rose asks.

"I spoke to my parents many times before they passed," Porter says. He declares every word with so much dryness. It is hard for Rose to discern when he is joking.

"Pretend, for my benefit, there's someone controlling all of this," Rose says, lifting her arms and spreading them across the vast expanse of land before them. "What would you say to Him?"

Porter takes his time in answering. When he speaks, his answer is not much louder than a whisper.

"I'd say thanks."

"Thanks?" Rose repeats. "For what?"

"For this moment."

Rose is touched. "Do you think someone is responsible for this moment?"

"Yes."

"Who?"

"Us."

"No one else?"

"No."

"That's bleak."

"Why?"

"It lacks…romance."

"I left a war and ended up here. You left your mother and did the same. It wasn't divine intervention; it was human decision."

"I don't believe that," Rose says. "Something…bigger brought us to this moment."

"That's convenient."

"How so?"

"It recuses you of any responsibility for your actions," Porter says. "You can always blame or give credit to God."

"Does He not deserve the credit?"

"Do you forsake your own accountability?"

Rose sighs and gets to her feet. She paces the porch. "Suppose God exists. He is everything we've been told He is. Does it not frighten you to think of the punishment that awaits you for the things you are saying?"

"What am I saying?"

"That He doesn't exist!"

Lightening flickers in the distance. A thunderclap follows, shaking the porch. Rose clutches a nearby pillar. Porter does not move.

"Did that frighten you?" Porter asks.

"It startled me," Rose says, returning to her chair.

"Zeus must be upset," Porter says.

Rose ignores his joke.

"Indulge me, Porter," Rose says. "Pretend there is a God, and you must stand before Him in judgment. What will you say when He asks why you denied Him?"

"I will say 'can you blame me'?"

"You will not. The courage you display now will escape you."

"Why would God bless me with the ability to think and then punish me for doing so?"

Rose contemplates Porter's answer. It contains a logic she cannot help but admire. "I fear what He may do with such ignominy." Rose stands and straightens her dress. "I need to put the children to sleep," she says.

"Have I upset you?"

Rose searches for how best to answer him. Several times she opens her mouth to speak, but she halts her thoughts and keeps them unspoken. She starts for the house. At the door, she pauses and turns to Porter.

"I cannot decide what I think of you," she says.

Porter nods. "Maybe it is time I left this place."

"I'm not sure I want you to leave,"

"You're also not sure if you want me to stay."

"I want you to be something you're not."

"No," Porter says. "I'm fine how I am; it's everything else that you want to be different."

Porter stands. He walks to the door and opens it for Rose. She hesitates before stepping into the house. The door slaps shut behind her. She turns, expecting to see Porter in her wake, but he has remained outside. She walks to the window and pulls back the curtain. Porter remains outside with his head turned to the sky. The rain is falling. Porter walks into the storm, his head turned upward to the heavens. *He almost seems happy,* Rose thinks. *Almost.*

CHAPTER 11

Quinn and Porter arrived at James's ranch nine days ago. During that time, other than retiring to Rose's bedroom to sleep, Porter can count on one hand the occasions that required him to enter the house. He has no business in the house. The neglected ranch had enough chores to keep Porter occupied. He has repaired all that needed repaired. He has split logs and planed wood and mended fences. Now he is bored. Which is why he is now standing in the living room of James's house—awkward and out of place.

Claire sits alone at the kitchen table knitting. Glaze blankets her eyes, and she works the needles without much thought. She is solemn and obedient and a perpetual exhaustion has robbed her of life. She exists only to please her husband. Claire reminds Porter of his own mother before Porter resurrected her by killing his father. Porter cannot bear to look at Claire. He clears his throat to capture her attention. Claire lifts her head and gasps upon seeing Porter.

"Oh, my," she says. "You startled me."

"Is Quinn around?" Porter asks.

"She is upstairs in the boys' room."

As if on cue, the bedroom door swings open and Quinn appears on the landing. She sees Porter. He stares up at her and motions outside.

"Sure, son. I'll be right down."

Porter walks to the shed where a healthy plot of shade casts a welcoming shadow in the scorching sun.

"What is it?" Quinn asks.

"We've been here for nine days," Porter says.

"Has it been that long?"

"I'm all out of chores."

"I'm sure James could find—"

"I have no reason to stay here," Porter says. "If you want me to go back to your ranch, I will. I'll plow your fields, plant your harvest, repair what needs fixing. If you don't want me anymore, I'll head west. Either way, I can't stay here any longer."

Quinn contemplates Porter's offer. "I'd hate to lose someone who works as hard as you do," she says. "I'd like your help on the ranch. The sabbath is in two days. Can you wait until the day after? I'll go back with you."

"What about Rose?" Porter asks.

"I'll ask her to come with us."

"What if she says no?"

"I don't know, Porter," Quinn laments. "She's a grown woman. I cannot force her one way or another. I suppose I ought to let her make her own decisions."

"What are you two conspiring about?" Quinn and Porter and find Rose standing with a laundry basket balanced to her hip.

"Porter and I are leaving Monday," Quinn says. "We were hoping you'd come with us."

Rose looks from Porter to her mother. "You're both hoping I come to the ranch," Rose asks, "or just you, Mother?"

Quinn turns to Porter, hoping he will offer some encouragement. Porter glances at Rose and then starts in the opposite direction. Both women watch him go.

"It appears he doesn't care if I come home with you," Rose says, her voice breaking.

Rose's comment reaches Porter. He stops. Something weighs heavy with him. He pivots, hastens his step, and approaches Rose.

"Can I help you with the laundry?" Porter asks. Rose hands Porter the basket. Together they walk behind the house to the clothesline.

Rose pulls a shirt from the basket and pins it to the line. Porter does the same.

"What is wrong with you?" Porter asks.

"I beg your pardon?"

"You're beautiful."

"Thank you."

"Smart."

"Thank you again."

"You're an upstanding Christian woman."

"Is there a question in there?" Rose asks.

"You want to be married, so why aren't you?" Porter asks.

Rose chokes on the question and reflects how best to answer it. She takes another piece of clothing and pins it to the clothesline, hoping the task can mask her grief.

"Has my mother not told you?" Rose asks.

"No."

Rose's chest heaves. This is ground she has tilled too many times and wishes she could leave in the past. She wipes her eyes.

"Five years ago I had a man," Rose explains. "He was kind and warm and smart. Or so I thought. Everyone suspected he would ask for my hand. Then one night, without warning, he disappeared. Ran away with another girl. Rumors spread. His family claimed he could not marry me because I was unclean, that I had been with other men." Rose stops tending to the laundry to collect herself. "His father believed my grandfather had lost his way. They made it their mission to besmirch our name. In the end, they left to start their own church. Took half of my grandfather's flock and my reputation with them." Rose's breath is heavy. She yanks a shirt from the basket. "People think I'm something I'm not."

"That's why you want to go to Utah?" Porter asks. "Because no one here will have you?"

"Utah would be a fresh start," Rose says. "My name isn't ruined there."

"You'd have to share your husband."

"If I stay here, I'll never get a husband."

"That sounds like the better bargain."

Rose blinks away the invading tears. "That's easy for a man to say. My entire life the church taught me to cater to the whims of men. When Steven fled, no one questioned *his* integrity. It was me who received the judgmental stares. The hushed and hurried gossip. This life is not a pleasant one for a woman." Rose lifts her head and meets Porter's eyes. Her chin quivers. "I don't want to be alone anymore, Porter. Can you understand that?"

A tear escapes Rose's eye. Porter steps to her, and with a gentle thumb, wipes the tear from her cheek.

"A marriage is not a solution to a problem," Porter says.

"It is my calling."

"That's absurd."

"It is written. I cannot pretend otherwise."

"And what about love?" Porter asks. "Could you love someone you had to share?"

"Love?" Rose repeats and stifles a laugh. "Love only happens in books, doesn't it? I used to live inside my novels."

"What happened?"

"I grew up. I cannot expect love. Only forced companionship."

"You will be miserable in Utah," Porter says.

"I will endure it, and I will be with my sister."

Porter says nothing else. There is nothing else to say. His eyes cut straight into Rose, daring her to choose a different life. She cannot handle it any longer. She turns and runs into the house, getting as far away from Porter as possible.

CHAPTER 12

Porter sleeps. He does not hear the door open. He does not see Rose enter. She closes the door behind her and moves without making a sound. She pads to the bed and sits down on the edge of it. Porter opens his eyes.

He does not react to her presence. She is nervous; he is not. She tries to speak, cannot, and tries again. Her voice is soft and full of fear.

"Did I wake you?" she asks.

Porter shakes his head.

Rose looks about the room. She knows why she has come, but she does not know how to ask for what she wants.

"I've never been with a man," she says. "Not in a…romantic way," she adds.

Porter stares at her.

"I shouldn't be here," she sighs.

She wishes to stand, to leave before making a bigger fool of herself. To escape the fantasy that has been playing in her mind since Porter arrived. Porter lifts the blanket, an invitation to be next to him, to consume him. This is what she was hoping for. This is why she came.

"I just want to be held," Rose whispers and Porter nods.

Rose turns from Porter and slides into the bed. She backs into him until her body meets his. It is warm; it is inviting. Porter receives her and pours his arm over her and pulls her into him. She shudders and closes her eyes. He buries his head in her hair and closes his own eyes.

.   .   .   .   .

Rose wakes before Porter. She slips out of bed without disturbing him. She edges to the door and stops. On the table, under the window, Porter's bindle spills open. Rose spies an envelope.

Rose turns to Porter. He still sleeps. She creeps to the table and inspects the envelope. The envelope has an even incision on its seam. Inside is a letter. She pulls the letter from the envelope. The white paper is yellowing at the corners. She reads.

Her eyes read the words, her heart digests them, gets lost in them, absorbs them. She finishes and reads the letter again. Moved and heart-broken, Rose looks to Porter. Wishes to hold him again, to press his body against hers and tell him all the things she cannot. Instead, Rose returns the letter to the envelope and exits the bedroom. Once she exits, Porter opens his eyes.

.   .   .   .   .

Rose stands at the clothing line taking down the laundry. In the distance she spots Porter. He walks with purpose away from the house. A pang strikes Rose's heart, and she wonders where he is going. Wonders why he did not think to invite her.

She pulls a bedsheet from the line and folds it, keeping her gaze on Porter as he continues away from the house. Quinn appears on the porch. She meets her daughter's eyes and offers a hurt smile. Panic swells inside Rose. Quinn approaches. She stands next to her daughter. Unclips a shirt from the clothesline and folds it. The laundry is a welcomed distraction. Keeping mother and daughter occupied while Rose steals glances at Porter. Watches as he disappears on the horizon.

"He'll be back tonight," Quinn says.

"Did you send him on an errand?"

"No," Quinn says. "There's nothing for him to do here. He said there's a nice reading tree next to a stream a little ways out. He's gonna spend the day there." Quinn folds another shirt and then as an afterthought adds: "Probably gonna read one of your books."

Rose imagines how it would be to sit under a tree with Porter reading a book. She imagines the discussions, the debates, they would have. And she imagines holding him and being held by him. And she imagines other things. Things she should not think but cannot escape. The fantasy is too much to comprehend. The weight of it makes her knees buckle.

"He's a…peculiar man," Rose says to fill the silence.

"The way you're staring after him makes me wonder if you want to spend the day by the creek, too."

Rose takes a dress from the basket and pins it. "I have my chores," Rose says.

"I could see to your chores, honey. Chase after him."

Rose scoffs. "And what would I say when I caught him?"

"Why must you say anything? He never does."

Rose laughs.

"James is grateful for all that you've done these past months," Quinn says. "He wasn't sure how he was going to juggle the kids and Claire's sickness."

Rose reaches for a clothes pin, and Quinn places her hand over hers.

"They don't need you here anymore, Rosie," Quinn says. Rose understands what her mother is saying. Her eyes ask what her voice cannot.

"And what would become of my life back home, Mother?" Rose asks.

"You would help me."

"I don't want that."

"Would it be worse than what it is here?"

"What do you mean?"

"Will you find a husband here?" Quinn asks.

Rose pulls her hand away from Quinn and returns to the laundry. Quinn's remark hangs with the laundered items.

"So it's settled," she says. "I should go to Utah."

"No, Rosie. You should come home."

"To what?" she cries. "Barren fields and a cold bed?"

Quinn has no response to this. She knows her daughter is right, and it stings to accept this truth.

"And what about Porter?" Rose asks. Her question comes out innocent, but Quinn notes the desire within the question.

"He has promised to help me until winter."

"And then what?"

"I can't say. He doesn't tell me much." Quinn studies her daughter, senses her confusion. "Do you want him to stay longer?" Quinn asks.

Rose sighs and turns away, but she knows how transparent she appears. She desires Porter. It is nonsense to pretend otherwise.

"He fascinates me," she says. Her admission sounds like a confession. "He doesn't look at me like the others. I told him of Steven, about how he abandoned me and ruined my name. Porter did not pass judgment."

"Do you love him?" Quinn asks.

"Love him?" she laughs. "I don't know him."

"The heart knows."

"Spare me the platitudes, Mother," Rose says. "I've known him less than two weeks. What I know about him frightens me. Besides, I would think you of all people would not want me involved with a man like him."

"A man like him?"

"An atheist," Rose says.

Quinn nods. "I dislike entertaining the possibility that you could settle for a pagan."

"But he's better than a Mormon?" Rose sneers.

"An atheist can always find God. A Mormon, I would guess, would have a harder time of it."

"Mormons believe in the same God as you and me, Mother."

"Sammy tell you that?"

"Yes."

"I have no idea what they believe," Quinn mumbles.

"I could teach you," Rose says, but Quinn dismisses the offer with a wave of her hand.

"Be slow to judge, Mother," Rose advises.

Quinn tightens and changes the subject. "Has it occurred to you that maybe you can bring enlightenment to Porter?"

"Yes, it has," Rose says, nodding.

"Maybe he's just confused. Lost. War does that to a man."

"He seems strong in his convictions."

"And what of your convictions?" Quinn asks. It is an innocent question, but Rose does not interpret it as one. She turns indignant.

"You question my convictions?" Rose asks.

"I meant nothing by it."

"I am a good Christian woman," Rose proclaims.

"I know you are, Sweetie."

"Then why say such a thing to me?"

Quinn trembles. "I've lost so much, Rosie. Your father, your brother, your sister, and my father. I don't want to lose you, too."

Rose lowers her head and Quinn takes her into her arms.

"Come home with me, Rosie" Quinn says. Rose rests her head on her mother's breast and looks for Porter, but the horizon has swallowed him.

CHAPTER 13

Porter returns with the dusk. A black silhouette outlined with the fiery sun. Rose sits on the porch, waiting. A plate of food rests on the table next to Porter's chair. When Porter appears, her heart stops. She will admit to no one how worried she was that he would not return. She buries her joy and assumes a false air of indifference. In his left hand he carries something. Her book.

He arrives at the porch and stops, sees his food plate, and flashes a brief, appreciative smile.

"It's getting cold," Rose says.

Porter sets the book on the table and takes up the plate.

"Did you need an escape from us today?" Rose asks.

Porter chews.

"Did you finish my book?"

Porter nods.

"Did you not think I would enjoy an afternoon reading beside a creek?"

Porter nods.

"Was I not worth inviting?" Rose asks.

Porter swallows a piece of chicken and licks the grease from his fingers. "I worried if you came, you'd spend the afternoon talking." The glint of merriment in Porter's eyes does not go unnoticed.

"One would think with how much time you take to speak that you would not say things so unbecoming," Rose says.

Porter takes a healthy bite from the chicken and chews. He will never tell her how much he wishes she would have accompanied him earlier. Her fantasies are his fantasies. The pride of lovers too often keeps them silent.

"Are you going to tell me what you thought of the book?" Rose asks after a long silence.

Porter swallows and screws his face up into deep contemplation. He exhales and resumes eating. Rose has grown accustomed to his mannerisms. This is not avoidance; it is deliberation.

"I suspect my opinions should remain my own," he says after a moment.

"You did not like it?"

"I did not say that."

"You did like it?"

"I did not say that either."

"Well, then, say…something," Rose exclaims.

Porter reflects for another minute and then answers: "I think it's…fitting."

"Fitting?" she repeats. "In what way?"

"In every way."

"Would you care to elaborate?"

"No."

"Why not?"

Porter finishes his food and places the empty plate on the table beside his chair. He wipes his mouth and turns to Rose.

"Do you really want to get into this?" he asks.

"Yes."

"You asked for this," he says.

"I did."

"Do you see the parallels between your life and Catherine's?" Porter asks.

This analysis has never occurred to her.

"Bronte could have taken our conversation at the clothesline yesterday and inserted it into her novel," Porter says.

"How so?"

Porter's face twists into pure bewilderment. "You cannot be this dense."

"I beg your pardon!"

"You are Catherine."

Rose scoffs. "Catherine?"

"Yes."

"Are you mad?"

"Are you not considering going into the Salt Lake Territory to wed a man for convenience?"

"My reasons for going into Utah are…are…"

"Ridiculous."

"They are to ensure my salvation."

Porter expels a healthy guffaw.

"Do not laugh at me!"

"I could not help it."

"Catherine did not follow her heart."

"And neither are you."

"I do not have a Heathcliff to follow!" Rose cries. "You call me dense? What about you? You see things through a lens that does not exist for a woman. I cannot walk and find work on some widow's ranch. I am confined to the lot I drew in life, Porter!"

Porter opens his mouth to speak, but a sigh escapes in place of a sentence. What he wants to say, he does not. What Rose wants to hear, Porter will not say. He cannot proclaim himself her Heathcliff. That is a responsibility he cannot carry.

"You're right," Porter whispers. He turns away from Rose and stares into the night.

"You don't believe that," Rose says. "You do not believe I am right."

"It doesn't matter what I believe."

"It matters to me," Rose says. She edges to the lip of her chair, hoping to detect Porter's countenance. His voice registers sorrow. *What does it mean?* She wonders. *What is he concealing?*

"Will you not look at me, Porter?"

Porter turns to Rose, locks her with his gaze. They remain arrested, swallowed by each other, hoping their eyes convey what their unspoken words cannot.

"I need a walk," Porter says.

He attempts to stand, but Rose places her hand over his and looks up at him.

"Please don't leave me," she says. Her eyes are pleading. Porter does not understand her fear. "I was so certain when you left today, I would not see you again. I fear if you leave now, it will be for good."

Porter looks at her hand on top of his. Rose follows his eyes and quickly removes her grasp. Porter wishes she would have left her hand where it was. Rose wishes the same. How frightening love is when it must be suppressed. Porter settles back into the chair and for the next five minutes, only the crickets speak.

Riddled with their thoughts, Rose grows anxious and burdened by something. She glances to the front door, checking for any interlopers. She drops her voice and avoids Porter's glance.

"I want to apologize for last night," she says. "I do not know what came over me."

"Will you be returning tonight?" Porter asks. Rose turns away, embarrassed.

"I will not," she says. "My Christian values won't allow it."

Porter stares into the night.

"I need to confess something," Rose says. "I read the letter you keep in your bindle."

Rose glances at Porter. He remains inscrutable, and she suspects he already knew of her snooping.

"Who was she?" Rose asks.

Porter's jaw clenches and his features sharpen. "Just a girl," he answers.

"Why did she leave?"

"She didn't," Porter says. "I did."

"You mean the war?" Rose asks, but she does not need him to confirm this. The country is riddled with soldiers leaving sweethearts to fight. "I imagined that hurt. Losing her," Rose says. "Her words moved me. I understand the woman's heart."

Porter shifts in his chair.

"Is she why you left the war?"

Porter crosses his arms.

"Is this too painful to talk about?"

Porter rubs his chin.

"Have I said something so awful you will not speak to me?"

"I could no longer fight for the confederacy," Porter says. "That's why I left."

"So you are an abolitionist?"

"I'm a humanist," Porter says. Rose senses this conversation is hard for him. She has never seen him on edge like this before. She wonders if his lost love causes his discomfort or if their earlier conversation is the reason.

"We don't need to talk about her if it is too painful," Rose says.

Porter says nothing.

Rose cannot discern if his silence is permission to continue with this discussion or confirmation that he wishes it would end. She thinks to reach for him. To place a comforting hand over his like she did a moment ago, but she senses he would not welcome the gesture.

"You frighten me, Porter," Rose says. "I worry what the next life may have for you."

Porter's intense eyes dart to her. "And I worry what this life holds for you," he says.

"What do you mean?"

"You're so worried about the next life that you're not living this one."

"That is an ignorant thing to say," Rose says. "Your comment hurts me."

"'The wicked take the truth to be hard'," Porter says.

Rose mulls over Porter's words. There is a familiarity to them, but their context escapes her. "Is that from your book?" she asks. "*Frankenstein*?"

"It's from *your* book," Porter says. "*The Bible*."

Rose blanches, embarrassed she did not recognize the reference.

"It appears I know your book better than you do," Porter says.

"Oh, you have a lot of nerve quoting *The Bible* to me," Rose says. "I am very much alive."

"Prove it."

"How?"

"Last night you came to my bed because you've never been with a man," Porter says. "You haven't lived."

Rose blushes and glances over her shoulder to make certain no one overheard Porter's recounting of the previous night.

"Must you remind me of my shortcomings?" she whispers.

"They are not shortcomings, Rose. They are desires."

"Yes, and we must control them!" Rose cries. "*The Bible* says—"

"It's natural…wanting human touch."

"I…I cannot…deny that," Rose stammers, flushed. "But when two people have not been joined in a union before God—"

"God would punish two people for succumbing to their natural desires simply because they are not wed?"

"Yes."

"Then to hell with your God."

"Watch your tongue!"

"Why punish people for acting on the instincts he cursed them with?"

"The iniquities of the world tempt us to strengthen our resolve. To show we can resist our impulses."

"You sound ridiculous."

"My devotion is not ridiculous!"

"To deny yourself the faculties that give you life is ridiculous."

"You do not know what you are saying. And I will repeat what I have already proclaimed: I am alive!"

"Kiss me."

Porter's demand stifles the air and knocks it from Rose's body.

"What?" she asks.

"Kiss me."

"Are you mad?" she asks. Her eyes shoot to the door. "I will not…kiss someone who is not my husband."

"You are a coward," Porter says.

"I am not!" Rose cries.

"I've seen your bookshelf. You don't want to know what the characters in your books feel?" Porter asks.

"I left my books at home so they could not tempt me," Rose says. "They were childhood fantasies, and God punished me for indulging them."

"Punished?"

"A fellow church member gave me a copy of *The Scarlet Letter*. Shortly after, Sammy and I came down with the scarlet fever."

Porter laughs.

"It is not funny!" Rose cries. "Within weeks the man who gave me the book died and so did my father. My grandfather proclaimed it was because of me. Because for a moment I believed I could find more truth in literature than in *The Bible*."

"You can."

"I cannot."

"Your books give you life. *The Bible* robs you of it."

"It does not!" Rose exclaims.

"Kiss me," Porter says again.

"No!"

"Why?"

"My morals—"

"Don't mask your cowardice as morality."

"I'm not!"

"Do you want to kiss me?"

"I…that's beside the point."

"No, that is the point," Porter says.

"Do you want to kiss me?"

"Yes."

Rose struggles to catch her breath. *How can Porter speak so openly about these things,* she wonders. *He is not nervous or scared.*

"I would…it would need to mean something," she says.

"It would," Porter says.

"Would it?" Rose asks. "Or would I just join the litany of whores you have bedded?"

"I have slept with whores," Porter says, "but I never shared a soft word with them."

"Is that what you call this? Sharing soft words? Your words could cut iron."

"Prove to me you're capable of living, Rose. Kiss me."

Emotion overcomes Rose. "You…are not…my husband," she says, her voice breaking. She stands. "I must help clean up."

She reaches past Porter to retrieve his plate, and Porter takes hold of her wrist. Now it is his turn to detain her. His touch is stern but somehow soft. She is confined, suspended between Porter and his dinner plate. She fights, with little effort, to free herself from his grip. Porter leans toward her, his lips inches from hers. She is terrified and excited and wants nothing more than to have his lips on hers. The moment is spellbinding, and she cannot break free to see if anyone has exited the house to witness this interaction. She does not want to escape his clasp, yet she knows she must.

"Tell me last night when you came to my bed, you did not feel alive," Porter whispers.

She takes in his breath, warm and welcoming. It runs through her body, causes her to shudder. He inches closer.

"Tell me you did not enjoy your body pressed into mine," he says.

Rose takes in his scent. Drunk with the pleasantness. He touches his cheek to hers. His stubble is coarse and inviting. If she turns less than an inch, her lips will meet his.

"It was a mistake," she trembles. "I should not have come."

"Last night is the most you have ever lived," Porter whispers.

"That…that is not true," she says.

Porter hovers his lips over hers. She cannot handle the anticipation any longer. She cannot resist the moment another second. Damn her morals! This is what she wants! She cannot deny this moment.

Her eyes close, and she waits for Porter to kiss her, to bridge the gap between his lips and hers. But he does not. He releases her wrist and sits back in his chair. Rose's eyes shoot open, confused.

Porter stares past Rose and into the night as if nothing had happened. She nearly collapses under the weight of her fleeting desire. Somehow, she manages to stand straight. Her reddened face struggles to regain its natural color. She checks the door and turns back to Porter. He will not look at her. He is done with the moment and with her. A single tear escapes her eye and runs down her cheek.

"I hate you," she cries. "Damn you for coming here. Damn you for surviving the war."

Porter offers no response, no reaction. Her words echo inside him, repeating through her voice what his own has proclaimed many times.

"Please," Rose says, wiping her eyes, "stop playing with my emotions."

She reaches across Porter and snatches his plate. She steals one more glance at him and then turns and walks into the house.

Porter takes in a long breath and holds it. He releases it slowly, wondering how he came so close to her kiss just to let her escape the moment. Even he cannot explain the rationale behind that absurd act.

CHAPTER 14

Porter knows she will come. He knows she will come just as he knew the other one would leave when he enlisted to fight. People have told him his entire life women are impossible to understand. They are not. Humans are simple. Men want power, and women want connection. The war proved both, while highlighting the heartbreak when neither is achieved.

Some women, desperate for a connection, will sleep with a man and foolishly believe the act will lead the man to her same desires. This works until it does not. This is how Porter knows Rose is coming to his room tonight. She will regret it later. If Porter were not a man plagued with his own desires, he would leave before Rose can arrive. A gentleman would escape before she comes to spare her the shame she will experience later. A shame rooted in the absurd notion that God only serves to punish. This is why Porter prefers whores. They reveal nothing. They expect nothing. He does not know if they feel anything or if their chosen life has beaten all the life from them. They are purely transactional. They are more dead than the men Porter has killed.

So Porter knows she will come, and he knows he is too weak to escape before she does. He wants her as much as she wants him. Maybe more. He cannot remember ever wanting something as much as he wants Rose. Tonight will haunt him forever. What is about to happen must happen, and it should not.

He sits at the small wooden table in the room's corner. Through the open window, the moon casts just enough light for Porter to read. He is thinking about her—not Rose, the other one—the one he refuses to name now. He believed he loved her, but he is not sure anymore. She had told him she loved him, but now he is not sure of that either. He does not care that Rose read her letter; he cares that he continues to keep it. The war, not the letter, is why he fled. The letter, just like the war, was inevitable. Which left him more damaged, the war or her abandonment, he does not know. Had she not sent the letter, had she remained faithful while he fought so he could return to her once the war had ended, their relationship would not have worked. Hindsight has proven as much. He was weak. So was she. Sending him the letter was the greatest gift she ever gave him. Perhaps that is why he keeps it. A reminder of the life he is grateful for escaping.

He closes his book. Reading is useless. He cannot concentrate. His conscience tells him to rise, take his knapsack, walk through the door, and never return. Exit Rose's life so she can retain a virtue she wishes to part with yet assumes doing so will damn her. But Porter does not move. Instead, he stares at the door. Then it opens.

Rose does not notice Porter sitting in the corner. She is too worried about waking the others to give the room a proper overview. With a delicate step, she creeps to the bed and sits on the edge of it. She runs her hand over the covering, expecting to find Porter's body. The bed is empty. She is confused, relieved, and saddened. Her virtue will stay intact, but her yearnings will remain unchallenged and heightened. *He must have known I would come*, she thinks. *This is why he fled*. She loves and hates him. Exhausted with the contradictions, she wonders if such paradoxes plague all lovers.

She looks to the window. The moon's muted glow penetrates the darkness. She finds Porter in the corner.

His presence does not startle her. Porter stares at her, and she returns his stare without flinching. He casts his eyes, deep and unforgiving. She rises. Studies him without a trace of sorrow. She walks to him, takes his hand, and leads him to the bed.

"You will regret this," Porter tells her.

Rose nods. "I'll regret it if we do, and I'll regret it more if we don't."

This, Porter knows, is the most honest thing she has ever said.

"I'm nervous," Rose says. Her breath is hot and arduous. "Will you guide me?" she asks.

"No," Porter says. "Whatever happens has to be your doing."

Rose appears to have expected Porter's recusal. She extends a shaking hand toward his belt. A struggle ensues. She cannot navigate the clasp. Porter watches her effort without helping. She forsakes the task and steps away from him. Her trembling hand fumbles with the lacing on her nightgown. She cannot work the knot, so she pulls the gown over her head. She holds the clothing to her chest for a moment before letting it fall to the floor. Her skin is milky, unblemished. No scars traverse her untouched body, leaving traces of a past. Porter has seen only one other body like hers. A body he wishes he could forget. Rose's body is the antithesis of Porter's. He wonders how she will react to his scarred and tarnished flesh. Will she recoil or accept his disfigurements? He pushes the fear from his mind. He is a man of war. His mended skin is a symbol of a world infested with men spouting ideologies designed to bruise.

Standing naked in front of Porter, Rose does not feel exposed or vulnerable. She reads in Porter's face an unchecked longing. He is enamored by what he sees. He has the same yearnings as she. This pleases Rose. Gives her the affirmation she sought by coming tonight.

Rose steps to Porter. She reaches again for his belt. Now her hand is steady and sure. The buckle frees easily from its latch. She snakes the worn leather free from the stained dungarees. She lifts her head, takes in Porter's scent, and asks him if he will kiss her. He does. It is soft and tender, and she imagines for an instant that maybe some things in her books are real.

CHAPTER 15

The sun peaks through the window and casts its light onto Rose's face. She wakes with a start and rushes from the bed. Porter sleeps. Rose fumbles with her nightgown, manages to pull it down onto her body. She steals a glance at Porter, who has not stirred, and steps outside the bedroom.

She closes the door to Porter's room and turns. James stands alone in the living room, Bible in hand, watching her exodus. She turns and their eyes meet. The sudden tension sucks the air from Rose's lungs. The criminal accosted by the law without warning.

James understands what has happened. His face hardens. Rose cowers. James shakes his head, disgusted that his niece has turned his Christian home into a house of iniquity. Rose opens her mouth to speak but does not. What could she say? She is a sinner brought before her mortal judge and condemned. Words are unnecessary. Words are for the innocent. James turns and disappears into his den. Rose stifles her guilty tears and climbs the stairs to her bedroom.

An hour later Rose returns to Porter's room. Her Sunday dress is pressed and hangs off her body how it should. She steals glances over both her shoulders, stands erect, and knocks on the door. She fidgets and tries to settle her breathing. Then Porter opens the door. Upon seeing him, Rose is thrust back into the previous night. The wild wonderment they shared, the excitement of the sin, and the remorse she has now for feeding her lust. She loses her breath for a spellbinding second. How badly she desires to push him back into the room and be with him like she was eight hours earlier. To live in the bedroom forever and never leave it. Life does not exist outside the walls of the bedroom. Her impure thoughts bring the blood to the surface, blushing her skin and quickening her pulse. She pushes the desires from her head and again stands upright, proper.

"Good morning, Porter," she says. Her dignified air is off-putting. Porter sneers at her propriety. He does not want this version of her. He wants her impulsive and adventurous. The prude before him offers nothing for him.

"I've come to ask you to accompany me to church," she says.

For a moment Porter assumes she is joking. She is not. He wishes he would have left before the morning, before she forced this interaction upon him. Her guilt has assailed her. This is her repentance—bring her fellow sinner to the light and hope God will save them both.

"No," is all he says.

She lowers her voice and says, "It is the first step to repentance."

Porter says nothing.

Rose swallows hard. Her eyes plead. "I am fearful of God's wrath," she whispers. "My uncle caught me this morning exiting your bedroom. We must atone for what we did."

"We must not."

"Porter, please…"

"Your demons are not mine, Rose."

His comment strikes Rose. It is an effort not to buckle from the weight of his words. Her chin quivers. Porter, too, wishes he could pull her into the bedroom and hold her like he had the previous nights. Close the bedroom door on the rest of the world and live with Rose unencumbered by her religious absurdities. He thinks to tell her this but knows she would not hear it. Not with the weight of the guilt pressing down on her.

"Do you love me, Porter?" she mutters.

Never has she ever spoken of love with a man. Porter is always navigating her into unchartered territory. She wants to retreat to safer ground where risks do not exist, and all answers are known without their questions even being asked. Her heart cannot waver in so much uncertainty. Porter opens his mouth to answer, but Rose, fearful of what he may say—fearful of what she knows he will say—cuts him off.

"Please don't make me choose between you and my God," Rose whispers. "That is a battle you cannot win."

"I can accept you for being Christian," he says. "Can you accept me for not?"

"Porter, please," she cries.

"Would not a true Christian accept me and my trespasses?" Porter counters.

"I cannot be with a man at odds with my faith."

"I am not at odds with it; I am indifferent to it."

Rose analyzes his words, but the more she replays them, the less she can make of them. "I cannot distinguish the difference," she says.

Porter contemplates if there is a way to help her see what she will not. He remembers leaving the war hospital. He kept to the back roads, hiding in ditches at the sound of approaching horses or men. On the third day of his exodus, he spotted smoke billowing into the sky. He followed the black plumes and soon heard crying. He quickened his stride and came upon a church house. It was a tinderbox engulfed in flames. An army of confederate soldiers astride languished horses stood outside the church doors. They had barricaded the worshippers inside and then placed torches to the splintered, clapboard meeting house. A handful of men trapped inside hoisted a bench and tossed it through a window. It crashed to the dried grass among shards of glass. A man followed, jumping from the burning edifice. He stumbled to his feet, his shirt blazing. He thrashed about, trying to extinguish the flame. A soldier raised his gun to shoot the man, but a fellow soldier told him to wait. "Let him burn," the soldier ordered. The worshiper dropped to the ground and rolled about and snuffed out the flame. He returned to his feet and made for the woods, running right at Porter. He did not make it ten feet before a soldier shot him dead. Others spilled out from the window—men, women, children. Most were black; some were white. All were slaughtered.

Had Porter witnessed the burning church a year earlier, it may have made an impression. He may have even intervened. But as a scarred war veteran, newly educated in the gross habits of man, he simply turned from the smoldering church and resumed his journey. The stench of charred wood and seared flesh filled his nostrils for nearly a mile. He came upon Quinn's ranch a week later.

Porter needed no explanation why the soldiers set the church house ablaze. It was obvious—the church housed blacks *and* whites. God's superiors co-mingling with His inferiors. It was an infraction suitable for death. Anyone strident enough to question this assertion could consult *The Bible*. The Good Book would confirm the lawfulness of murder committed in the name of the father. Purging the world of rebellious negroes and sympathetic whites was a task not to be ignored.

Porter spent many nights during the war trying to make sense of the senseless. Hoping an epiphany would strike to justify and explain the ridiculousness of the southern ideals the men of war tasked him with protecting. In the end, an epiphany did strike. While in the hospital, convalescing from the wound that would lead to his desertion, the scales fell from his eyes, and it became clear he was on the wrong side of the war.

It was in the throes of another senseless battle when he took aim at a Yankee soldier. He fingered the trigger and then, at the last moment, lifted his muzzle and fired, knowing the round would get lost in a tree. The spared soldier fired back and struck Porter in the chest. Another round penetrated his shoulder. Porter fell to the ground and hoped the bullets would do him in. They did not. But his wounds did take him out of commission. In the hospital more epiphanies occurred, and he resolved that if he could not exit the world, he would at least exit the war.

Religion and land. Had a war ever been fought over anything else? Porter denounced God. If he were honest with himself, he would recognize that he had abandoned God years before the war.

If Rose knew of the things he did, could she fault him for swearing off God? If she could spend one minute ricocheting inside his head, would she understand? Would she forsake her mission in converting him to her misguided theology?

Porter thought to explain this to Rose, but he did not think it worth the effort. It is damn-near impossible to reason with the religious. Regarding one's faith, reason, Porter learned, is a trait in short supply. It cannot be any other way, for if it were, the faithful would have a harder time finding recruits.

"Please, Porter," Rose says, returning Porter from his reverie. "Come to Sunday service with me. James is a wonderful vessel to God. God will forgive us for what we did last night if we repent."

"What we did last night needs no forgiveness."

Rose restrains the tears forming at the corners of her eyes and asks one last time. "Will you come with me to church?"

Porter tells her again: "No."

Rose trembles, stares at the floor, at a loss. She cannot escape her guilt, only the man instigating it. She offers Porter one last painful glance and shuffles away.

CHAPTER 16

The children run ahead, ignoring their mother's pleas to slow down. Claire worries her children will dirty their Sunday clothes. She is the preacher's wife. The unspoken expectation to always appear perfect is one she takes with unremitting pride. She does not want her fellow parishioners casting judgmental stares at her children because dirt outlines their collars.

Quinn and Rose walk in Claire's wake. Rose is distant, despondent. Quinn thinks to ask what is wrong, wants to ask, but does not. Rose is a grown woman. Quinn does not think it her place to meddle. She fears if she becomes too involved it will hurt her campaign to have Rose return home. Instead, Quinn extends her arm as an invitation. Rose considers it for a moment and then threads her own arm through her mother's. This was their custom years ago when they would walk to church and watch Quinn's father preach. Quinn enjoyed the trek to the church house more than the sermons. A truth she always kept concealed. She feels the same now accompanying her daughter to worship. Basks in this simple repose. Wonders if Rose relishes the moment as much as she does.

"Can I ask you something?" Rose says.

"You can ask me anything," Quinn replies.

"When you think of God, is He vengeful or compassionate?"

Quinn ponders the question. "He's both."

"How so?"

"He is whatever the situation requires, whether it be vengeance or compassion."

"That's my fear," Rose says. She chews on a fingernail, a nervous gesture from her childhood that does not go unnoticed by her mother.

Quinn stops. "Is something the matter, Rosie?"

Rose cannot help it. Without warning, she falls into her mother, crying. "I'm certain I have shamed God."

"What has happened?" Quinn asks.

"Can you forgive me, Mother?"

"For what?"

"I've fallen for Porter," she says.

Quinn sighs and refrains from laughing. Her daughter may be a woman by definition but in many respects, she is still a child.

"You do not need my forgiveness for falling in love, and I'm sure God can overlook such a common transgression."

"Porter would scoff at such sentiment," Rose cries. "He blasphemes with no fear of reprisal. I do not know how I have fallen for such a man."

"Many women before you have fallen for the wrong man. His disbelief is not your burden."

"He will never be the man I want him to be."

"You don't know—"

"I do, Mother," Rose says. She casts her tear-stained eyes to her mother. Quinn detects the seriousness in her daughter's gaze, and something more serious lies underneath her daughter's countenance. It is stronger than a silly infatuation.

"I asked him to come today, and he would not," Rose explains. "His heart is hard, and there is no getting through to it. I cannot have a life with him."

"Has he hurt you?"

"No. Not intentionally."

"And you love him?"

"Despite all my efforts."

"What do you want?"

"Only what I cannot have."

"He will not have you?"

"He does not want me."

"That is ridiculous," Quinn scoffs. "I see how he looks at you."

"He wants me but not my faith."

"You cannot abandon your faith in pursuing love, Rose."

"I know, and I have told him as much."

"I have asked him to return to the ranch with me," Quinn says. "With us. I'll tell him he is no longer welcomed. Not if you don't want him."

"That's the problem," Rose cries. "I do want him. I want him so badly that my bones ache."

"Oh, Rosie," Quinn says, taking her daughter in her arms again. "My sweet child."

"Repentance, mother," Rose says. "It is a gift reserved for all, is it not?"

"Of course it is."

Rose cries a moment longer and then pulls away from her mother and straightens her dress. She wipes her eyes and stands rigid, with new resolve.

"Then that is what I'll do," Rose says. "I will repent."

"God does not require repentance for falling in love with an atheist."

Rose shakes her head, incredulous by her mother's ignorance. All her books share a common thread that a mother always knows a child's heart. Quinn does not. She will not see what is so obvious. Paternal affection, weighed by the millstone of unconditional love, can blind parents to the harsh realities of their children.

Rose forces a painful smile and nods. Her grief will remain her own. Admitting her sin to Quinn would not absolve her from it.

Quinn cannot grant Rose absolution. That pardon is God's to give. Rose also knows if she were to confess her carnal abomination to Quinn, her mother would not allow Porter back onto her ranch. Porter should not suffer for the spell he has cast on Rose. She handles her own heart and the actions it inspires. Rose lifts her chin and resumes her familiar position next to her mother, and together they approach the church house.

CHAPTER 17

The chapel is sweltering. Devoted members sit in the pews fanning themselves. Rose sits next to her mother. Claire and her bevy of children fill out the rest of the bench. James stands at the pulpit. He is at a fever pitch. Consumed with the spirit and meting out judgment with righteous indignation.

"Brothers and sisters, I stand before you today on this glorious Sabbath afternoon to tell you that Satan is near. I know he's near because the Second Coming is near. We are in the last days."

Heads nod. Fans pump.

"The more powerful the devil's presence, the closer Christ is to returning. To saving us," James proclaims. "That is why I must implore you, brothers and sisters, I must implore you to be stringent in your morals. To be upright and steadfast. Do not succumb to the temptations of man. Do not let Lucifer get his hooks in you and force you into a life of sin and depravity. Abstain from sins of the flesh. Refrain from the carnal desires that have consumed man since Lucifer tempted Adam and Eve to eat the forbidden fruit."

James pauses and levels his eyes on Rose. She shifts in her seat.

"Remember what *The Bible* warns about fornicating. Heed the words in First Corinthians that instruct us to 'Flee from sexual immortality. Every other sin a person commits is outside the body, but the sexually immoral person sins against his own body!' God has cautioned us, brothers and sisters. We have been warned!"

A series of "amens!" fill the clapboard house. Rose trembles.

"Recall the whore that was Sodom and Gomorrah. Recall what God said about it in Jude: 'Just as Sodom and Gomorrah and the surrounding cities, which likewise indulged in sexual immorality and pursued unnatural desire, serve as an example by undergoing a punishment of eternal fire.' Yes, brothers and sisters. If you fornicate with one who is not your spouse, you will burn forever! God will thrust you down into the depths of hell where you will burn for your transgressions! God will have no remorse, no mercy for your shortcomings! We cannot balk at God's divine precepts. In Deuteronomy we're instructed to kill those who commit sins of the flesh!"

Rose clenches her clammy hands into impenetrable fists. Her cheeks flush. Beads of perspiration dot her upper lip and forehead. She shifts in her seat again and wipes her brow.

"The scriptures command us to mete out God's justice to fornicators. 'But if the thing is true, that evidence of virginity was not found in the young woman, then they shall bring out the young woman to the door of her father's house, and the men of her city shall stone her to death with stones, because she has done an outrageous thing in Israel by whoring in her father's house. So you shall purge the evil from your midst.' That is our calling!"

James halts for a dramatic pause. He casts challenging eyes over all in attendance. His rage builds. His self-proclaimed righteousness gives him permission to cast judgment to his congregation. He is God's vessel.

"Stoned to death!" he shouts. "That is the proper punishment for whores! That is the only way to rid the earth of those who cannot bridle their sexual indiscretions! When we call out the unclean, when we shine the light of Christ onto those who have sinned, we are doing God's work! He instructs us to purge the world of any man, woman, or child who forsakes His commandments!"

The temperature continues to rise. Rose can sense her Savior's wrath. Her misdeeds have not gone unaccounted for. She has sinned. God witnessed it. Watched as she crept from her own bed into Porter's. He must have placed James outside the door the following morning. The King sending his sentinel to the threshold of evil to witness the departure of his fallen child. When Rose emerged from Porter's bedroom and found her uncle at the ready, it was as if God Himself had discovered her.

Rose tightens even more. Her uncle will not relent. He continues to spew spiteful scripture and doctrine directed at her. The congregation lifts his words into a chorus of agreement. Rose cannot hear another word. She bolts from the church house. Quinn watches her go, perplexed and confounded. James beams from the pulpit. He lifts his head to the rafters and smiles. A nourishing ray of light shines through the splintered rafters, casting its warmth onto James. The chosen basking in his calling.

Had James taken a moment to shift his gaze from Rose to his own wife, he would see that she too had fallen pale from his sermon. It was not the heat; it was her own carnal transgressions that forced the blood from her face. She could not understand how her husband could spout such invective language from his pulpit, when Claire knew, as well as James, that their own wild youths, saturated with unbridled desires, made them guilty of all he proclaimed.

CHAPTER 18

Rose rounds the corner of her uncle's house and halts when she spots Porter. He sits on the porch reading. He looks up from his book and his eyes meet Rose's. Something is wrong. Rose's breathing is heavy, labored. Porter closes his book and stands. He knows he must go to her. He takes a step to do so, but Rose backs away.

"Don't," she says.

Porter stops.

"It's nothing you can fix," Rose says. She mounts the porch and pushes past him, calling over her shoulder, "Leave me alone."

She enters the house and takes the stairs two at a time up to the children's bedroom. Porter wants to go to her, feels that he should, but something deeper convinces him not to interfere. He remains on the porch weighing his options when he hears horses. He squints in the distance and lifts his hand to shield the sun.

Five men on horseback appear on the horizon. Porter appraises them. It is difficult to tell, but he does not believe them to be Home Guard hunting for runaway soldiers. They ride with purpose; they ride straight for the house. Porter goes inside and retrieves his gun. He tucks it in his pants and steps back onto the porch. He awaits the men's arrival.

They ride straight for the house and then halt. They see Porter but pretend not to. He is not worth their time. Each man is armed, and Porter knows each man can work his weapon. One man, the leader from the looks of it, dismounts. His eyes survey the property. He glances past Porter, sees him, and ignores him. Porter knows these men are not looking for soldiers. Their plight is something different. The dismounted man spits into the dirt and says something to his men before settling back to Porter. The man's name is William Bath.

"Afternoon," he says. This sounds like a greeting, but Porter knows men like this do not offer friendly salutations. "I was wondering if my men could water our horses at your trough?" the man asks.

Porter ponders the request but does not offer an answer.

"We've been riding for three days straight," William says. "Our horses are spent, and we are too."

"It's not my trough," Porter says.

"Whose is it?"

"Preacher's."

"The preacher around?"

"No."

"This is not your property?" William asks and Porter remains silent. William takes a step towards the porch. A newfound interest with Porter. "This preacher," William says, "he's not a Mormon, is he?"

Porter says nothing and William rests his hand on his revolver.

"He'll be back shortly," Porter says. "You can ask his affiliation when he returns."

"Well, seeing how he isn't around to grant permission to his trough, I suspect we can take advantage of his Christian charity and help ourselves."

William turns to his horse and takes hold of the reins.

"Can't let you do that," Porter says.

William turns back to Porter. "Why's that?"

"I don't have permission."

William studies Porter for a beat and laughs. "I'm not the kind of man you'd want to say no to," William says. His hand returns to his gun.

"I'm not telling you no," Porter says. "I'm telling you to wait."

The men murmur. Each reaches for his gun, but no one draws. They know not to act unless William gives the go-ahead. William squints at Porter and walks to the bottom of the porch.

"Is this a fight you really want to have?"

Porter's eyes shift from William to the four mounted horsemen, contemplating his strategy. He suspects he could fire off three shots and get inside before the men could react.

"It's just water," William says. This is his last peace offering. If Porter does not stand down, the outlaw and his men will fire.

A child's sudden laughter penetrates the quarrelsome air, breaking the heated interaction between the stubborn men. The laughter grows, and another child joins in the merriment. Scattered voices fill in the gaps. Two running children appear around the blind side of the house and stop once they see the men on horseback. William takes his hand from his gun and motions to his men not to pull their firearms. Four more children round the bend along with Claire, Quinn, and James.

Everyone freezes. James takes in the scene, unsure what he just encroached upon. He looks at Porter. Sees something beneath his gaze he cannot fathom. Whatever it is, it frightens James.

"You must be the preacher," William says, breaking the silence.

"I am," James says, shifting his stare to William. "Can I help you?"

"Yes, you can," William says. He shoots Porter a menacing glance before addressing James. "My men and I would be grateful if our horses could use your trough."

James again spies Porter standing erect and ready on the porch. He suspects he has just walked into something, but he does not understand what. The unforgiving Oklahoma heat must have everyone on edge. James forces a smile.

"Of course, gentlemen," James says. "Help yourselves. I wouldn't be a Christian if I didn't give drink to those who thirst."

"Appreciate it," William says, tipping his hat.

He ambles towards James, his spurs chiming, and holds out his hand. The hand is coarse with a mix of earth and dried blood lining the cracks. James accepts the handshake and tries to mask his fear.

"Tell me, preacher," William says, "you preachin' Mormon doctrine?"

The suggestion hardens James's features. "Absolutely not," he says.

William smiles. "Glad to hear it," he says.

William motions for his men to water their horses. They turn their tired steeds toward the trough. William makes for his horse when Quinn steps next to her brother.

"What has you so interested in Mormons?" Quinn asks.

William stops and looks to Quinn. Lifts a hand to shield the sun and flashes a cryptic smile. "We're huntin' one," William answers.

PART II

CHAPTER 18

James passes the tintype to Quinn. Quinn studies the photo. The innocent face staring back at her, foreign yet somehow familiar, reminds Quinn of her own daughter. The girl in the photo looks about the same age. She is the same age. Same age with the same story. The recognition is slow, but it arrives. Quinn has met the young girl in the picture.

"That's Hester Martin," William says. He sits at the table inside James's house. James and Quinn sit too. William's men stand on the fringes. All the outlaws are doing the same: surveying the home, appraising its worth, searching for anything worth stealing. Nothing catches their attention other than a polished crucifix nailed to the wall. William is not religious but he is superstitious. Claiming a religious token is not worth the mental discomfort it would cause.

"Who is she?" James asks, pointing to the picture of the girl.

"That's who we are after," William says. "I've never met her."

"I have," Quinn says. "She stopped by my ranch a few months ago. Came with a Mormon claiming to be her husband. Man had three wives with him. Two of them were so young I thought they were his daughters." She passes the picture back to William. "What do you want with her?"

"Hester's father hired me to bring her back home," William says.

"Who's her father?" James asks.

"Noah Martin," William says. "Rich plantation owner in Arkansas. The story goes his childhood friend, a guy named Henry Dawkins, converted to Mormonism. After his conversion, he took young Hester to be his new wife. Claimed God commanded it and married her in secret. Her and another girl. Henry's first wife found out and ratted him out. Of course, when Noah pressed Henry about it, Henry denied everything. Then one night he lit out with his three wives. Headed to Utah with the other Mormons."

"He has four wives now," Quinn says under her breath.

"What did you say?" William asks.

"He has four wives now."

"That so?"

"He married my daughter in a similar fashion."

"Took your daughter too, huh?"

"Just like you described," Quinn says.

"How long ago was that?"

"Few months."

"Yeah," William says. "Time frame seems about right. Mr. Martin hired another man to go after Hester few months back. He met up with his people from Arkansas on their way to California. Mormons ambushed them out at Mountain Meadows. Killed everyone but the children."

"I heard about that," James says.

"What did they do with the children?" Quinn asks.

"I heard it told they're raising them," William explains. "Actin' as if the massacre didn't happen and pretendin' the Arkansas kin is their own. Bringin' them up to be Mormons."

"You're not serious," Quinn says.

William laughs. "I am serious, ma'am. These Mormons left New York and been makin' their way across the country. They fled the states for the territories and marryin' up unsuspectin' girls along the way. Takin' children as their own believin' they're doing God's will. They're buildin' an army."

James looks at the men who are accompanying William. They are hard men, rugged but outnumbered. "You'll need more than five men if you're taking on an army," James says.

"We're not lookin' to fight the Mormons," William says. "Just one—Noah Martin—and he is a coward. He won't put up much of a fight."

"Brigham Young might," James says. "I've heard the rumors about Mountain Meadows. The Mormon prophet ordered the killing of that entire caravan from Arkansas."

"That's not how he tells it," William says.

"How does he tell it?" Quinn asks.

"He blamed the Indians and then appointed his own fall guy. Another Mormon by the name of Jon Lee."

"You know about Young's bodyguard?" James asks. "The Rockwell fella?"

William rubs his chin and nods. "His reputation is worth considerin'. But we ain't after anyone other than Hester. If Rockwell or any other Mormon wants to put up a fight, well, then we'll fight."

"Hester may not want to leave," Quinn says. "Those Mormons are pretty persuasive. They're good at convincing young girls of falsehoods."

William flashes a smile that chills Quinn. "We can handle the women."

"What about the others?" Quinn asks.

"What others?"

"His other wives? The other girls he stole from unsuspecting parents?"

"What about 'em?"

"Are you reclaiming them?"

"They ain't my business," William says.

"What if you made them your business?" Quinn says.

William leans back in his chair and casts a discerning eye on Quinn. "Now why would I do that?"

"I don't have much," Quinn says, "but I'll give all I have."

"You askin' me to kidnap your daughter and bring her back here?"

"It ain't kidnapping," Quinn says. "It's returning what he stole."

"I doubt you can afford my services."

"What's your price?"

"$1,000."

"I don't have $1,000."

"Then your daughter is not my problem," William says. He takes the tin cup from the table James had given him earlier and downs the water inside like a man taking a shot of whiskey. He makes to stand, but Quinn lifts her hand, asking him to wait a minute.

"I have land," Quinn says. "About twenty miles back. I'm sure you rode past it on your way here."

"We passed a ranch 'bout twenty miles back," William says. "It had dusty fields where it didn't have neglected crops."

"It has value," Quinn says.

"That's dad's land," James says.

"Dad is dead," Quinn says.

"You have no right," James says.

"It's for Samantha, James," Quinn pleads. "Imagine if one of your children—"

"I was going to sell some of that land to help build a new church," James says.

"It isn't yours to sell," Quinn says.

"He was my father too, Quinn."

"You left, James! You abandoned—"

William rises from his chair, pausing the sibling rivalry playing out before him. He spits a string of tobacco juice that lands in a brown puddle in the room's corner. James feels to demand more decency from the mercenary but thinks better than to tell this man what to do.

"I'll tell you what," William says. "If I find your daughter, I'll bring her with us. And when I return, we can negotiate, and if you don't have anything to my likin', well, I guess I'll just have me a Mormon wife." William releases a sinister laugh. His posse laughs right along with him.

Upstairs a door is flung open, and footsteps penetrate the silence. All heads turn up to find Rose. She looks down at the congregation, taking in each man. She overheard the conversation between William and her mother, and now she has come to help plead for her sister's return. But she cannot think of what to say. All the menacing eyes that have landed on her have frightened her silent. None more than William Bath's.

"Now who is that?" William asks.

"That's my other daughter," Quinn says. "Rosie."

William spits another string of tobacco juice onto the floor and wipes his mouth.

"Well now, if your other daughter looks anything like that delicate thing, I may reconsider my services."

Porter bolts through the front door with his gun drawn. Before anyone can understand what has happened, Porter is standing before William, the barrel of his gun pressed against William's forehead. A beat too late William's men pull their guns and take aim at Porter.

Time stops. William looks beyond the gun barrel pressed to his forehead to Porter. For the first time in his life, William fears he may die. He knows killers, and he can tell Porter is one. If they were outside the house, he is certain Porter would have pulled the trigger already. William bridles his fear, knows he cannot put it on display for Porter or his men to witness. He does not flinch, and he does not reach for his gun. Doing so would do him in. It is what Porter wants; it would give him reason to pull the trigger. William's eyes meet Porter's. He detects rage and not much else.

"Careful, son," William says. He lifts his hands to show he has no inclination to make for his own gun.

"Porter, what in God's name are you doing?" Quinn asks, her voice frantic.

"These men are bounty hunters," Porter says. "They'd rape your daughter twice before they thought of bringing her back."

"Take it easy, cowboy," William says. "We're civil men just hired to do a service."

"There's blood on your boots," Porter says.

William forces a smile. "That's pig blood," he lies. "Slaughtered him last night for supper and cooked him over our campfire."

"Porter, please put your gun away," Quinn pleads. "We're just having a conversation."

Porter turns to Quinn while keeping his gun pressed to William's forehead. Quinn is all fear, confounded by Porter's sudden outburst. Porter pities Quinn. She does not understand the men she is negotiating with. Porter shifts his gaze to the landing where Rose stands, mouth open, staring down at Porter with her own heightened sense of perplexity. She shakes her head, begging him to holster his gun. Porter's features tighten. Rose understands that if she were not here to bear witness, Porter would have already pulled the trigger. She is the only thing saving William Bath's life right now. Porter lowers his gun and walks out of the house.

William's men look to William, awaiting orders to follow Porter outside and put a bullet through his brain. William shakes his head, wordlessly commanding his men to stand down the way Rose commanded Porter.

"Who is that man?" William asks.

"I don't know," James says. "He just showed up here with my sister a couple weeks ago." James shoots an accusatory glance at Quinn and then Rose.

"Well, you best put a leash on him," William says. "My men just about caved in his skull."

"*They* almost caved in *his* skull?" Quinn asks. "From my vantage it looked like your head was the one about to be run through."

"He may have gotten me, but if he had, he warn't leavin' here alive," William says.

"If I had it my way, he never would have stepped foot in this house," James says.

"He's a good man," Quinn says.

"He's immoral, Quinn."

"Moral enough to dig dad's grave," Quinn argues.

"Yeah, and he fornicated with your daughter last night," James says.

Silence.

The accusation penetrates the room. Quinn stares hard at her brother, wondering why he would make a claim so blatant and untrue. James sighs and looks away, unapologetic for what he said. Quinn lifts her gaze to her daughter. Rose's expression confirms James's allegation. The knowledge deflates Quinn, and all life escapes her. She lowers her head and closes her eyes, mutters a prayer. When she looks back to the landing, Rose has disappeared into the bedroom. Quinn takes in a long breath and exhales it slowly. She does not know what she feels. She does not know who she is more upset with—her own daughter or Porter. Perhaps even herself.

"I caught her this morning sneaking out of his room," James says.

"It's…not true," Quinn says, her maternal instinct arriving to defend her daughter from what she knows she has committed.

"I want them both out of my house in the morning," James says. "I will not give shelter to fornicators."

"Settle down, Preacher," William sneers. "No amount of religion could keep a man from a girl like that."

William's men laugh. They appreciate the remark, the truth to it, and the tension it frees from the room. Quinn settles her crestfallen eyes to the ground.

James turns to William. "In my home, we do not succumb to temptation," James declares.

William shrugs and puts on his hat. "Thanks again for the water, Preacher," William says. He spits another wad of tobacco sap on the floor. He spies James and Quinn, begging either to question his manners. They remain silent. William is a man among cowards. He laughs and shakes his head before exiting the house, his men following.

CHAPTER 20

From the bedroom window, Porter watches William and his men mount their horses and ride away. He does not hear Quinn enter the room, nor does it surprise him she has come.

"Is it true?" Quinn asks.

Porter knows what she is asking, but he ignores the question.

"Is it true, Porter?" Quinn asks again. Her voice wavers on the edge of fear and anger. "Did you…fornicate with my daughter?"

Porter turns. "Yes," he says.

His answer stings. Quinn burrows her eyes deep into Porter, hoping to break him, hoping to convey to him the magnitude of his actions. But he does not stir. Porter feels no compunction for what he has done. He made love to a woman he loves. It is nonsense to feign guilt for such a natural act. He is stone. Quinn takes in a heavy breath and exhales it. She paces the room.

"Do you know what it means to be moral?" Quinn asks. "Do you have any idea?"

"Morality is for the fearful," Porter says.

"Enough!" Quinn shouts. "I don't need to hear anymore of your broken dogma! How can you be so selective with your words only to choose the wrong ones when you finally speak?"

Porter returns to the window. He traces the plains searching for William and his men, but they have vanished.

"Do you love her?" Quinn asks.

Porter does not answer, so Quinn asks again and adds: "I need to know that there is good in you, son. If you laid with my daughter to satisfy a carnal urge, I will shoot you between the eyes. But if there's more there, if you can admit love, I may find understanding enough to forgive you. So tell me true, son, do you love her?"

"What I know of her," Porter answers.

Quinn nods. "Will you make an honest woman of her?"

Porter remains silent.

"I'm picking my poison here, Porter," Quinn says. "I'd rather her be with an agnostic than...than join up with some cult."

Porter expels a weighted laugh.

"I say something funny, son?"

"I have a hard time distinguishing what constitutes a religion and what makes up a cult," Porter says.

"Truth," Quinn answers.

"As you see it?" Porter counters.

Quinn's face demonstrates her confusion. "You're sticking up for Mormons now? Do I need to remind you they stole my daughter?"

"No," Porter says. "I'm just trying to determine how your beliefs are less absurd than theirs."

"Goddamn you, Porter," Quinn says, her voice rising. "You rob my eldest daughter of her virtue and now you mock my faith? Today you've made me wish I had never asked you to dig my father's grave. If it weren't for Rosie, I would skin you right here." Quinn goes to the door and stops. "Please, make an honest woman of her. She is as close to God as anyone I know. She may save you."

"I don't need saving," Porter says.

Quinn scoffs and shakes her head. "Son, you need it more than you know."

CHAPTER 21

Porter stands on the porch inspecting the landscape. He witnessed William and his men ride away, but he does not trust they have left the valley. Porter knows men like William. Understands that even when they leave, they are never gone. They have no reason to return. James is not a man of wealth. He has nothing worth stealing, but William's presence lingers. Teasing Porter with the prospect of bloodshed. If Porter were to consider his pondering, he would discover the real reason he assumes his nocturnal watch—Rose. William looked at Rose the way a man should not. Porter saw the glint in his eye, recognized in William what he had unearthed in other men during the war. Men are not tamed. Their vices dictate their actions. Porter does not trust William. Rose's unrivaled beauty may be enough to incite his return. Porter will end him if he chooses such a reckless path.

The front door opens and slaps shut behind Porter. He recognizes the foot pattern on the porch boards. Rose. He does not move, but he can feel her eyes on his back. She has rehearsed what to say, but now that she must voice her desires, she cannot find the words. Porter turns because he believes it is what she wants. It is not. What she must say is easier said to his back. It will break her to find another sliver of rejection in his face.

"I'm returning with my mother tomorrow," she says. Her voice is distant and hollow. "James doesn't want me here anymore. Not after..." she trails off. The thought does not need finishing. She studies the ground between her feet, scavenging for the right words. She folds her arms across her chest, protecting herself from the answer she may receive when she asks: "Do you want me, Porter?"

"If you'll have me," he answers.

He would take her into his arms right now if he knew she would permit it. She would not, though. Her faith, along with her uncle and mother's judgment, has racked her with too much contrition to permit Porter to touch her again. Porter understands they will not touch again unless they marry.

"If I'll have you?" she repeats. "It seems I don't have a choice."

"You always have a choice."

"You claimed my virtue."

"I did not force you."

"I was seduced."

"As was I."

Rose's chin wavers, and a tear escapes her eye. "We must pay for our sin."

"I am. Your guilt is my sin."

"You must atone to God," she says.

"I must atone nothing."

"I will not marry an agnostic," Rose says. She lifts her pleading eyes to him, soaked in tears. Porter cannot stomach her pain knowing he is the one instigating it. "What if your woman were to return?" Rose asks. "The woman in your letter."

"She does not mean to me what you think she does."

"She means enough to keep her letter," Rose says, and Porter falls silent. "I cannot share your heart."

"You cannot share my heart, but you could share your sister's husband?"

"That would be different. A union borne out of necessity. It would not involve love. I love you, Porter. I need your heart and your devotion to God. It can be no other way. I must have both."

"You already have one," he says. "You will never receive the other."

Porter's answer robs Rose of her wits. She swallows hard and wipes her eyes. She wishes Porter would sweep her into his arms and offer soothing words he does not own. What would it take for him to resign his way of thinking and adopt hers? Oh, the life they could create if Rose could dismantle his obstinance. Such a joyous life. One worth living. One even worth writing about. Rose knows she must not entertain the fantasy. Dreams hurt less when they shut off upon waking.

Rose has nothing left to say. She stands straight, collects all her wits, and nods. Porter does not know if she is nodding acceptance or conceding defeat. She is inside the house before he can ask.

CHAPTER 22

The morning has not yet broken. Porter retrieves a book and exits his room and goes to the porch. He surveys the ground, foraging for signs of William's return. The ground appears untouched. Porter sits in the porch chair and opens his book, tries to read, but cannot—the muted light is too weak, and his thoughts will not allow him to concentrate. He gets to his feet, paces the porch, and awaits Quinn. She is always the next to rise followed by James. Porter must speak with both.

Quinn appears in the kitchen thirty minutes later. James appears shortly after. They help themselves to coffee, neither acknowledging the other. They are family, so the things said yesterday will linger and haunt, but they will reconcile. Maybe.

Porter enters the house. He glances at the landing and wonders if he can say what he must before Rose wakes and exits the children's bedroom.

"I was hoping I could have a word," Porter says. It is not clear if he is addressing James or Quinn. They both give him their attention.

"I want to apologize for what I've done," Porter says. "This is your home. You have rules, and I should have been mindful of them, regardless of my faith, or lack thereof."

James stares hard at Porter and says nothing. It is not he who needs the apology but God.

"I appreciate the kindness you've extended to me," Porter continues. "Last night Rose laid out certain conditions for me to return to the ranch. I'm…I'm not the man she needs me to be. I think it best if I continue to California. Being at the ranch with her would be difficult for everyone." Porter pauses. This admission is difficult for him. "I was hoping you could tell this to Rose," he says.

"You rob her of her virtue, and now you want us to explain where you're running off to?" James says.

"James, please…" Quinn says.

Porter pulls a folded piece of paper from his back pocket. "I wrote her this note. It explains everything."

He holds the note out to Quinn. She stands and strides past Porter. "You can give it to her yourself," she says. She stops at the bottom of the stairs and calls up: "Hey, Rose! Rosie! Come down here please."

Porter exhales, and his shoulders fall under the burden of what he must now do. He faces the landing knowing that the moment he sees Rose, he may break. She will appear strong, but underneath, in the depths where she believed love might exist, she will harden and let loose any notion of romance for herself.

Porter and Quinn wait. Quinn taps the banister. Porter shuffles his feet. The bedroom door remains closed. Quinn calls again. Levi, James's oldest son, steps out from a bedroom. He rubs the sleep from his eyes and looks down at his aunt.

"Levi," Quinn says, "tell your cousin to come down here, please. Porter needs to tell her something."

"Rose isn't here, Aunt Quinn."

"What?" Quinn asks.

"She isn't here," the boy repeats.

"Where is she?"

"She left."

"What?"

"In the middle of the night," Levi says, suppressing a yawn. "She said she was going to Utah to be with Sammy."

Porter bolts out the door and runs to the barn.

James rises from the kitchen table and draws alongside his sister. "What did you say, Levi?"

"She said she was going to Utah," Levi repeats.

Porter returns. "Horse is gone," he says, panting.

"Goddamn it!" Quinn cries.

Porter rushes into his bedroom to retrieve his knapsack and is out the door running to the barn before anyone else can say another word.

CHAPTER 23

Frost blankets the valley. The dying cinders of a fire emit a small ribbon of smoke. William sits on a rock drinking coffee, thinking. He and his men will enter the Salt Lake Valley today. He senses the inevitable bloodshed. This morning, like so many others, contains the ominous promise of murder. William once feared this prognostication; now he embraces it. All men, he believes, have a calling. He counts himself fortunate he found his. He spits a wad of tobacco juice into the red coals and wipes his mouth. The spit hisses, and his men wake.

They rub the sleep from their eyes and help themselves to the coffee. One man, Owen, rolls himself a cigarette. His back aches from the cold, frigid ground. He cannot wait to return to Arkansas where he has a feather mattress and fireplace. He touches his cigarette to the red coals, brings it to his lips, and takes a long drag.

"How'd you sleep?" he asks William.

William did not sleep well; none of them men did. William had heard tales about Utah winters. It was late September now and the cold morning chilled his bones. He envies no one who must inhabit this godforsaken valley in January. He wants to return to Arkansas as much as any of his men. Maybe more so.

"How much farther?" Owen asks. Owen always wants to know how far something is. He spends his life arriving at destinations. He despises journeys.

"Settlement should be right over that ridge," William says. He does not indicate which ridge, but Owen can deduce the correct one. Another man, Francis, has risen. He ambles to the muted fire rubbing his hands together and cupping them and blowing his stale breath into his palms. He pours himself coffee and sits next to Owen.

"What do you reckon the odds are that this Henry guy will give us any trouble?" Francis asks.

"We're goin' in there to take his wife," William says. "What would you do if someone took somethin' that belonged to you?"

"She belonged to Noah Martin first," Owen says. "He stole her from her daddy before she belonged to him."

"And it falls to us to make certain he sees it that way," William says.

"We gonna bring back that preacher's daughter?" Francis asks.

"The daughter weren't the preacher's. It were his sister's," Owen corrects him.

"Mr. Martin hired us to bring back his daughter," William says. "No one else is our concern. That lady don't have no money, and I don't want any godforsaken Oklahoma land."

Francis sits up straight. "Does that mean…" Francis begins. A hopeful smile prevents him from finishing his thought. It does not need finishing. William gleans what Francis wants to know.

"No one is to touch Mr. Martin's daughter," William says. He casts a serious eye towards Francis. He holds Francis for a beat and then turns away. "The rest of the women, you can do what you'd like."

Francis's smile widens. The other men awaken with delightful murmurings. William dumps his coffee on the coals and stands.

"Keep your minds clear of that until we've accomplished what we're bein' paid for," William says. He looks each man in the eye to emphasize his seriousness. The men fall silent and nod, regaining their focus.

"Gather your gear," William says. "I wanna be out of here 'fore the sun gets too hot."

"Hell, I'd welcome the sun right about now," Owen says, and the other men second this notion.

"This valley is peculiar," William says, surveying the land. "I don't like it here. The sooner we can finish our task, the better. Gather your gear, and let's go."

Less than a hundred yards away, Rose hears William and his men talking and wakes from her own restless night. She turns onto her stomach and spies the men's camp through a thicket of bushes. She has been following them for three days, keeping a safe enough distance to remain undetected but close enough to cry out for help if she were to encounter any blood-thirsty natives.

Fifty yards behind Rose is her horse. Each night she ties the horse to a tree and then sneaks closer to the men's camp, worried that if she keeps the animal too close, she may become easier to detect. She believes this will be her last morning waking in this fashion. From the broken conversations she has overheard, she knows the men expect to enter Salt Lake by this afternoon. Rose has considered returning to Oklahoma every day since she fled three nights ago. Pride keeps her tethered to the bounty hunters. She uses them to drive her further from Porter and closer to a man she has never met and will never love. A woman's life, she has decided, is endured, not lived.

Rose does not see the rattlesnake until it is slithering over her boot. She cannot keep from screaming. It is instinctual. She kicks the snake away and scrambles from the bush. The snake hisses and slithers away into a cache of rocks. The ruckus drives all five men to draw their guns and take aim at her hiding place.

"Seems someone is followin' us," William says. He keeps his gun trained on the thicket of bushes. "Whoever is hidin' behind those bushes," William yells, "we've got five guns trained in your direction. Come out now or we'll start shootin'. I want to see your hands."

Fear freezes Rose. William aims high and fires a shot. It grazes the bushes and spits debris all around Rose. She cowers closer to the ground.

"The next shot won't be high," William warns.

Rose lifts her hands and gets to her feet. "I'm coming out," she yells.

Rose emerges from behind the bush. Once the men make out who she is, all but William lower their guns. William spits into the dirt. Watches, listens for anyone else who may have followed Rose. Rose steps into the clearing and stops. She keeps her hands raised and awaits further instructions.

"You alone up there?" William asks.

"Yes," Rose answers.

"You sure? That hothead back at your ranch isn't hidin' up there, is he?"

"No."

William fires a shot into the heart of the bushes. Rose flinches and cries and then lifts her hands higher. William turns to Owen. "Go make sure she's alone," he tells him. "Tie her hands and bring her down here."

Owen pulls a length of rope from his satchel and draws his gun. "Cover me," he says and starts up the hill.

"Owen is comin' to get you," William says. "I've ordered him to put a bullet between your eyes if you give him any trouble. Start walkin' this way. Keep your hands raised."

Rose does as William instructs. When she reaches Owen, he holsters his gun, looks over her shoulders for anyone lurking, and ties her hands. "Head on down there," he tells Rose and then kicks her in the back for good measure. She stumbles to the ground and the men laugh. She shoots Owen a sharp glance, but it goes undetected. With his gun drawn, he hikes to the thicket to investigate. Rose looks past Owen to the tree line where she tied her horse. Unless Owen grows a notion to investigate further, Rose's horse should remain undetected. Rose gets to her feet and wanders down the mountain. She stops two feet from William.

"Why are you followin' us?" William asks.

"I'm going to Utah to be with my sister."

William looks past Rose to Owen. He is circling where Rose spent the night, looking for any signs that she is not alone. He bends down and picks up her knapsack. Inside is nothing of value besides some dry biscuits.

"What do you see?" William calls to Owen.

"Nothing much," Owen calls back. "Just her knapsack."

"She have a gun?" William asks.

"No," Owen answers, rummaging through the sack's contents. "Just a couple books and some stale food."

"Bring it down with you," William tells him. He turns to Rose. "This land is crawlin' with savages. Damn foolish to follow us."

"I know the risks," Rose says. Past William she spies Francis. He smiles at her. His eyes cloaked with lustful ideas.

"You on foot?" William asks.

"I am now," Rose says, hoping her voice does not reveal the truth. "My horse quit on me yesterday. Had to leave him to the buzzards."

Owen returns carrying Rose's bindle. He hands it to William. William turns the sack upside down and dumps the contents onto the ground. He filters through the mess with his worn boot.

"Damn, woman," William says. "You followed us out here with nothin' more than a couple books?"

"I don't need much more," Rose says.

William shakes his head, incredulous. "What do I do with you now?" he asks.

"Salt Lake is right over that ridge, isn't it?" Rose asks, nodding to the west.

"Yeah."

"Just ride ahead," she says. "Let me walk the rest of the way."

"Why would I do that?"

"Why wouldn't you?" Rose counters. "There is no sense in killing me, is there? I'm just a naïve girl trying to get to my sister. Why not let me?"

William weighs his options. A gust of wind kicks up and pushes Rose's hair into her eyes. William removes a strand of hair from Rose's face and smiles. She recoils but tries to appear indifferent to his touch.

"You can ride with me," he tells her. "If I untie your hands, will you be civil?"

She thinks to offer a better argument to letting her travel alone, but she knows it would only fall on deaf ears. "Yes," she answers.

William draws his knife, and with a simple upward motion, frees Rose's hands. "Let's go to Utah," he says.

CHAPTER 24

The Salt Lake Temple comes into view as they descend the valley. It looms, magnificent and near completion. Several men work. Carving stone and hoisting blocks. It is a formidable endeavor. Even William takes a moment and appreciates its design, studies the edifice with quiet reverence. Any group of people that can erect such a majestic structure deserves the world's attention. He did not suspect Mormons capable of such fine craftsmanship. He wonders if the same ingenuity extends to their gunslinging skills. Perhaps he underestimated them. He tells his men to be ready for anything, and then they ride into the capital.

Women, their faces fixed to the ground, shuffle to and from their clapboard houses, chasing children, hanging laundry, and completing other necessary chores. An ominous note seems to accompany William and his mercenaries. The temple workers and sister wives halt their tasks and draw their mouths tight, appraising the visitors and wondering what sort of evil they bring.

William relishes the fear he elicits. Basks in it. He is a man to be reckoned with. He advances to a man lugging buckets of drinking water for the parched workers. The man senses William and stops. Lifts his gaze to meet William's. He sets his buckets to the ground and awaits William's approach.

"Good afternoon," William says to the man, tipping his hat. The man offers a skeptical nod. William's men encircle the Mormon. "Lookin' for a man from Arkansas named Henry Dawkins," William says. "You know where I might find him?"

"What do you want with him?" the Mormon man asks.

"Just to talk."

"Where you from?" the man asks.

"Arkansas," William answers. "Same as Henry."

"He had nothing to do with Mountain Meadows," the man says. "None of us did."

"That's not why we're here," William says.

"Then why are you here?"

"I already told you. We just want to talk."

"You brought four men just to talk with him?" the man asks.

"Yeah," William says.

The man knows William is lying. William knows the man knows.

"He isn't here anymore," the man says. "He left about a month ago."

It is obvious the man is lying. A certain inflection, William has learned, a change in stance always reveals when a man is lying. Men intensify these traits when they believe they will soon die. A small Mormon crowd has congregated. William does not pay the onlookers much attention, but his men do. All hands come to rest on their pistols.

"He left, huh?" William asks. "Where did he go?"

"West," the man says. "California, I believe."

"He take his wives with him?" William asks.

"Believe so," the man says. Small sweat beads prickle his forehead. William has killed many men. The ones that know they are about to die always sweat.

William squints at the man and spits a string of tobacco juice at the man's feet. "You're lying."

"We're simple people," the man stammers. "We just want to be left alone. Leave us be. We ain't hurtin' nobody."

"I don't care about your people," William says. "I don't care nothin' about whatever nonsense you want to subscribe to. You can return to your simple ways just as soon as you tell me where Henry Dawkins is."

"I already told you—he left."

William sighs. He now takes stock of the crowd, targeting anyone who may have the nerve to draw against him. None look threatening. The ones who do not appear fearful only look curious.

"Your kind ain't welcome here," the man says. The gathered spectators have restored his confidence.

"My kind?" William sneers. "What is my kind?"

"Butchers," the man says.

William nods, appreciating the analysis. "Well, if you don't want to get slaughtered, I suggest you cooperate."

"We are a holy people here," the man says. "We just want to be left alone to worship freely."

"Is there an echo around here?" William frowns. "You've already said all that. Next, you're gonna tell me Henry Dawkins isn't here."

"He ain't."

William pulls back his coat, revealing his gun. "You sure he ain't here?"

The man eyes the gun. Swallows hard. "You don't scare me," the man says, his voice does not match what his words claim. "God will protect me."

"Let's see if He will."

William pulls his gun and shoots the man between the eyes. He falls to the ground dead. William already has his gun holstered before it registers with the crowd what has occurred. A few spectators, none louder than Rose, cry out. William's men all have their guns drawn, ready to retaliate if anyone tries firing on them.

William faces the crowd. He pulls his gun again and keeps it at the ready.

"We don't want no trouble!" he declares. "No one here has to get hurt. We just want to know where we can find Henry Dawkins. Tell us where he is, and there will be no more bloodshed."

William scans the crowd, looking for anyone who may cooperate. He notices a boy, about fifteen, standing on the fringe of the crowd. The boy looks terrified and willing to talk. William steers his horse toward the boy.

"What's your name, son?" William asks the boy.

The boy looks about sheepishly. "Ben," the boy says, fear soaking his voice. "Benjamin Smith."

"Benjamin Smith," William says. "Where might I find Henry Dawkins?"

Benjamin scans the crowd for guidance and finds none. "He has a house," Benjamin says. He extends a shaking finger. "Half a mile that way."

William tips his hat to Benjamin and starts in the direction of the house. William's men fall into place. Rose looks down at the dead Mormon as they pass and wonders why God does not seem to have any footing in this foreign land.

CHAPTER 25

A pregnant girl sits in the corner knitting. She is solemn and forlorn and a month beyond her fifteenth birthday. Another girl, also pregnant though she shows no sign of it yet, sits opposite the first girl. She also knits. She also appears solemn and forlorn and pubescent. A woman, much older than the others, enters through the front door carrying a basket overflowing with dirty clothes. Her name is Fanny. She casts a critical eye to her husband—all the girls' husband—as she scavenges the house, picking up discarded clothes and adding them to her basket. The husband sits in the farthest corner of the room hunched over his scriptures. His name is Henry Dawkins.

Henry lifts his head when his oldest wife enters the house. Their eyes lock. Fanny gives her husband the sharp stare she has perfected over the years. All her stares are sharp, but the ones Henry receives could cut glass. This is not the life Henry promised her after the Free Masons murdered her first husband. Henry did not want to take Fanny as a wife. She was too old and too coarse. Fanny accepted the union because she had no other prospects; Henry accepted because the church authorities demanded it. Fanny despises Henry; she despises her life and the shared commonality of it. Personal introspection makes her question her decisions every day.

The moment Henry's eyes catch hers, he cannot look elsewhere quick enough. This is his custom, as if he always means to look at something beyond her. Henry and Fanny seldom speak. When they do, Fanny voices her displeasure at the life Henry has provided. Henry accepts her criticisms without protest. He tells her she is free to return home if she desires. Head east to the land Joseph Smith cultivated before gentiles forced the Mormons west. Fanny scoffs at the suggestion. The only place worse to live than Utah would be home. When she abandoned her family for the Mormons, her kin made it clear—she was dead to them.

Fanny treks across the room and throws open a bedroom door. A moment later she returns with her laundry basket stacked higher. Henry shifts in his chair and studies his scriptures. He will not lift his eyes again until he is certain Fanny has gone to the wash creek.

Three more girls emerge from the upstairs bedrooms. Two of the girls carry babies pressed to their breasts. The girl without a child, Samantha, is expecting one. Fanny's eyes dart to the landing where she shoots accusatory stares at the three sister wives. She despises everyone she must live with. All the girls have provided Henry with an offspring. All except Fanny. The girls, like Henry, avoid Fanny at all costs. Sometimes, when Fanny permits herself to consider her life, she wonders if Joseph Smith's first wife—Emma—viewed her in the same fashion Fanny observes Henry's plural wives. These meditations, when entertained, suffocate Fanny to the point of near compassion.

She turns on her heel and strides toward the door when it is suddenly thrust open and five men—led by William Bath—enter.

Fanny halts, inconvenienced at having her exit blocked. One of the girls shrieks while the others stare dumb and mute. Henry glances at the door and observes the intruding men. They do not look like Mormons. A young woman, Rose, follows in the men's wake. A bout of recognition seizes Henry, but he cannot place where he has seen her before. He removes his reading glasses and stands.

"Good afternoon, gentlemen," Henry says. "Can I help you?"

"We're lookin' for Henry Dawkins," William says. "Is that you?"

"Did Brother Brigham send you?" Henry asks, but he knows the prophet did not send these men. He conjures the church leader's name hoping it will elicit respect and fear.

"Nope," William says, inspecting the room. "Brother Brigham did not send us." In the far corner he spots Hester Martin. A smile spreads across William's lips. "Her daddy sent us." William gestures to the young wife sheltering in the corner.

Henry swallows hard and buries his now-quivering hands into his pant pockets. "I…see," he mutters.

"Rose!" a girl on the landing cries.

Rose lifts her head and spots her sister at the top of the stairs. "Sammy!"

Rose pushes past the men while Sammy runs down the stairs. They embrace at the base of the landing. After a moment, Rose pulls herself away and inspects Samantha's pregnant belly, rubbing it with jealous affection.

"My word, Sammy! You're really gonna be a mother, aren't you?"

"It's a blessing," Samantha says. Tears hang on the corners of her eyes.

"It certainly is," Rose says. Her voice does not hide her envy. Rose scans the room. Henry has taken more wives since he passed through Oklahoma.

"Have you come to join our cause?" Samantha asks. "Did you read *The Book of Mormon* I left?"

"Ladies," William interrupts. "Quiet."

Samantha looks at William and then the rest of the men standing in her home. "What is going on, Rosie?" Samantha asks under her breath.

"Just do what these men say," Rose cautions, patting her sister's hand. "They aren't here for you."

"Why are they here?" Samantha asks.

"Enough!" William shouts. "Your reunion will have to wait. We have a business matter to discuss with Mr. Dawkins."

With a measured step William strolls toward Henry. A line of nervous sweat moistens Henry's eyebrows. William took him for a coward the moment he laid eyes on him. He is almost disappointed; he was hoping for a struggle, and it is clear Henry will not provide one. William arrives at Henry. Looks him over with disgust before turning to the harem of girls who have spilled out from all corners of the house.

"I'm here for Hester Martin," William says. William turns toward Hester. "I've come to return you to your father."

"You cannot take her," Henry says.

William pivots back to Henry and for a fleeting moment catches a modicum of courage in his countenance.

"We were hired for a service," William explains. "My employer would not react kindly if I did not return his daughter to him."

"She is my wife," Henry says.

"Yeah, one of many, I see."

"It is an ordinance for men to take plural wives," Henry says. "Passed down from God Himself."

Fanny scoffs, forcing all eyes to her. She returns all stares with her own, cold and calculated. Outlaws do not scare her. Fear is for those with something to live for. William appraises Fanny and smiles.

"She must be your first wife," William says. "I hear the first wife is always the…least compliant with God's ordinances."

"She is my first plural wife," Henry says. "She is devoted and upstanding in the eyes of God." Henry glances at Fanny, hoping his proclamation soothes her. It does not.

"Well, before Hester Martin was your wife," William says, "she was Mr. Martin's daughter. He wants her back."

"She does not want to return," Henry says. "She is happy here."

"She don't look happy," William says. "She looks like a frightened kitten."

"Her demeanor is in response to this intrusion."

William steps closer to Henry, daring him to insult his presence again. Henry lowers his head and studies the floor.

"I…I…have money," Henry says.

William lifts his eyebrows. "How much?"

"Will you promise not to take her?"

"I have already made a promise to Mr. Martin," William explains. "But money has a tendency to change my mind."

"I will go and get it," Henry says, turning toward a back bedroom. He does not take one step before hearing a gun click. Henry freezes and turns back to William. William aims his gun at Henry's head.

"I can't have you runnin' off and getting a gun," William says.

"I do not own a gun," Henry says.

"That is an error in your judgment," William says. "Any man who kidnaps little girls and marries them oughta own a gun."

"I do not kidnap—"

"Her," William says, pointing his gun at Fanny. "Send her."

Henry's eyes dart to Fanny and then quickly shift elsewhere. She frightens Henry more than William's posse.

"She…does not know where I keep it."

"Well, tell her," William instructs. "Your hidin' place no longer matters since you'll soon have nothin' to hide. You," William says to Fanny, "what is your name?"

Fanny stands straight and answers: "Francis Ward Alger Custer."

"That is a mouthful," William says.

"People call me Fanny."

"That is a horrible name," William sneers, and his men laugh.

"Not *the* Fanny Alger?" Rose asks.

Fanny glances at Rose. "You know me?"

"I know *of* you," Rose exclaims.

"Are you someone worth knowing?" William asks Fanny.

Fanny slouches. "If I am known, I suspect it is for reasons I do not wish to repeat."

William turns to Rose for an explanation. Rose glances at Fanny. She casts her eyes to the floor. Rose feels Fanny's embarrassment although she does not understand the root of it.

"Fanny was Brother Joseph's first wife," Henry explains, having never understood Fanny's indignity to the claim.

"His first *plural* wife," Fanny corrects her husband.

"Brother Joseph?" William asks.

"Joseph Smith," Henry says.

"Well, you Mormons are a close-knit community, aren't you?" William says.

"It was my honor to accept her as my companion after the mob killed Brother Joseph," Henry says.

"Mr. Dawkins," William says, "it appears she doesn't share your enthusiasm for…sharing."

"I do not support plural marriage," Fanny says, her voice full of conviction.

"But you were the first," Rose says.

"I wish I were the last," Fanny says. "It is heartbreaking to share a husband."

"Fanny—"

"Do not silence me, Henry," Fanny says. "It is an abominable practice, and I regret having ever takin' part in it."

Henry falls silent. The domestic tension lingers. William laughs and shakes his head at the absurdity of the situation.

"Fanny," William says. "Be a good sister wife and fetch your husband's money."

Fanny considers protesting, but William has his gun aimed at her. She strides past William and Henry toward the bedroom.

"Let me tell you where I've hidden it," Henry says.

"I know where you hide it, Henry," Fanny says. "Not a night passes where I do not think to take it and leave this life."

Fanny disappears into the back bedroom and returns a moment later carrying a small wooden box. She hands it to William. William throws open the box and pulls out a stack of bills and a few gold coins.

"It's not much," Henry says. "I…I gave most of what I had to the church. For the temple."

"You are right," William says. "It is not much. Certainly not enough to justify returnin' to Mr. Martin without his daughter."

Henry goes flush. "Please, sir. She is my wife under the banner of heaven. You cannot take her. Trust me when I say you do not want God's wrath for doing this."

"God's wrath?" William says.

"God commanded I take Hester as a wife," Henry says, his voice quavering.

"God has abandoned you, Mr. Dawkins," William says.

"God is my strength," Henry says, his voice heavy under the weight of the words he does not believe. "He will protect me and my household. He will cast those out who oppose His work."

"Will He now?" William asks.

"Y-y-yes."

William looks hard at Henry. Burying his stare into Henry, conveying without words that he is about to die. A sudden epiphany strikes Henry. William's mission is twofold—return Hester and kill Henry. Henry swallows. He shakes his head, and mouths "please" under his breath. William smiles. He will extend no mercy. The killing is what he enjoys the most. He lifts his gun and fires a bullet between Henry's eyes. Henry falls to the ground dead. Blood seeps from the wound and stains the floor. The sister wives shriek. Fanny stares down at her dead husband in a trance. She marvels at the blood. Cannot fathom how dark it is, how much there is.

William faces his men. All hands rest on their firearms but none have drawn. The women are too shocked to retaliate.

William looks at each of his men. He knows what depravity grips them. They shuffle their feet in eager anticipation.

"Hester is not to be touched," William says. "Make it fast. It's best we don't linger."

William's men break into lustful grins and advance on the sister wives. Once the wives understand what is happening, they come to life, screaming and crying to a God who, for reasons they cannot comprehend, ignores them. Fanny remains indifferent. She is old and uninviting and assumes she will remain untouched—an assumption that will prove faulty. A man's carnality, at its height, does not discriminate.

Rose and Samantha huddle together. They spot Francis crossing the chaos, striding in their direction. His ravenous eyes frighten them both. Rose slaps him across the face when he reaches for her. The slap stuns him for a second and then he lifts his hand to return the blow. Rose flinches in anticipation, but the blow does not land. William catches Francis by the wrist before he can strike.

"She's mine," William says. "Don't touch her."

Francis jerks his wrist free, disappointed. He looks past Rose to Samantha. She will suffice. He moistens his lips.

"No!" Rose screams, shielding her younger sister from Francis.

William steps in front of Francis and lunges for Rose. She thrashes madly, striking William about the head. He ducks and lifts her over his shoulder. She thunders blows to his back. She kicks and screams and strikes him with targeted condemnation, but her blows do little to stop him. William spins and carries Rose into the back bedroom, stepping over Henry as he goes.

CHAPTER 26

Rose fought. With reckless abandon, she swung her crazed fists. She kicked and thrashed and pleaded.

And lost.

The struggle excited William. He smashed her face with his fists. Hit her until her nose broke. Blood blurred her vision, and she still fought. When William finished, she recoiled and cried and cursed God and then admonished herself for having done so. If she withheld any virtue from her encounter with Porter, it was now stolen by William.

It does not eclipse her that two men have now known her—the first with a gentle hand, the second with a forced one.

Now she lay on the bed motionless while William dresses. His gun, fit tight into its holster, rests on a chair five feet from Rose's reach. She wills herself to lunge for it. Pull it from the worn leather casing and empty it into William's chest. Maybe save a round for herself. If only she could summon the strength to move. To pitch forward and end everything.

William, as if sensing her plan, walks across the room and takes his gun. He fits his belt around his waist and leans down and whispers into Rose's ear. "You fuck better than a whore," he says and presses his palm onto her cheek and pushes himself upright.

He walks to the door and throws it open. "Let's go, boys!" he yells.

Hester sits in the corner, trembling and untouched. William approaches her.

"You're coming with us," he says.

Hester does not move. William extends his hand. Hester hugs herself tighter and closes her eyes. William grabs her arms and lifts her to her feet.

"You'll be safe with us," William promises. "Your daddy paid for that guarantee."

The bedroom doors of the house all swing open and William's men emerge situating their belts. Inside each room is a sister-wife, prostrate and naked, biting their tongues to keep from crying. For some, this is not their first time on the damaging end of a man's desires. Their wedding nights marked that distinction. It is not uncommon for Mormon husbands to violate their teenage sister wives when consummating their wedding vows. Some of the sister wives now question the difference between the desires ordained of God or the devil. To them, the indignity is impossible to differentiate.

The posse descends the stairs and congregates at the landing. Their spirits are high, their dispositions boisterous. They bask in the spoils of being a man in a world populated with oppressed women.

Their celebratory demeanor breaks when, without warning, Fanny tears open a nearby door and emerges. Her hair is in tangles, and her torn dress exposes a wild breast. In her right hand is a gun. She takes aim at the cluster of men and fires. The ball hits Francis in the shoulder. He cries and spins toward Fanny. He draws his pistol and shoots Fanny in the chest. She drops the gun and slumps over dead.

"Goddamn whore!" Francis yells, clutching his wounded arm. He bellows and then turns and puts his fist through an unsuspecting wall. The men laugh, grateful Fanny's haphazard shot hit Francis and not them.

Once the excitement dissipates, the men look up at the landing where Francis had emerged. They find Samantha, trembling and determined, holding Fanny's gun. She has it pointed at Francis—her violator. Tears stream down her cheeks, cutting clean paths through the blood and dirt that mark her face. Her quivering mouth is a pool of red. Tiny white specks—her teeth—powders her lips. Earlier Francis had tried thrusting his penis down her throat. She resisted, and at one point clamped down so hard that he smashed her teeth with the butt of his gun.

The men raise their hands. Samantha feels powerful behind the gun, respected. With a careful step, she descends the stairs, her dead eyes fixed on Francis. She must get closer to ensure she does not miss. She will put a round between Francis's eyes and watch his spirit leave his body.

"Lower your gun, miss," William says, but Samantha pays him no mind. Francis has her complete focus. Samantha stops less than ten feet from the men. Her hand steady, poised. She pulls the trigger and the gun jams. She looks at it, confused by the malfunction, and in the brief lull, William pulls his gun and shoots Samantha in the head. She falls dead and tumbles down the remaining stairs to the men's feet.

William and his men watch as blood trickles from Samantha's head and crawls toward them. William notices Owen staring past him. He follows Owen's gaze over his shoulder and turns. Rose stands in the doorway of a bedroom. She looks from William to her dead sister. The knowledge seeps in. She screams. She bolts to her sister, collapses, and cradles Samantha's head in her lap.

"You animals!" Rose wails. "She was pregnant! You murdered a pregnant girl!"

Francis spits. The saliva lands inches from Rose's feet. He grabs his injured shoulder and turns toward the door. The other men follow. Rose spies Samantha's gun. She scrambles for it, retrieves it before any of the men can determine her cause. She picks it up and fires a shot into Francis's leg. Francis yells and turns and fires a shot into Rose's chest.

"Goddamn it!" Francis screams. In a fit of hysteria, he takes aim at the other sister wives who have congregated to watch the slaughter. Francis empties his gun, and pulls his second, and empties it too. A moment later, all the wives, save for Hester, lay dead.

Francis's agonized breathing cuts into the looming silence. His shirt and pants are stained red. William approaches Francis, taking stock of his wounds.

"Can you ride?" William asks.

Francis grunts.

"Let's go before a mob forms," William says.

"It's forming now," Albert says. He stands at the window. Owen and Clay stand on either side of him watching the Mormons congregate outside the house.

"They armed?" William asks.

"It doesn't look like it," Albert says.

"Time to go," William says. He grabs Hester by the arm and pulls her to the door. As William forces her outside, she examines the lifeless faces of her sister wives. Her expression a mixture of fear and jealousy.

Outside a small crowd has gathered. Some have guns, most do not. The ones who do, keep them lowered, concealed behind long shirts and coats.

With guns drawn, William and his men mount their horses. On the edge of the crowd, William sees a man holding a gun at his side. His eyes lock with William's. The man raises the gun but does not fire a shot before William lifts his own pistol and takes aim.

"Don't even think about it," William says to the Mormon. "Drop it," William commands. The Mormon freezes, appreciates the situation, and drops the gun.

Owen rides to a Mormon carrying a torch. He yanks the torch from the man and hurls it through a window of the house. The torch clatters to the floor and the flame finds the curtains and catches fire. Clay, Francis, and Albert all follow suit, stealing torches from the onlookers and setting fire to the house.

They do this because they can. Because some men do not know how to build; they only know how to destroy.

Flames engulf the house. No one dares move. William keeps his gun fixed on the spectators as he and his men ride toward the blood-red sun.

CHAPTER 27

Porter's horse did not last more than a day before it stopped. It staggered fifty feet and then dropped dead. Had the horse lived another hour, had Porter not urged it forward when it had nothing left to give, Porter may have caught Rose.

Porter continued the rest of the way on foot. On the third day he found Rose's horse behind a mass of rocks. The animal assessed Porter and then lowered its head in deference as Porter stroked its mane. Porter whispered in its ear, asking where Rose had gone, subscribing to the intuitions of animals like others presume the power of Gods. Porter swung one leg over the animal and set off toward Utah.

* * * * *

The temple's foundation causes Porter to pause. The white marble stands stark against the desert plains. Porter cannot help but question why a people so certain the Second Coming is near, would relegate so much time and effort to build an edifice that will prove irrelevant when Christ returns.

Past the temple Porter eyes the smoldering remains of Henry Dawkins' house. His instincts tell him what he does not want confirmed. Porter contemplates steering his horse away and departing the Salt Lake Valley as he exited the war. He no longer has the stomach for death, and he knows death awaits him if he rides further into the settlement. Common sense tells him to detour and continue to California. Common sense is reserved for the man who is granted a long life. Porter is not that man, so he rides toward the ashen house.

Smoke swirls from the charred foundation. A handful of men cluster about. They stare at the destroyed house with inscrutable faces. Outside the smoldering remains, Porter spies three dead sister wives placed in a neat row. The ruthless stench of death hangs heavy. A man exits the house carrying another body. He places it at the end of the line enumerating the deceased.

Porter dismounts his horse. He studies the dead, notes Rose is not among them, and starts for the house. An onlooker grabs Porter's forearm and asks who he is. Porter pulls his arm free and enters the smoking home. His instincts lead him to Rose. She lies dead under a pile of debris. Porter tosses the cinders about until he can pull her free. He carries her from the house. He walks to the row of the dead and places Rose at the end. His eyes fall to the girl next to Rose. Porter assumes the girl is Samantha. Her face is swollen and dried blood sticks to her ashen cheeks. Porter crouches toward her and opens her mouth, studies the dental shards outfitting her gums. His face screws up in confusion. *Why break her teeth?* he marvels.

He kneels over Rose and inspects her. Her teeth are still in place, but her eyes and nose are swollen. Her face is not hers. Porter fills in the spaces, in his mind he witnesses the struggle. He frowns and lifts her dress. Her delicate parts are bruised and violated. Porter's eyes tighten, his jaw tenses.

Then a gun clicks.

"Lower that dress," a voice behind Porter instructs. Porter pulls down the dress but not because he was ordered to do so. He does not want passerby to see Rose's damaged parts.

Porter gets to his feet and turns. Two men with heavy beards stand before him. Porter deduces one man is Brigham Young. The other, Porter divines, shares his name. He is right on both accounts.

The second man settles his gun on Porter. Porter discerns he knows how to use it, and he uses it often. He stares at Porter through long, stringy hair. His eyes are hollow and trained to push all the world's ugliness to places few men have ever visited. He does not frighten Porter, but his presence is formidable. They have more in common than a name.

"Who are you?" Brigham Young asks.

Porter does not answer.

"Were you with them?" Young asks. "The posse from Arkansas?"

Porter shakes his head, and the prophet discerns he is speaking true.

"Who are you?" Young asks again.

"I suggest you answer the prophet," the man with the gun says.

"I know the mother of two of the girls," Porter says, nodding to the line of charred dead girls.

"They took one girl with them," Young says. "Hester is her name."

Porter nods.

"You know anything about that?" Young asks, and Porter shakes his head. "They are from Arkansas. I think they came for revenge. For what happened at Mountain Meadows."

Porter stares into the distance, bored with the interrogation.

"You know what happened at Mountain Meadows?" Young asks.

Porter nods. He had read about the slaughter at Mountain Meadows in the Union papers. Nothing about it surprised him. At the time, it seemed the entire world was at war. Seems that way still, Porter reasons.

"I had nothing to do with it," Young answers. "Jon Lee ordered the killings."

"So you say," Porter whispers.

"It is the truth!" Young proclaims.

"I'm not here because of Mountain Meadows," Porter says.

"Then why are you here?" Young asks.

"To try to stop what I could not," Porter says.

Brigham Young and his gunman value Porter with skeptical eyes, but they understand something in his demeanor registers as truth. Porter is not an enemy; he is a man, bereaved and numb.

"What's your name, boy?" Young asks.

Porter ignores the question. He looks back to the ground and studies the dead. A crowd assembles. They approach with cautious steps, hoping to overhear the prophet's examination.

"I asked you a question," Young says.

"Answer the prophet!" the gunman says.

Porter sighs. No sense in dying over something as trivial as a name.

"Porter," he answers.

Brigham Young and the gunman exchange a furtive glance.

"Porter?" Young says. "Your name is Porter?"

Porter nods.

"Well," Young says, addressing the gunman. "It appears you two have the same name."

"Seems that way," the gunman says and spits. The spittle lands on Porter's boot. "Middle name, at least," the gunman adds.

Brigham Young flickers an ominous sneer. "Porter," Brigham Young says to Porter, "meet another Porter—Orrin Porter Rockwell."

CHAPTER 28

Porter sits at Brigham Young's table staring at the heap of fried chicken and mashed potatoes placed in front of him. Porter does not eat. He wants to, and all his faculties are begging him to, but he will not. His pride restrains his hunger. He will not break bread with a man whose moral code is at odds with his own.

Young sits at the head of the table. He gnaws on a chicken bone before dropping it onto his plate and licking his fingers. Rockwell stands behind Young. A sentinel at the watch. He eyes Porter. Porter does not fear him, but he appreciates his talent for murder.

The house is infested with women—Young's sister wives. They congregate with downcast eyes and somber expressions. Some appear like beaten dogs, afraid to make sudden movements and risk disappointing their master. They keep to themselves, performing a variety of domesticated tasks without rousing attention. Others sit proud and erect. Basking in the knowledge that God chose them as companions to the world's only true prophet. When Young calls to them, they float across the room, dignified and unapologetic. The latter-days are near, and because they submit to the prophet, God will bless them in the next life as He has in this one. This belief, however nonsensical, sustains them.

Young motions to one of his wives, and she drops her sewing and hustles to the table and clears her husband's plate. She looks at Porter's dinner. He has not touched it. She turns to her husband for guidance.

"You're not hungry?" Young asks Porter.

Porter slides his plate toward the obedient wife. Young nods and the wife gathers Porter's plate and hurries into the kitchen. Perpetual hunger tempts her to steal the uneaten chicken. To feast on the bounty that the stranger did not accept, but she, like Porter, resists the desire. No morsel of chicken is worth the inevitable punishment awaiting her if the prophet learns she ate without permission.

Young motions to Rockwell. The bodyguard strides across the room and takes a dirty bottle from a nearby cabinet and returns to the table. He uncorks the bottle and pours the prophet a drink. Young lifts his eyebrows to Porter—an offering—Porter looks away.

"This is the best whiskey in the valley," Young proclaims. He downs the spirit and motions for Rockwell to pour him another. "My congregation thinks it's a sin to drink. I think it is a sin not to." He downs his second shot. He nods to Rockwell and Rockwell returns the liquor to the cabinet.

"I plan to make a distillery," Young says. "Rockwell will run it."

A distillery? Porter ponders. He had heard tales of Joseph Smith and his disdain for liquor. Young seems to sense Porter's confusion. He pats Porter's arm and smiles.

"Brother Smith would approve, I think. He did not oppose hearty drinks unless his wife was in shouting distance. He appreciated an inebriated state as much as the next man." Young glances at Rockwell. A knowing smile spreads across the murderer's chapped lips. Porter glances at the assassin, and Rockwell's tough demeanor returns.

Young nods to Rockwell to bring more liquor. He does, and Young takes a nip from the bottle and winces at its strength.

"What do you plan to do?" he asks Porter.

Porter prefers to remain silent, but he knows providing answers is the quickest way to escape Young's den of iniquity.

"I plan to return the bodies," Porter says. "The mother will want them buried at her ranch."

"They were Mr. Dawkins's wives," Young says. "We can bury them. Give them a proper Mormon funeral."

"Only the younger sister married Mr. Dawkins," Porter says.

"It was my understanding the other came here to wed him," Young says.

"You were misinformed," Porter says. "The older sister had no intention of marrying into this…ideology."

"Ideology?" Young repeats. "Young man, this 'ideology,' will usher in the latter—"

"I'm taking the bodies to the mother," Porter interrupts. Beyond Young, Rockwell places his hand on his pistol. Porter catches the gesture but does not react. Rockwell is a trained killer, but his movements are too obvious. Porter knows if he must, he could lodge a bullet into Rockwell's skull before the bodyguard could even draw.

"Fair enough," Young says, respecting the intensity in Porter's demands. He nods to Rockwell who drops his hand to his side. "And after you bury the bodies, will you venture on to Arkansas?" Young asks.

Porter does not answer, but Young perceives a glint of confirmation in Porter's countenance.

"Take Rockwell with you," Young says. "He's good at killing." Rockwell almost blushes at the compliment.

"No," Porter says.

"We want vengeance as much as you do," Young says. "We are a close community here. Those butchers killed a fine man and raped and murdered his faithful women."

"Girls," Porter corrects Young.

"Excuse me?" Young says.

Porter stares him square in the eyes. "Girls," he repeats. "There wasn't a woman among them. They raped girls…just like you do."

Rockwell's hand rushes to his gun. He would have pulled it and taken aim at Porter had Young's own hand not landed on top of Rockwell's, keeping him from drawing. Young shakes his head to his loyal servant. Rockwell nods to the prophet, but he remains rigid, ready to pull if needed.

"We do not rape girls here," Young says.

Porter spies a young girl sitting in the corner knitting. Her knitting materials rest on her pregnant belly. Her eyes meet Porter's for a moment. She whimpers and averts her gaze, fearful for having looked at a man who was not her husband. She knits with newfound vigor.

"That girl cannot be more than thirteen," Porter says.

Young looks at the girl in question. "Clarrisa?" Young says. "She just turned fifteen."

"And she's with child," Porter observes.

"It's a blessing," Young says.

"Did she consent, or did you force her under the guise of God's will?"

"They all consent," Young says.

Porter stares at the young sister wife, but the girl will not look at Porter.

"She's more timid than a beaten horse."

"She is a vessel for truth and called to bring about God's plan."

"She is a pawn. Used to bridle your lust. You bed these girls under the false claim that God has chosen you to bring about his plan."

Rockwell's building rage can no longer remain unchecked. His loyalty to the prophet forces his hand. He draws his gun intending to silence Porter with a bullet through his throat, but before he can act, Porter is already out of his chair. He dodges Rockwell's arm and pulls his own gun. Porter smacks Rockwell on his temple with his gun, and slams Rockwell's head onto the table. He forces

Rockwell's arm behind his back while pressing his head to the table. Porter twists Rockwell's arm until he drops his gun. It clatters to the floor and Porter kicks it under the table. Porter drills his gun into the side of Rockwell's head. Rockwell grunts and tries to free himself from Porter's hold but cannot. The exchange took less than two seconds.

Silence fills the room. The harem of sister wives freeze. Their domestic hobbies forgotten.

"Easy, boy," Brigham Young says. He sounds calm, but Porter reads the fear in his face.

"I have no quarrel with you," Porter says. "I just want to return the bodies to their mother."

Young catches Rockwell's eye. His disjointed arm aches, although he tries to pretend otherwise. Porter could snap it with ease. It registers with Young that Rockwell knows this, and Young sees something in Rockwell he has never seen before: fear.

"Take the bodies," Young says. "You will encounter no resistance from us."

Porter releases Rockwell. Rockwell stands straight and tries to mask the pain in his arm. His pride is shot, and he looks anywhere other than at Porter. He wants to retrieve his gun and fire a bullet between Porter's eyes but knows if he tried, Porter would beat him to the task.

Young stands and puts a consoling hand on Porter's shoulder. "Believe what you will about us," Young says, "but we *are* God's chosen. He has called on us to usher in the latter-days." Young tries to determine if his words impact Porter. They do not. "I'll have someone prepare the bodies," Young says. "I wish you a safe journey back to Oklahoma."

Young turns to one of his sister wives and tells her to bring him the bundle. The wife scurries from the room and returns holding a charred knapsack. Porter recognizes the sack as Rose's. The wife hands the bundle to Young, and he passes it to Porter.

"The woman who came with the posse, Samantha's sister, she had that with her," Young says.

Porter opens the sack and pulls a seared copy of *Frankenstein* from inside. He drops the book back into the sack and starts for the door.

"If you continue on to Arkansas," Young calls after Porter, "I hope your vengeance is swift. I will pray for your success."

Porter pushes open the door and exits the house. He cannot leave the Mormon country fast enough.

CHAPTER 29

Quinn sits on her porch examining the dusty prairie. This is how she has spent the past week. Waiting for the harsh reality of what she knows is coming. When Porter materializes in the distance, he confirms her greatest fear. She knows because if things were otherwise, riders would be next to him. There are no riders next to him. Just a riderless horse carrying two lifeless bodies. The distance is too great to make out who the horse carries, but Quinn knows. A mother knows.

She rises from her porch and starts toward the lone rider. Her stride increases and soon she is running at Porter. Twenty feet from him she collapses in a heap of parental sorrow. Porter stops his horse and dismounts. He goes to Quinn, kneels, and lifts her to her feet. Their eyes lock. This is all the confirmation Quinn needs. She clutches Porter and wails into the dusty Oklahoma landscape.

Porter releases her and stands rigid. He is not the man who left for the Utah Territory last week. He steps past Quinn and, towing his horse, heads for the barn. When he exits the barn, he is carrying the dull spade.

Quinn stumbles toward the horse carrying her children. With a shaking hand she removes the white linen covering her daughters' faces. Deep purple bruises make the girls almost unrecognizable.

Quinn must squint and tilt her head to see her daughters' faces hidden deep beneath the savage marks desecrating their faces. She caresses her daughters swollen and disfigured features. Buried under the grief of her daughters' murders lies a deeper grief: her failings as a mother. Trembling lips come to rest on Rose's forehead. They curse God, admonishing Him and His damned order of things. Why is it that He always expects His children to do what is right, yet the same standards do not apply to Him?

When Quinn pulls the horse toward the house, she finds Porter under the massive oak digging the graves. Quinn guides the horse to the oak. She takes Samantha's body, nearly buckling from the weight, and places her on the ground with a softness she never extended to her while alive. She does the same with Rose. Porter digs, and Quinn dissolves to the ground and watches Porter work.

"Can I help?" Quinn asks, but she knows Porter will not answer. She asks because her Christian character requires it. She does not have the strength to help. How Porter has the fortitude to drive the spade into the dirt is a mystery. Yet he does it. He plunges the tool into the callous dirt and tosses the shovelfuls beyond the oak. Quinn, broken with sorrow, falls to her side and falls asleep, whispering to God never to wake her.

She wakes an hour later. She sits up and winces, her back aching from the unforgiving ground. The graves are dug, and Porter lifts Samantha over his shoulder and places her body into her grave. Next, he goes to Rose. He crouches to lift her but stalls for a moment. His lips draw thin, and he swallows hard. He holds out his hand. Like Quinn's, it shakes—the tremors of the bereaved. He clenches the hand into a fist, confused with the tremor, and lifts Rose from the earth. He carries her to the grave and sets her gently inside.

"I fear I may have caused this," Quinn says. Her voice is empty and stripped of all life. "I wasn't a very good mother. Lord knows I tried, though." A soft breeze kicks up little eddies of dirt. "After my husband died, I just...I was at a loss. My father told me the Lord was testing me. Like a modern-day Job. Looks like I failed, huh? Every test the Lord gave me I failed. I drove my son to a senseless war and drove both my girls away. One to the arms of a Mormon and the other to the bed of an agnostic."

Quinn spies Porter to determine if her words land the blow she desires. Porter is stoic, unmoved.

"I deserve this," Quinn continues, "but my girls didn't. Why did they have to suffer for my shortcomings?" Quinn pauses, contemplates the hard truth she has never voiced. "I was bitter," she says, her voice cracking with the admission. "That's the truth. I was bitter, and I was angry when my father got sick. Why should James reap the benefits of his illness? It should have been me—at least that's what I thought, and God rebuked me for having such thoughts. For thinking a woman could lead a church. For questioning a patriarchy that exists simply because tradition dictates it must. People cannot see past their ancestors' ways. So, my father's followers flocked to James while I got a crippled father, a dead son, and two neglected daughters. It's no wonder Sammy left and Rose followed. Hell, I would have too if someone came along with the prospect of a better life." Quinn wipes her nose on her sleeve. She looks to the sky and cries: "I'm sorry, Father! Forgive me my trespasses!"

Porter takes his knapsack and retrieves his scorched copy of *Frankenstein*. He places it on Rose's breast, again noting his trembling hand as he does so. Quinn cannot make out the book's title but presumes it to be a Bible. She smiles with great pain and affection.

"A Bible." Quinn says. "Thank you, Porter. She would like that."

Porter lets the oversight go unchallenged. He takes up the spade and begins filling the hole. Soon, Porter has filled both graves. Quinn tries to stand but cannot. Porter helps her to her feet.

She falls into Porter. Porter staggers backwards from her weight but manages to remain upright.

"What do I do now?" she whispers into Porter's ear.

Porter scoops her into his arms and carries her into the house and upstairs to her bedroom. By the time he places her on the bed, she is already asleep.

CHAPTER 30

The next morning Porter rises before the sun. His plan is to leave before Quinn wakes. When he exits the bedroom, he finds Quinn at the kitchen table huddled over a cold cup of coffee. She lifts her head when Porter enters. From the lines drawn on her face, Porter knows she did not sleep the previous night. Until this moment, Porter never charted how much Rose resembled her mother. It breaks Porter to look at Quinn now.

"I need a horse," Porter says.

"To go to California?" she asks.

"I'll return it," Porter says, ignoring the question. "It won't be more than a week."

"Where are you going, Porter?" Quinn knows where he plans to go. Porter does not have time for an interrogation, for trivial quarrels. "It's best to go to the authorities," Quinn says. "They broke the law. You're not a bounty hunter, Porter."

"You don't know what I am."

"There's five of them."

Porter starts for the door. "A week," he says over his shoulder.

Quinn jumps to her feet, knocking her chair against the wall. Porter halts and turns. Quinn's chest is heaving.

"They were my daughters!" Quinn cries. "They raped and murdered *my* daughters!" Quinn strikes her heaving chest, punctuating her claim to motherhood. "Goddamn you for coming into my life," she cries. "Goddamn you for coming into this world."

Porter remains expressionless. He will let Quinn curse and reprimand him if that is what Quinn needs to accept what has happened. Porter will not begrudge her that luxury. She has earned it.

A minute passes and Quinn runs a dirty hand through her dirty hair. When she looks up, James is standing in the door.

"I came to offer my condolences," James says.

Quinn sinks into her chair.

"Was it the Mormons?" James asks. Quinn looks at Porter for confirmation.

Porter shakes his head.

"The men from Arkansas?" James asks. Porter nods.

James approaches his sister and places a hand on her shoulder. "I know you are hurting. I can understand and appreciate your grief, but God has a plan."

"You know nothing of my grief," Quinn says. She pitches forward, tossing James's hand from her shoulder.

"Rose was my niece," James says.

"She was your chore girl," Quinn counters. "Did you ever speak a kind word to her?"

"She knew she was appreciated."

"Us women always are."

"What is that supposed to mean?"

"It means you can't appreciate what it means to be a woman in a man's world, James. We live at your constant beck and call."

"Don't be ridiculous, Quinn."

"Ridiculous?" Quinn repeats. "You strip a woman of her wife and mother status and what is she?"

James's face is pure confusion. "What are you talking about, Quinn?"

"What is she?" Quinn asks.

"Who?" James asks. "I'm not sure what you're asking."

"I'm asking what is a woman if she is not a wife or a mother?"

"I...I don't know."

"A damn disgrace, James," Quinn says. "An embarrassment. We are nothing else but ignorant if we pretend to be surprised when Sammy and Rose left for Utah."

"Quinn—"

"What other choice did Rose have than to run away to be a sister wife to some Mormon? I caused this. Every time I seconded dad's wisdom that a woman's place is in the home, I drove Rose further from who she was. Every time I asked her to put down a book and pick up *The Bible,* I drove her further away."

"That's ridiculous," James says.

"She was strong and smart and we cursed her for it!" Quinn cries. "We told her it was better to be soft and submissive. Find a husband. That's all women are good for."

"She had her agency," James argues, "and she employed that agency to sleep with an atheist." James casts an accusatory glance at Porter. Porter gives no reaction.

"She had the agency of a slave who can pick her master," Quinn cries.

James is incredulous. "Are you comparing companionship to slavery?" he asks.

"What kind of companionship requires unwavering obedience to one party?" Quinn asks. "Rose felt trapped. She felt what I felt in my marriage and what Claire feels in hers."

"Claire does not feel trapped," James says.

"Look into her eyes, James," Quinn says. "Your ways have sucked all the life from her."

"She is a righteous, upstanding woman."

"She is as dead as my daughters," Quinn says.

James raises his hand to strike Quinn, but Porter grabs his wrist before he can land the blow. They exchange a hateful glance. Porter dares him to try to hit his sister again. James pulls his hand free from Porter's grasp and paces the kitchen and reclaims his composure.

"I curse you for making such claims," James says to Quinn. "Do not conflate what happened to Rose and Sammy with the union I have with my wife. Rose's choices led to her death. God punished her for her iniquities."

Quinn crosses to her brother and strikes James hard across his mouth. The pain is manageable, but it is the shock that silences him. He did not see Quinn move. She advanced on him before he could even process the words he uttered that forced the action.

"You are not my brother," Quinn says, her chest again heaving. She dares James to speak again, to proclaim more false gospel so she can end his blasphemy for good. "If you speak ill of my daughters again, I will take you out back and hang you from the oak."

James studies his sister. She is more foreign to him now than a new language. Her hand makes a pink outline on her brother's cheek. He massages the tender spot and turns for the door.

"I'll pray for you," he whispers. James pushes past Porter and exits the house. The door slams shut after him, and a silence penetrates the room. Quinn waits a moment before breaking it.

"I'm coming with you," Quinn says.

Porter nods and steps outside the house.

• • • • • •

They spend the day riding. Quinn steals glances at Porter, watching him watch the horizon, wondering what he is thinking, contemplating. Neither speaks for which Porter is grateful. The silence makes Quinn grow fretful. If asked, she could not explain what she expects to get from this trek. Justice maybe? What does justice look like? She is not a killer. She is a daughter of God. When faced with confrontation, she turns the other cheek, or tries at least.

These thoughts rack her. It is not until hours later she knows why she asked to follow Porter—she did not want to be alone. She did not know what else to do with herself. Being alone in her house haunted by the ghosts of her father, husband, son, and daughters. She could not fathom it. Her home has become a sarcophagus. To stay would mean accepting her own death.

Quinn wonders how long they will ride. The sun will soon set, and Porter gives no indication of stopping. Quinn calls to him, tells him she needs to relieve herself. Porter pulls on his reins and stares at Quinn as if seeing her for the first time.

"Are we planning to ride through the night?" Quinn asks.

Porter lifts his gaze, stares into the darkening night. He dismounts and retrieves a blanket from his bundle. He drops his blanket onto the ground and sets off to gather wood for a fire. An hour later he and Quinn are under the stars watching the fire's dancing flames. Quinn is restless but curbs her budding inquiries. If the circumstances were different, the night would pass as pleasant. Idyllic. Half an hour later, she can no longer restrain herself. She needs answers.

"Why are we going to Arkansas?" Quinn asks. She knows the answer, and Porter knows she knows, but Quinn needs a verbal confirmation. "You're going to kill those men, aren't you, Porter?"

The fire is dying, and Quinn can barely make out Porter over the gasping flames. Quinn hopes for an answer but knows Porter will not extend one without more prodding.

"I suspect you've killed before, being in the war and all," Quinn says. "I could count on one hand how many times I've fired a gun. The few times I did, it was always to put an animal out of its misery or for food. Even then, it wasn't easy to do. My dad did most of the slaughtering. I wouldn't even watch if I could help it. When I got married, I tended to the home while Benjamin did any necessary killings." Quinn sees if her words impact Porter. They do not. The fire crackles. A comfortable chill cools the night.

"What's it like, Porter?" Quinn asks. "Killing a man?"

A mosquito lands on Porter's arm. He watches the insect bury its nose into Porter's skin. Its sac fills with blood and then Porter swats the bug dead, leaving a red blotch on his arm.

"I can't condone killing, Porter. The right thing to do, the lawful thing, is to hand the men over to the authorities."

Porter likes to pretend God, if one exists, swats at humans with the same indifference humans swat at mosquitoes. *How insignificant we all are*, Porter thinks. The thought almost elicits a laugh. He would like to run this hypothesis past Rose. Present it to her so she can dismiss it and tell him why he is wrong. Argue men are not the same as mosquitoes. He loved talking with her. Debating, disagreeing with her philosophies while promoting his own. He pushes the fantasy from his mind and wipes his eyes, shielding Quinn from his vulnerable moment.

"Can you tell me what you're thinkin'?" Quinn asks, breaking the silence. "What is your plan?" Porter notes the frustration in her voice.

A new mosquito lands on Porter's arm. This one takes its fill and Porter watches it without taking action. The mosquito flies into the night, ignorant to Porter's benevolence.

"For crying out loud, Porter!" Quinn cries. "Talk to me! I deserve to know what you're thinking. They were my girls!"

Porter lifts his head. The fire outlines his cold, rigid features, highlighting his edges and anger. Quinn notices a spark in his eye. It chills her.

"You know what empathy is?" he asks.

The question throws Quinn. She runs the word through her mind. "You mean like putting you in another man's shoes to better understand him?"

"Yeah."

"What about it?" Quinn asks.

"That's my plan."

Quinn digests Porter's answer, but it only leads to more confusion. "How do you mean?"

"I'm going to make those men feel empathy for your daughters. Turning them over to the authorities would rob them and me of that privilege."

Quinn contemplates this. "You intend to rape and then murder them?"

"In a manner of speaking."

"I'm curious how you will accomplish that, but I'm too fearful to ask," Quinn says. "God will judge them and make them pay for their trespasses in the next life, Porter. If you kill them, you're no better than they are. Let's go to the authorities and let God do His job."

Porter scratches his chin and stares at the fire.

"Your beliefs frighten me, Porter. They frighten me more that they don't frighten you. I'm not a killer."

"Then go home," Porter says. He turns onto his side and rests his head on his arm.

The last flame dies. Porter's words hang in the air, heavy against the listless night.

"I wish I could go home," Quinn says. "Ever since we left the ranch, I've wanted to turn back, but something keeps me here. I haven't decided yet if it's God or the devil."

"It's you," Porter says over his shoulder.

"What?"

"You're here because you want to see me do the things you're too afraid to do. If you were honest with yourself, you'd admit you want those men dead."

Quinn opens her mouth to speak, but her rebuttal remains locked in her throat. Porter is correct, and Quinn prays God cannot access the part of her that hopes to witness Porter's vengeance come to pass.

CHAPTER 31

Quinn wakes. Porter is gone, but his bedding is not. A pot of coffee rests over fresh coals. Everything hurts when Quinn moves. It is an effort to rise and pour herself the coffee. She ambles to a dead log and sits against it. In the distance she hears the trickling of a stream. She marvels how she did not hear it the previous night. She surmises Porter knew of it and stopped here because of it. Quinn suspects coincidences are not a common occurrence with Porter.

Porter stares into the stream's black moving water and dwells on death. He recounts how he killed his father, ruminates on Rose's murder, and contemplates the killings he will commit later. Porter does not believe Rose exists anywhere. Logic tells him her life, cut short at the hands of a madman, is extinguished and cannot be reclaimed. However, deep in the recesses of his heart, he ponders if she might exist in some other realm, some other…form. He scolds himself for having these ridiculous thoughts, yet when they haunt him, he is slow to drive them away. He embraces them, allows them to tease him with the prospect he may one day hold Rose again. That he may argue with her over the merits of different books. Debate her on theology, philosophy, and love. These phantom fantasies dance inside his head, and although he does not trust any of them will happen, he indulges in the fictions because they comfort him, if only for a moment.

Porter does not pretend to divine what happens when someone dies. Nonsensical certainties are for the foolish. He only knows what he knows, and what he knows is Rose is dead. But he still talks to her as if she were not. He tells her what he plans to do, and he knows she would not approve. He hears her rebuttal. She speaks to him in cliches, tells him two wrongs do not make a right. Turn the other cheek. He dismisses her platitudes. She is gone while he must stay, so she does not get to enforce her tired ideologies. If he must exist without her, then he must find comfort within himself. Killing will comfort him. At least he imagines it will. She cannot rob him of that, and he will not give her the privilege of trying to do so.

He apologizes to the stream for who he is, for what he is, and then gets to his feet.

Quinn has fallen asleep perched against the dead log, her coffee mug tipped onto its side, its contents staining the earth. Porter taps her on the shoulder. Quinn jumps, startled, and looks up at Porter. Porter says nothing, and Quinn reads in his expression that they need to go. An hour later, they ride to the Arkansas border.

Twenty miles into Arkansas they come to a town. Porter sweeps the terrain, examining the surroundings. In the distance he spots a tavern. He pulls on his reins and halts his horse. Listens. The town is quiet, ominous. Quinn does not like it, but Porter welcomes it. Something is brewing. Vengeance.

Quinn asks Porter why they have stopped but receives no answer. Drunken laughter invades the silence. A hundred yards ahead Albert and Clay stumble into the street. Each carries a half-empty bottle of whiskey. Porter lowers his hat and places a stable hand over his gun and squints at them. They are too drunk to pay him or Quinn any attention. Their step falters as they cross the street and enter the tavern. Porter directs his horse down a grimy side street. Quinn follows. They come to an old, splintered outhouse. Flies circle. The stench is strong.

Porter dismounts and unstraps his bundle. He notes its contents and retrieves a second gun. He checks that it is loaded. Past the outhouse is a horse post. Porter walks his steed to the rail and ties the reins to the post. Quinn draws her horse next to Porter's.

"What's your plan?" Quinn asks.

Porter starts past Quinn, and Quinn grabs him by the arm. Porter stops, pulls his gun, cocks it, and points it between Quinn's eyes. The soldier awakened and ready for battle. Porter performs the gesture before Quinn can even register the barrel is between her eyes. Acknowledgement settles in and fear floods Quinn's face. She removes her hand and steps back. Porter holsters his gun, and lowers his head, ashamed. The action was instinctual. He mumbles an incoherent apology.

"How do you see this playing out, Porter?" Quinn asks. Porter does not think on the question. Too much deliberation may rob him of his wits. He pushes past her and sets off toward the tavern. Quinn contemplates her choices before running after Porter. They round the corner together. The town is dead save for the horseflies circling a dog rotting dead in the street. Quinn stays at Porter's hip, fearful to be next to him, more fearful to be anywhere else. They arrive at the tavern.

Less than ten people are inside. The few customers drink watered-down whiskey and play poker. Clay and Albert sit at the bar, each with a woman on his lap. Porter enters the saloon like a shadow and drifts to the bar unnoticed. Quinn stands at the door, shaking, frozen with fear and excitement. She wishes she had a gun yet grateful she does not. She cannot keep score of her contradictions.

Porter grabs each woman and pulls them from the men's laps. They squeal and stumble toward the poker tables. Before Clay and Albert can register what is happening, Porter pulls each man's gun from his belt and shoots them both in their kneecaps. Albert falls to the ground clutching his leg. Porter grabs Clay by the collar, keeping him upright at the bar. He cocks his gun and places it between Clay's eyes.

"Where are the rest of your men?" Porter asks. Clay grunts and clenches his teeth. Porter repeats his question, but Clay does not answer. Porter asks again where the other men are; Clay remains mute. Porter shoots him through his boot. The bullet rips through the worn leather and a small splatter of blood lands to the floor next to Albert. Clay cries and curses and Porter tells him the next one is between his eyes if he does not answer the question.

"Brothel," he sputters. "Down the road."

Porter waves his gun at the saloon's entrance. "You see that woman," Porter says, pointing to Quinn. Clay looks at Quinn. He remembers her. "She had two daughters," Porter explains. "One was at her brother's ranch. The other was in Utah. Pregnant girl about fourteen years old. Did you rape either?"

Clay grimaces and shakes his head. Porter looks down at Albert. He is squirming about, trying to drag himself to the exit. Porter points his gun at Albert, and Albert raises his hands in surrender.

"Was it you?" Porter asks.

"No," Albert says. He can sense Porter does not trust him. "I swear," he adds. "I didn't rape no teen. I took the older one."

"Who raped them?" Porter asks.

Both men stare at each other, too afraid to answer. Porter puts a bullet into Albert's other kneecap.

"Goddamn it!" Albert cries, clutching his knee.

"Who was it?" Porter asks. His voice is even, but his patience is wearing thin. Quinn thinks to do something, but she does not know what.

"William," Albert screams. "William raped the older sister. The one at your ranch." Alberts twists his chin towards Quinn.

Porter's face tightens. He suspected William would choose Rose. "Who raped the younger one?" he asks.

"Francis," Albert says.

Porter places the guns on the bar and takes a length of rope from around his waist and ties Clay's hands. Using the rope, he pulls Clay from the barstool. Clay hobbles onto his good leg. Porter crouches and strings the other rope end around Albert's wrists. He checks his knots, satisfied, and reaches into Albert's shirt pocket. Porter had spotted the bulge when he approached the men. He finds what he expected—a wad of bills. He stands and tosses the money on the bar. From the end of the bar, the bartender spies the bills. Porter finds another wad of cash in Clay's pocket. That too Porter pitches onto the bar.

"Sorry 'bout the mess," Porter tells the bartender. The bartender nods, panic flooding his own gaze.

Using the rope, Porter drags the men from the tavern. They leave a trail of blood out the door, struggling to keep pace with Porter. Quinn follows the three men into the street. Porter pulls the men to where he and Quinn tied their horses. Clay and Albert shout obscenities the entire way, and when these go unacknowledged, they resort to pleadings. Porter ignores them. He also ignores Quinn who appears more terrified than the bound prisoners. She begs Porter to find a lawman and hand the mercenaries over to the authorities. Quinn's words cannot reach Porter.

Once they arrive by the horses, Porter drops the rope. The men fall to the ground, stumbling over each other like drunken buffoons.

Porter takes his gun and aims it at Clay. He pauses and turns to Quinn. "You may not want to see this."

"You're fucking crazy," Clay cries. "William is gonna find you. He'll kill you, you crazy son-of-a-bitch!"

Quinn does not turn away. She is stupefied. Porter wishes she would turn around. What he is about to do, she will never forget.

"Quinn," he says. "Turn around."

"I wish it were me," Clay says.

Porter looks at Clay. "What?" Porter asks.

Clay smiles, looks past Porter to Quinn. "I wish I had raped your daughters," Clay says to Quinn. "William and Francis said they were the best fucks of their life."

He cackles, flashing rotten yellow teeth. If he must die, he may as well ensure his place in hell. Porter cocks his gun and steadies his aim. Clay releases one last hearty chortle and closes his eyes to wait for the bullet.

Porter's trigger finger snaps, but it only catches air. Quinn has snatched his gun and is standing over Clay pistol whipping the life from him. Her blows are fast and forceful. His nose breaks, his eye sockets crack, his skull splits.

Clay cries and yelps and begs her to stop, but Quinn's blows keep coming and soon Clay cannot speak. Quinn cannot be contained. She breathes fire and curses Clay and unleashes a rage only known to grieving parents. The scene becomes so gruesome that even Porter must turn away. It is not until fatigue clutches Quinn that she stops the flogging. Clay lays broken and nearly dead on the filthy road. His face is a mashup of broken skin, bone, and bloody tissue. Somehow, he clings to life. His shallow breathing escapes his lungs in disheartened gasps, painful and apologetic. Albert stares at what remains of Clay. It sickens him. He turns away from his friend and vomits onto the ground.

Quinn stands straight. Her hair covers her face, plastered there by Clay's blood and her own sweat. She pulls the strands from her eyes and stares down at Clay. He is unrecognizable. *Did I do that?* she admires, but the reality will not manifest. She shifts her gaze to the bloody gun in her hand. A relic confirming her chaos. She inhales and drops the weapon. Clay emits a painful moan, wishing for one more blow strong enough to end his life.

Porter bends and picks up his gun. He wipes the bloody handle on his shirt. "Do you want to finish it?" he asks Quinn.

A fog has claimed her. She gazes forward, dumfounded and hypnotized. Porter touches her shoulder. She jumps and looks at

Porter. He mouths something she does not hear. He motions to the ground. Quinn follows his finger to Clay. He looks dead but is not.

I did that, Quinn thinks. The shock absorbs her, but she feels no remorse. If anything, she feels…alive. Justified. She turns to Albert, willing him to disparage her daughters in the same fashion Clay did. All she needs is another reason to claim Porter's gun and unleash her maternal fury.

Porter cocks his gun and again raises it to finish Clay.

"No," Quinn says. "Don't shoot them."

Porter frowns and lowers the gun.

"In the outhouse," Quinn says, but it is not clear what she means. "Put them in the outhouse," she explains.

Porter does not understand.

"Empathy," Quinn says. She walks to the outhouse and throws open the door. The rancid air penetrates her nostrils. She covers her mouth and coughs. Albert hacks. Porter remains indifferent.

"Get inside," Quinn tells Albert. "Drag him with you," she says, pointing to Clay.

"What are you going to do?" Albert asks.

"Get inside."

"We have money," Albert says.

"Get inside," Quinn repeats.

"Take us to the sheriff."

"Get inside!" Quinn yells.

Albert does not move. Quinn walks to Porter and holds out her hand for his gun. Porter recognizes what has awakened inside her. He saw it in the war; he felt it in himself when he killed his own father. Quinn has arrived at the place where reason does not exist. All her demands must be met, lest you find yourself on the receiving end of her wrath.

Porter hands over his gun. Quinn turns to Albert and raises the gun. "Get inside," she tells him.

"We can't both fit," Albert says, scrutinizing the wooden box.

Quinn fires a bullet that wheezes past Albert's ear.

"Okay…okay," he cries. He struggles to his feet. He reaches down and pulls Clay to his. Somehow Clay remains conscious, but he is dead weight. Albert drags himself and Clay to the outhouse. He studies the wooden box, doubts they will both fit. Quinn fires another bullet. It splinters the outhouse.

It is difficult, but Albert somehow manages to get himself and Clay inside the outhouse. Quinn slams the door shut and jams a nearby plank into the door's seam, locking the men inside. Albert pounds on the door. He coughs and hacks and pleads for Quinn to let them out.

Quinn pulls a book from Porter's bundle and tears several pages loose. Porter remains silent. He is just a spectator. Whatever Quinn is doing, she has the right, and he will not interfere.

Quinn takes a book of matches from Porter's sack. She strikes the match, and it blazes to life. She touches the flame to the torn pages. They catch and shrivel towards the flame. Some dried weeds sit at the base of the outhouse. Quinn drops the burning pages to the dead brush. It catches and the flame spreads to the wooden outhouse. It is a tinderbox, and soon Albert understands his fate. He cries louder, pounds harder, begging Quinn to open the door and put a bullet in his brain. The flames and smoke consume Albert and soon he is silent. It is not until he is dead that the spell imprisoning Quinn releases its hold.

CHAPTER 32

The stench of fire and shit and death stings their senses. It is an effort not to double over coughing from the putrid smell. Porter stands at his horse organizing his effects. Quinn stands at her own horse, ruminating on what just occurred. She killed a man. Two men. Beat one nearly to death. Behind her the outhouse smolders. She turns to it, watches the dying flames spit black streams of smoke into the sky.

"Quinn?"

Quinn turns. Porter stares at her from atop his horse. "We need to go," he says. Quinn nods. She takes hold of the saddle horn and wills herself to mount her horse, but she cannot move. Her breath feels heavy; she clutches her chest. Porter recognizes what is about to follow. He dismounts, and Quinn is in his arms before she can process what is happening. Her breath is cut short. Her lungs will not fill. Her panic increases. Porter tightens his grip and whispers for her to breathe, but she cannot. It is a futile request, he knows this, yet he continues making it.

"I got you," he whispers. "Breathe."

"I...I...can't," Quinn gasps.

"It'll come," he says, holding her upright. "Don't force it. Relax."

"What's...happ...en...ing?" she huffs.

"Get it out, Quinn," Porter says, "Release it."

And at his command, something takes hold of Quinn. Her lungs fill as if rising to the surface of a lake after being submerged for her entire life. She inhales her take and then releases a great wail. Screams and cries and curses and sobs pour from Quinn into Porter's chest. Her legs give way, and Porter clutches her to keep her upright. Her breath returns in full force as she purges all the pent-up emotion that has spent a lifetime trapped inside her. Porter holds her and watches as the shock of what she did to Albert and Clay absorbs her. She must feel this so she can escape it. This is part of her resurrection.

.   .   .   .   .

The brothel is two floors. The main floor houses poker tables and a bar overflowing with cheap spirits. Bedrooms are upstairs. A drunk sleeps in the corner. The madam steps out from behind the bar. She is older and struggles to hide her age behind too much makeup and a disposition that exudes wisdom obtained through hard living. She approaches Porter and extends a customary smile that goes unreturned. Porter's eyes scan the bottom floor, his hand hovering over his gun. He shifts his gaze to the second floor and counts five bedroom doors.

"How many men you got upstairs?" he asks the madam.

"Two."

Porter eyes her. "You're sure it's not three?"

"I always know who's in my establishment," she says. "You want a girl?"

"No."

"I got two unaccounted for," she says. "I can fetch them. I got boys too. Whatever you want."

Porter pulls his gun and starts for the stairs.

"Hey, cowboy," the madam calls. "I don't want no fighting in here."

Porter stops, turns. "You may want to step outside."

She curses and asks him to reconsider, but Porter is already mounting the stairs. The madam swears a hundred more times under her breath and heads towards the door.

"Don't hurt my girls," she cries. Somehow, she divines Porter will honor this request. She steps outside, away from the gunfire.

Porter sidles to the first door and presses his ear to the polished wood. Inside he can hear a man and woman having sex. Porter tightens his grip on his gun and slowly opens the door. The musk of sweat and sex permeates the bedroom. Owen is on top, pushing hog-like into the girl. The invading light forces Owen to turn. His eyes meet Porter's. Porter does not react yet. He waits for Owen to register who Porter is. He must process who is about to kill him. Understanding floods Owen's face. His gaze shifts from Porter to his gun resting on the chair next to the bed. He makes a slight move for it.

"Don't," Porter says. Porter does not want to kill Owen in front of the girl.

Owen remains still. Porter looks at the girl, half buried under Owen. Her eyes big with confusion. Porter puts his finger to his lips, warning her to remain quiet, and motions for her to get out from the bed. Owen must move for the girl to escape, and in the arrangement, he lunges for his gun. Porter's bullet is through his skull before he reaches the chair. The girl is painted with Owen's brains. She screams and pulls the bedsheet tight to her body. Porter steps inside the bedroom and slams the door behind him and waits. The whore cries and begs Porter not to kill her. Porter ignores her and keeps his ear pressed to the door.

Two rooms down, Francis throws open his brothel door. Francis, naked at the waist, steps into the hall, carrying a gun in each hand. The brothel is still. He takes a cautious step, the floorboards creak and he halts. Listens. Francis cannot remember which bedroom Owen was in. He believes it was the one next to his.

He squares up and kicks in the neighboring door, his guns ready. The room is empty.

Porter ducks into the hall and unloads two balls, each missing Francis. Francis turns and fires a shot that grazes Porter's arm. Porter drops back into the bedroom. Francis delivers three more shots, splintering a railing but missing Porter. Porter sits against the doorjamb. The whore unleashes a new series of screams and hides under the bedding. Porter inspects his wound. It is not bad, and he knows the bullet is not inside his arm.

Francis freezes in the hall and listens again. He reckons he may have hit Porter, but he does not know how bad. He takes a delicate step, hoping to hear the strenuous breathing of a wounded man. Another slow step. Porter rotates against the doorframe and spills into the hall. He fires a bullet into Francis's shin. Francis's legs buckle. He shoots two wild shots as he falls to the ground. Porter fires another shot into Francis's arm. He drops one of his guns and fires his final round at Porter but misses. He pulls the trigger three more times, but he is out of rounds. He tosses the empty gun and tries for his fallen gun, but his wounded leg makes it impossible to reach.

Porter gets to his feet. He retrieves the gun Francis is trying to recover. Holds it steady and surveys the landing, making sure no one else is hiding behind any of the doors. Beneath Francis's heavy breathing, Porter hears a floorboard groan. He cocks his gun and waits. No one emerges. He approaches Francis.

"Who else is up here?"

Francis spits. Porter cocks his gun and points it at Francis.

"No one," Francis says. Sweat breaks all over his body.

From the bedroom, Porter hears a floorboard creak.

"A girl in there?" Porter asks, nodding to the nearest door.

"Yes."

Porter approaches the bedroom door. He kicks it open and finds a girl cowering in the corner. She lifts two shaking hands into the air. Porter surveys the room. It is empty save for the frightened girl.

"Stay here," he tells the girl and then he steps back into the hall with Francis.

"Where's the man you take orders from?" Porter asks.

"I don't take orders from no man," Francis heaves.

Porter kneels next to Francis and sticks his finger into Francis's blown-out shin. Francis cries.

"Where is he?" Porter asks.

"He had to return the girl," Francis yells. "The one the Mormon married."

Porter takes his finger out from the splintered shin. "Where did he take her?" Porter asks.

"Back to her daddy's plantation," Francis says. "'Bout thirty miles from here."

"What's the plantation owner's name?"

"William will kill you."

"What's the plantation owner's name?"

"You will not survive this."

Porter jams his finger back into Francis's wound.

"Noah!" Francis cries. "Noah Martin."

Porter removes his finger and wipes it across Francis's cheek.

"You raped the pregnant girl," Porter says. Francis cannot tell if this is a question or an accusation.

"What?"

"In Salt Lake. You raped the pregnant girl." Porter aims his gun between Francis's eyes.

"A man has needs," Francis says, trying not to sound afraid.

"Why'd you break her teeth?"

Francis casts a maniacal smile. "Bitch wouldn't stop biting."

Without warning, Porter smashes the butt of his gun into Francis's grinning mouth. Francis yelps and spits out a wad of blood. Porter takes hold of Francis by the back of his head and smashes his gun into his mouth again. Francis writhes and spits shattered bits of teeth onto the floor. Porter takes another handful of hair on the back of Francis's head.

"Show me your teeth again," Porter says.

Francis keeps his mouth closed. Tears stream from his eyes.

"Show me your teeth."

Francis turns his head away from Porter. He hears Porter's gun cock. His head swivels back to Porter.

"Please…" Francis cries. A dribble of blood escapes his mouth and runs down his chin.

"Show me your teeth."

Francis forces a pained smile, exposing bleeding gums and loose remnants of teeth. Porter slams the butt of his gun into Francis's mouth again. Francis cries and spits out more dislodged teeth.

Porter stands. "Open your mouth," he says. Francis shakes his head. "Open your mouth."

"Please," Francis cries.

"Open your mouth," Porter instructs again.

Francis sobs and opens his mouth, his jaw quivering. Teeth fragments line his lips and swollen gums. Porter grabs hold of the back of Francis's head again and shoves his gun barrel into Francis's mouth. Francis gags and tries to dislodge the barrel, but Porter pushes the gun further down his throat. Francis's gag reflex flexes, and he vomits. Chunks of sickness splatter out and around the gun barrel.

"Suck on it," Porter says.

Francis's eyes screw up toward Porter with confusion.

"Like you made her do to you."

More tears spill out from Francis's eyes. Porter tells him again to suck the gun's barrel. Francis does as instructed. Porter clutches the back of Francis's head and forces the barrel even deeper.

"This is what she felt," Porter says.

Francis weeps and struggles for breath. Porter watches with stoic eyes. Francis gags and is about to vomit again when Porter releases his hold and pulls the trigger. The bullet travels through

Francis's throat and exits through the other side. He falls dead at Porter's feet.

It takes a minute for the echo of the gunshot to disintegrate into the brothel's walls.

Porter walks into the first bedroom where Owen's girl sits motionless on the bed staring at Owen's dead face. Porter kneels next to Owen and closes the man's eyes. He takes a tablecloth from a corner table and goes to the girl. She keeps her eyes on Owen, the shock of what happened suspends her. With the cloth, Porter cleans the girl's face. Porter tears the cloth, separating two clean sections from the portion he used to clean the girl's face. He wraps the clean fabric around the girl's eyes. What she has seen cannot be unseen, but he can keep her from witnessing Francis's massacre. Shielding her from one less gruesome act is the most charitable thing he can do.

"Don't move," he tells her. "I'm going to get your friend."

Porter finds Daisy still cowering in the corner of her bedroom. She is half naked and shivering. Porter takes the bed covering and wraps it around the girl's exposed shoulders. With the other torn portion of cloth, he covers her eyes. He takes her hand and leads her out the bedroom.

CHAPTER 33

Quinn waits outside the brothel with the horses. She is anxious and worries if Porter or a different man will exit the whorehouse. The brothel's madam stands next to her, a cigarette pursed between her red lips. She stares at her establishment in deep contemplation. Wishes her life had taken a different path, wondering if it is too late to take one now.

Quinn and the madam heard the gunshots. Quinn flinched with each shot. The madam remained rigid. She has lived too long to be surprised anymore. Now they wait for whomever emerges from the wreckage.

It is Porter who emerges. Quinn sighs with relief. She stops herself from running to Porter and embracing him. In his wake are two blindfolded girls. One appears numb. The other cannot stop shaking. Porter leads the girls to the madam.

"Did you hurt my girls?" the madam asks. Porter shakes his head. The madam removes the blindfolds from both girls and inspects them.

"Are you all right?" she asks the girls. They nod and the madam pulls them both into her.

"You kill all three of them?" Quinn asks Porter.

The madam turns to her. "There were only two men inside," the madam answers. "You were looking for three?"

"Yes," Quinn says.

Porter inspected Owen and Francis before he exited the brothel. He found their stash of money like he found Albert's and Clay's. He hands the crumpled bills to the madam.

"What did they do?" she asks, inspecting the money. Porter takes his horse and turns away from the women. He starts down the road.

The madam looks to Quinn for answers. "They raped and killed my daughters," Quinn says. "He was in love with one of them."

"Well, shit," the madam says, shaking her head in disgust. "That changes things, don't it?"

"How so?" Quinn asks.

"Now I don't feel so bad knowing I get to spend the night washing the blood off the floors."

"I tried making him go to the sheriff," Quinn says.

The madam laughs. "That wouldn't have done no good. Nearest lawman is fifteen miles away. Besides, if Sheriff Tate knew he was walking into a gun fight, he'd surrender his badge before running the risk of doing his job."

Quinn watches Porter recede in the distance. She mounts her horse, offers the madam a slight nod, and rides after Porter.

    •   •   •   •   •

Just outside the town, Porter stops at a stream to wash his hands. Quinn edges next to him and does the same. Neither speaks. Quinn watches the cool water rush over her hands. She spreads her fingers and the current flosses through her open palms, washing away her sins. She watches Porter from the corner of her eye. They have a kinship now. A bond forged by their killings. A mutual understanding seldom shared with others. Quinn has never felt more connected to another person. This reality nearly makes her weep.

Porter cups his hands and washes his face and neck. His knees pop when he stands straight.

"Now where are you going?" Quinn asks as Porter returns to his horse.

"There's one left," Porter says.

Quinn exhales sharply. She cups her hand, bends low and drinks from it. She walks to her horse, makes to mount the steed but cannot.

"I don't want to go with you," she says. "I can't…the killing…it's too much."

Her voice is low. Her admission contains no regret, no cowardice. She has killed, but she is not a killer. Rumination will haunt her if she follows Porter. Porter expected her to turn back at this junction. Quinn killed Albert and Clay because the moment required it. The ride to find William will be wrought with contemplation and deliberation. Her mind will be a burden. Quinn is not a methodical killer but an instinctual one. She had her breakdown, as most do the first time they kill, but it was just the first of many. She must weather the next one alone to test if she can survive the new demons she has created. Porter suspects she will. She may be the strongest person he knows.

Porter takes his canteen from his horse and returns to the stream. Quinn appraises him, and with the blood and dirt of their chores no longer staining him, she spies a man she cannot fault her daughter for loving. She approaches Porter and places a hand on his shoulder.

"Hey, Porter?"

Porter looks up at her.

"What happened to me back at the outhouse? I'm trying to make sense of the events."

"You atoned," Porter says.

"After that," Quinn says. "It was like…someone was standing on my chest. You knew what was happening. Like you expected it or something. How?"

Porter takes a pull from his canteen and then hands it to Quinn. "I've seen the ugliness of your God."

Somehow, Quinn understands what Porter means. A shaking hand lifts the canteen to her lips. She downs most of the water but some spills out the sides and trickles down her chin. She thrusts the canteen back at Porter and then returns to her horse.

"Hey, Quinn?" Porter says. "With what you did, how do you feel?"

Quinn contemplates how best to answer and then realizes Porter already knows how she feels. His eyes glisten and glint. Locked inside is a pain she will never know and an understanding she now does.

"You would have made a fine husband," Quinn says.

Porter hears this, absorbs it, and kneels to the stream again to refill his canteen. He is grateful Quinn is already riding for home before the weight of her compliment forces his own breakdown.

CHAPTER 34

Two miles outside the plantation, Porter comes upon an abandoned hospital. The windows are shattered. Paint falls away in great patches. Door hinges hang loose, ready to snap.

Stained and upturned mattresses fill the open area. Rusted bed frames and metal basins clutter the floor. Porter sidesteps the debris, treading on insects dead and alive. He tries not to remember his own hospital stay. Tries to forget that which he cannot.

Porter finds the supply closet near the back of the building. Not much remains, but what he finds, he can use—scissors, gauze, tape, scalpel, a half-empty bottle of disinfectant. He tosses it all into his knapsack and flees the building.

That night he sleeps in the brush and reads by campfire. He wishes he would have spent more time discussing books with Rose. Memories of her stepping out from James's house and onto the porch invade his sleep. In his fantasies she tells him to turn around and abandon his vengeance. He asks her to talk about something else. So, she outlines his flaws, just as she did in life, pleading with him to come unto God, so she can enter his bed as his wife and not his illicit lover. Marriage is the only way I can be with you without the guilt, she tells him. Porter smiles, tells her God does not care about their actions, that her guilt is a construct devised by man. She does not relent her opinions nor does he.

She stands several times to leave the porch, to reenter the house and disregard Porter and his backward thinking. But she cannot. She flirts with the prospect that maybe his analysis of God is right, and she feels a greater shame for having such thoughts. This makes Porter laugh. He goes to her, ready to sweep her into his arms. Bury his head in her hair. Take in her familiar scent. Then he wakes with a start.

The fire's dying embers glow, emitting a pathetic light. Porter curses the night and tries to return to sleep, return to Rose and their struggle. He cannot. He gets to his feet and walks into the brush to relieve himself. It is cold. His bones ache; he is too young to have his bones ache. He returns to the fire and tosses more kindling onto the warm coals. They catch, and he takes up another book. His reading is fitful and haunted by Rose's ghost. He drops the book after reading a page. He stares at the dancing flames and weeps.

■　　■　　■　　■　　■

Porter comes upon the plantation in the afternoon. It stands white and majestic at the base of cotton fields spanning miles. Large white columns adorn the home. Slaves work the surrounding fields, casting curious glances at Porter as he rides past. He tips his hat to each of them in reverent salutation.

On the home's veranda, Porter spies two women drinking iced tea and fanning themselves. A black woman stands behind them, rigid and at attention. The women watch Porter approach, their stares more confounded than the slaves.

Porter stops his horse and dismounts. He cranes his head to appreciate the enormous structure. Thousands of men have died, are still dying, for homes like this. For a way of life that benefits the few at the expense of the many. Porter spits into the dirt.

"Can I help you, mister?" the older woman calls from the porch. She is a proper lady who despises anyone beneath her. The disdain in her inquiry is easy to detect.

"I'm looking for Noah Martin," Porter says.

"That's my husband," the lady replies.

"Is he home?"

"That depends on why you're asking."

"I'm looking for someone he knows."

The lady frowns. She stands and steps to the edge of her porch and casts a stern glance at Porter.

"Are you a Mormon?" she asks. "Did they send you?"

"No, ma'am."

"They kidnapped my daughter," the lady explains. "We paid to get her back."

"I have no quarrel with you or your husband," Porter says. "I'm here on a personal errand."

"And what errand is that?"

"Looking for a man.

"What man is that?"

"William Bath."

"I do not know a William Bath."

"What do you want with William Bath?" a voice cuts into the conversation. Noah Martin appears outside the front door. He is short, stout, with a heavy beard and beady eyes. He wears a white linen suit and stands as if he means something.

"Can you tell me where he is?" Porter asks.

"The Mormons send you?" Noah asks.

"I already asked that," Noah's wife chimes in.

"I have no affiliation with the Mormons," Porter says.

"They stole our daughter. They—"

"I already explained all that, Noah," Noah's wife says.

"Your daughter does not concern me," Porter says. "I'm here for William."

Noah glares at Porter.

"What do you want with William Bath?" Noah asks again.

"I'd rather not say."

"I'd rather you did."

"He stole something from me."

"What did he steal?"

"That's not your concern."

"I'm making it my concern," Noah says.

Porter did not want it to come to this, but he suspected it would. "Mr. Martin, William may have returned your daughter, but other daughters were not so lucky."

Noah studies Porter with a critical eye. "You're a mercenary," he says.

Porter cannot construe if this is a question or a statement, so he remains silent.

"You go after William Bath, and he will kill you," Noah says.

"Where is he?"

"I think it would be in your best interest if I withheld that information."

"Surrendering that information is the only way you'll live."

Noah's face tightens. "You insolent bastard!" Noah says. "You have the audacity to come to my home and threaten me! In front of my wife, no less. Get off my property!" Noah pivots to return to his house.

Porter pulls his gun and fires a bullet into Noah's shoulder. Noah twists and stumbles backward. He glowers at Porter and wonders if another shot will follow the one that has already struck him. Porter remains inscrutable. Noah understands Porter's shot was not intended to kill but to warn. Noah observes his wound. A red crimson patch stains his fine white suit jacket. The blood spreads fast. Porter climbs the porch and points his gun between Noah's eyes.

"Where is William Bath?" he asks.

"You crazy son-of-a-bitch."

Porter cocks his gun.

"Up the river," Noah cries. "About four miles. Small hut with a green door."

Porter turns and walks down the steps. He mounts his horse, gives Noah and his wife another glance, and rides to the end of the plantation where a group of slaves work the field. Porter pulls his horse into the field. The slaves stop working and stare at the mysterious rider.

Porter reaches into his bundle and retrieves a box of bullets. He holds the box out to the nearest slave. The slave looks at the box and then the others, unsure if he should accept it. Porter nods and lifts the box higher. The slave takes the box. Porter pulls a gun from his bundle. Several slaves take a cautious step back. Porter hands the gun to the slave who took the bullets.

"You know how that works?" Porter asks.

The slave nods.

"Use it at your own discretion," Porter says.

The slave frowns, unsure what to make of the offering. Porter turns his horse and rides away.

CHAPTER 35

William enters his shack carrying his hunting rifle. He props the rifle against the wall and paces to his small wooden table. He takes a match and strikes it to life. A small flame fills the space. William touches the flame to a nearby lamp, bringing the room into view. Porter sits in the corner, his gun on his lap.

William spots Porter but does not react to him. It is almost as if he expected to find the runaway soldier in his hut. Stares at him with indifference, as if he is nothing more than a confirmed expectation. William pulls a chair from the table and sits, keeping his eyes locked on Porter's.

On a small table to the right of Porter rests the medical supplies he stole from the hospital. They appear dull and useless. Rust has discolored some spots. William appraises the medical tools.

"What's all that?" William asks.

"Surgical tools."

"For what?"

"Wounds."

"You're hurt?"

"No."

William does not understand. Does not care to. He spits onto his floor.

"How do you want to settle this?" he asks.

"Lower your pants," Porter says.

"What?"

"Lower your pants."

"Why?"

"So I can settle this."

"I don't understand."

"You must feel what she felt."

"Who?"

"The woman you raped."

William expels a frightened laugh. "You're gonna rape me?"

"No," Porter says. "I'm not like you."

"Then how am I gonna feel what she felt?"

"Lower your pants," Porter repeats. His voice is calm, almost…soothing.

"If you came to kill me, just do it and get it over with."

"I did not come to kill you."

"No?"

"You get to live."

"Why?"

"You don't deserve death."

"What do I deserve?"

"A fate worse than death."

"What's worse than death?"

Porter's eyes shimmer, emitting a glint of untapped happiness. "Dependence." Porter stands. "You're going to feel the same fear she did. The same disgrace and stolen innocence. You're going to suffer like she did."

"How?"

Porter takes a dulled scalpel from the table. "Every part of you that touched her, you're going to lose."

The seriousness of the situation finally makes its way to William. He is speechless. He has dealt with madmen his entire life, but he never feared them. They have always been inferior to him. Porter is the exception. He has nothing left to lose. All that remains is his life. For most, living is enough. But Porter does not cherish his life. It is an inconvenience. The sooner he can rid himself of it, the better. William realizes this, and his fear chills him.

Porter thumbs the dull blade. "I'm going to take your hands, your tongue, your eyes, and your manhood. Never again will you set eyes upon a woman. I will rob you of your lust. Of your ability to desire, to ever feel another woman again. You won't be able to feed yourself when you're hungry, walk to the privy without stumbling over your own furniture, wipe yourself when you shit. You will become completely dependent on others."

"I know men worse than me," William says. His voice cracks. "You do this to me, and they will come after you."

Porter raises his gun at William.

"Bounty hunters," William cries. "Like me but worse."

Nothing human is left inside of Porter. He cannot listen to reason; he cannot extend sympathy; he can only apply empathy.

"Take off your pants," Porter says again. His voice is still even, but it is clear his patience is waning.

"You're a…you're a monster," William says, his voice breaking. "A goddamn monster!"

A monster? William's words play back at Porter. *Monster.* The label echoes inside Porter's head.

"'I have love in me the likes of which you can scarcely imagine and rage the likes of which you would not believe,'" Porter recites.

William's face becomes tied up in confused consternation. He does not understand Porter's words.

"What-what are you talking about?"

"'If I cannot satisfy the one,' Porter continues with the recitation, "I must indulge the other.'"

"Wh-what does that mean?" William cries.

Porter steps to William, the surgical blade drawn. The room's muted lamp light outlines his harsh face. Porter has transformed, demon-like and without remorse. William balks and covers his eyes.

And then the monster strikes his creator.

PART III

CHAPTER 36

The door's rusty hinges creak when the trespasser pushes it open. The morning's rising light forces itself inside the hut. If Porter were to lift his eyes, he would find a gun barrel emerging behind the wooden door. It is cocked and at the ready to end anyone who may prove difficult. But Porter does not lift his eyes. He crouches in the corner, his eyes fixed on the ground. In his right hand, he clutches a bloody cleaver.

On the other end of the gun stands Orin Porter Rockwell. He enters the shack slowly, with caution. The light that follows Rockwell into the hut brings the room into focus. Rockwell's gaze lands onto William Bath. Or what remains of him.

"Jesus Christ," Rockwell whispers. The horror grips him. The carnage stuns him silent. He wants to look away, for he knows what he is observing will stay with him forever, but his eyes betray him. They remain frozen on William, disbelieving what they absorb.

When the invading light hits William, he flinches.

"Who's there?" he cries.

He jerks upright and shifts his bandaged head from side to side, listening. He is a caged animal. Driven to insanity with fear and torture. He cannot use his eyes. Porter took them. In their place is a bandage seeping with blood, covering his hollow sockets. Porter also took William's penis and fingers. They sit idle and useless on the table next to the bed. Bloody appendages taken as penance for the pain they once caused.

"Who's there?" William asks again. Rockwell continues staring at William, incredulous. "Please…make him stop," William shrieks. "Please…"

Rockwell peels his eyes from William and looks to the table. He takes an account of the discarded body parts.

"Jesus Christ," he murmurs again. He gags, almost doubles over with a sickness he did not anticipate. He dry heaves, lifts his eyes again to William, and then bends and vomits onto the floor.

Porter drops the cleaver. It clatters to the ground and Rockwell spins at the sound with his gun drawn. Porter does not move. He does not look up. His eyes stare without seeing.

Rockwell wipes his mouth and stands straight. Porter is almost unrecognizable to Rockwell. His clothes, hands, and face are bloodstained. What Rockwell observes is a crazed hostile, marred by a ravenous appetite for vengeance. An appetite Porter has, for the moment, exhausted. Even if Porter wanted to make a move against Rockwell, he would pose no match. Fatigue has robbed him of his desire to kill anymore.

Rockwell lowers his gun. "What have you done?" he asks Porter.

Porter lifts his head and looks at Rockwell. Stares at the Mormon assassin for a long time. He wonders if he has come to kill him. He hopes he has.

"Please," William whimpers from the bed. "Don't let him continue. Please…"

William's pleadings awaken Porter. Transport him back to this time, place, and purpose.

"I still need to take his tongue," Porter says.

He sounds hoarse and defeated. He needs to take William's tongue, but his toils have robbed him of the conviction to do so. What he has accomplished thus far has extinguished his desire to

continue. At least for now. He is famished and tired and did not
expect the physical and mental fortitude his endeavors required.
Killing is simple. Disfigurement is not.

Rockwell glances back at William, holds his gaze for less than a
second before turning back to Porter. "You've turned him into
a…eunuch."

Porter stands, falters but catches himself. "I did what required
doing," he says.

"Nothing requires this," Rockwell says, waving to William. "I
don't know how a man could do that to another man."

"Then you've never loved," Porter says.

Rockwell could argue the point, but he knows it is senseless to
refute a madman. He cannot imagine doing to anyone what Porter
has done to William. Even if someone were to have his way with
one of his wives, Rockwell would not resort to conscious
mutilation. Sure, he would seek justice, but no amount of love could
drive him to…*this*.

"God help you," Rockwell says.

Porter lifts his bloodstained hands and appraises them,
surprised with their uncleanliness. His fingers tremble. He wipes
his hands on his pants and reexamines them. They remain red and
unfamiliar, foreign. He looks at Rockwell, as if expecting him to
explain his cruelty.

"Are you armed?" Rockwell asks. Porter shakes his head. "Lift
your shirt," Rockwell instructs. "Show me."

Porter does not move, so Rockwell straightens his aim and
cocks his gun. Porter smiles at the absurdity of the threat.
Instruments designed to take life can no longer compel Porter to
obedience. Rockwell spots Porter's knapsack on the table. Keeping
his gun trained on Porter, he steps across the room to the sack. He
looks inside and finds Porter's gun.

"Go outside," Rockwell tells Porter.

Porter thinks to resist but the thought of leaving the hut and
clearing his mind is a welcomed respite. He recalls a nearby creek.

The sudden desire to wash in it, to rid himself of William's blood, consumes Porter. The cleaning will restore his resolve, allow him to return for William's tongue. Porter takes a step toward the door.

"You may want to put your hands up," Rockwell says.

Porter pauses. He understands what is about to happen. He wishes now he had his gun so he could pull on Rockwell. Kill him and then take William's tongue. He curses his stalled resolve. Rockwell has robbed Porter of his quest. He walks to the door, opens it, and steps onto the porch, his hands to his sides. The men waiting have their guns ready.

William hears Porter's footsteps recede from the hut. "What's happening?" he asks.

"Shh," Rockwell says.

"Did he leave?"

"He's outside."

"Please…you can't let him…he's crazy! He wants to take my tongue. You cannot let him! Please!"

"I won't," Rockwell says. "What do you need?"

"Can I have…some…water?" William asks, his voice shaking.

Rockwell surveys the room and finds a basin filled with water. In the kitchen he spies a tin cup. He dips the cup into the cloudy water and carries it to William. He holds it to William's lips and faces away, refusing to meet the two bloody stains pushing through the white gauze where his eyes once dwelled. Most of the water spills down William's chin and onto his chest. He coughs, and Rockwell sets the cup on the bed.

"Do you want to live like this?" Rockwell asks.

"What do you mean?"

"You have no hands, no eyes…no…" Rockwell looks at the discarded penis on the table. It is unnecessary for him to finish naming what Porter removed.

"He took them from me," William cries.

"Can you live without them? Would you want to?"

William thinks hard on the question. A minute passes. "No," he answers.

Rockwell nods and draws his pistol. He fires a shot into William's head and another into his chest.

Outside, Porter sits handcuffed atop a mangy horse. He hears the shots. The lawmen, a father and son duo, rise in their saddles at the gunshots. The father draws his pistol while the son looks on with wide eyes. A moment later, Rockwell steps outside, closing the door behind him.

"It's just me, Langston," Rockwell says, and the lawman lowers his gun.

"We heard gunshots," Langston says.

"That was me," Rockwell says.

"You killed him?"

"What he left of him. No man should have to live like that."

"Like what?" the boy asks. He is young and naïve and will one day replace his father as sheriff if he can live long enough. The boy's father, Langston, is rugged and full of conviction. He is everything the world requires of a man just as his son is not.

Rockwell strides down the porch and up to Porter's horse.

"Brother Brigham told me to follow you," Rockwell says. "Make sure you didn't encounter any resistance. I seen the outhouse and the whorehouse. It appears you've been successful in your endeavors."

"So why are they here?" Porter asks, indicating the family lawmen.

"Brother Brigham and I suspected you may have cause to return to Utah once you finished your slaughter," Rockwell explains.

"I have no reason to go to Utah," Porter says.

"Well, the prophet wanted to make sure of that," Rockwell says. "What you did in there," Rockwell jerks his head toward the house, "I ain't never seen a man do that to another man before."

Porter stares ahead. Rockwell drives a discerning eye into Porter that goes unnoticed.

The boy looks from Porter to Rockwell. "What did he do?" he asks.

"Leave it alone, boy," his father says. "Brother Rockwell told us not to ask questions. We're here to arrest this man for the murder of Owen Kirkman, Francis Blackstone, Albert Wilson, and Clay Taylor."

"Add William Bath to that list, Sheriff," Rockwell says.

"William Bath was meant to live," Porter says.

"Thank God he won't," Rockwell says.

"*The Bible* condones an eye for an eye," Porter says. "Doesn't your other book?"

It takes a moment for Rockwell to understand what book Porter is referencing. Then Rockwell smiles. "I don't know. Don't tell Brother Bingham, but I've never read the damn thing."

Rockwell and Langston laugh. The joke eclipses the boy. Langston reads the confusion on his son's face and looks away. His son is an embarrassment. He does not know how they share the same blood.

"Well, I must return to Utah," Rockwell says. He saunters to his horse. "Thank you for killing those men for me," Rockwell says to Porter. "The church is grateful." Rockwell climbs atop his horse and steers it over to Porter. "I hope when you hang, it hurts like hell."

Rockwell waits for Porter to offer some parting words, but Porter has nothing to say. Rockwell nods to Langston and his boy and rides away. Once he is out of earshot, the boy turns to Porter.

"What did you do to the man in there?"

"Don't talk to the prisoner, son!"

"Aren't you curious?" the boy asks his father. The father concedes the point.

Porter looks the boy straight in the face. "I castrated him and took his hands and his eyeballs."

"Jesus," Langston whispers.

"Why?" the boy asks.

Porter's eyes sweep the skyline. "I thought it would help me feel better."

"Did it?" The boy asks, but Porter has said all he intends to.

CHAPTER 37

The cell is three brick walls and an iron door with metal bars. A waste pot in the corner and a paper-thin mattress. When Porter sleeps, he sleeps well. He does not dream. Rose no longer creeps into his subconscious with promises of a life that cannot happen. He falls into heavy slumbers and remains for hours without moving. He wishes he could sleep forever. Waking hurts. Waking drives him back to reality where his demons remind him of what he lost and his hand in it all.

The boy who helped arrest him is kind. He is too young and cautious to understand yet how dark and ugly the world is. He is curious and ignorant. Often escaping his mundane world into books that offer more adventure and wisdom. He lives the life Porter could have were it not for the war and an abusive father. Porter dwells on this analysis, of how life is better or worse considering whom one must spend it with. It is another injustice, he decides—the power a person can have over another. This insight stings, for he knows had he not entered Rose's life, things would be different.

One day the boy sat perched at the desk reading Faust. Porter watched his eyes dance over the words with silent envy. The boy sensed Porter's gaze and took his eyes from the page to meet the killer's. The boy did not flinch, and Porter did not look away. When he and his father arrested Porter, the boy knew he was in the presence of evil. Now, days later, the monster he sensed hidden in Porter has fled. What remains is a contrite man. Porter does not mete out the contrition for the men he killed but for other things. Things unspoken but examined. Porter fascinates the boy.

Meeting Porter's stare, the boy lifts the Faust and asks if Porter has read it. Porter surprises the boy when he gives a slight nod. He has never known a killer, but all his assumptions pointed to them being ignorant and uneducated. The boy drops his feet from the desk and asks more questions—hundreds of them. Porter ignores the obvious ones but answers some. His answers often lead to more questions. The boy is inquisitive, and he quizzes Porter for insights no one else can provide. They debate, converse, engage in a level of civic discourse that if all men had the capacity to entertain, wars would cease. Thought would prevail. Porter speaks of themes and metaphors. The boy is a sponge, soaking up everything, even taking notes on occasion. Perhaps in another life, Porter wonders, he could have been a teacher. Injecting higher-level thinking into his pupils to save them from the life Porter could not escape.

Now the boy brings books to Porter. Books he has read, or tried to, but could not comprehend. Porter explains what eludes the boy. Uncovering hidden themes, highlighting sentiments and wisdom within the literary works. The boy has a habit of screwing his face up into deep concentration, processing what Porter relays, asks more questions—they are endless. His mind is curious.

His father does not approve. Wishes his son would learn lessons not found in books. He tells the boy to stop wasting time with novels. The only book worth reading is *The Book of Mormon*, his father says. He has not read it, so it is important his son does. It is necessary for their journey, the father says. He keeps reminding his son that soon they will trek to Salt Lake City with the other

Mormons. The final days are near, and they need to be in Zion with their own kind when the Second Coming occurs.

The boy explains this to Porter. Reciting his father's regurgitated proclamations and second-hand prophecies. Porter listens with silent judgment. Would prefer to speak of anything other than religion. Porter has moved past religion. He finds it boring and without purpose, but he does not voice his boredom. Just listens when the boy declares he does not want to go to Salt Lake. Neither does the boy's mother. Neither knows what they will say when the father demands it is time to make their exodus west. The boy hopes the mother will stand up to the father; the mother prays for the same from her son. They do not give voice to this, only wonder in silence if two weak people can coalesce and become strong.

When Porter returns to the cell the day he learns he will hang, the boy has left a copy of *Annabel Lee* on Porter's bed. Porter reads the poem, turns to the wall, and stares at the cold concrete for hours without moving.

Sometimes this happens. Porter will read something and become distant. The boy dares not ask why, but he assumes it must have something to do with his murdered lover. The boy is wise in this regard. When Porter reads something that beckons him to Rose, it is best to leave him alone. Let him return from the place where he exists with her and her alone.

The boy does not know the full details of Rose's death, but he has pieced most of it together from overhearing his father tell others. Hired men raped Porter's lover and then trapped her inside the house and burned it to the ground. The father weaves this tale to anyone who will listen. He regales any audience with the story because of his role in it—the prophet called on *him* to help bring the crazed murderer to justice. The boy scoffs at this examination.

Upon hearing the story, ignorant bystanders always label Porter a madman, yet the men who raped and murdered the Mormon wives exit the fable with their names unsullied.

The next day the boy returns carrying another book under his arm. Porter remains on his side facing the wall. The boy finds the copy of *Annabel Lee* on the floor. He knows not to ask questions regarding the story. Porter will not offer insights into Poe's dark prose. The boy retrieves the book through the bars and thumbs through the text. The pages appear wrinkled and stiff. Damaged from water.

The boy clears his throat. "I brought you another book, Mr. Porter," he says and waits for the prisoner to acknowledge the announcement. "It's one I have not read."

Porter does not stir, but the boy knows he is listening. When it is clear the boy's generosity will remain unrecognized, he kneels and slides the book through the bars. He tips his hat to Porter's backside and takes his chair behind the old oak desk. He kicks his feet up onto the desk—the way his pop does—and waits for Porter to roll over and notice the book.

While he waits, his eyes get heavy. Soon the boy's breathing becomes thick, heavy. Porter rolls over and looks at the boy. His head is kicked back, and his mouth hangs open in innocent repose. Past the boy, on a hook fastened to the wall, hangs Porter's knapsack. Porter deduces from the sack's formation that his gun is still inside. He imagines walking out from his cell, retrieving his gun, sticking it into the boy's opened mouth, and pulling the trigger. Porter pushes the thought from his mind as quick as it enters. The boy is good to him. Killing him would not please Porter. The murderous notion occurs to him because of their lots in life. Porter is a prisoner; the boy is his jailer. He reimagines his escape and replaces the boy's murder with the father's. Porter does not balk at this fantasy. The father is a hard man. A Mormon like Rockwell. Hellbent on bringing justice to the world without questioning what he is fighting for.

The father spits at Porter on the days he visits the jail. Tells him he is of the devil. Condemns him for what he did to William Bath and Bath's men. He never mentions what William and his men did to Rose or the sister wives. Porter wonders if the father even knows the full story. Which parts did Rockwell reveal and which did he keep secret?

Porter spots the book the boy brought lying on the floor. He cranes his head and reads the title—*The Count of Monte Cristo.* Porter takes up the book and begins to read.

CHAPTER 38

Quinn arrives the following week. Like an apparition, she appears inside the jailhouse. It takes a moment for Porter to recognize her. She is in her Sunday best with rouge darkening her cheeks and her hair tied up into a tight bun. When Porter last saw her, dirt and blood and sweat lined every part of her. Now she has rid herself of the atrocity of that day. It breaks Porter's heart to see her. She is breathtaking. She looks like Rose, like a reason to stay alive.

Outside Porter's cell is a wooden crate the boy has fashioned into a stool. He sits on it eating apple pie he brought from home. He offered half to Porter, and Porter ate it before the boy could reconsider his generosity. A book sits opened on the boy's lap to a marked passage he could not understand. He showed the text to Porter when he first arrived and has been asking questions about it ever since. The boy chews and asks another question that goes unanswered. He then bounces ideas and themes off Porter hoping to impress the prisoner. Porter, unmoved, continues staring at Quinn. His silence is not uncommon, but the boy pulls his attention away from the pie, ensuring Porter heard his questions and literary analyses. He thinks to repeat his inquiries and wisdom but can surmise something behind him holds Porter's attention. He follows Porter's gaze to the door where Quinn stands.

The boy gets to his feet. His book and pie tin clatter to the ground. He is embarrassed and mumbles an apology. First for his bad manners and then for conversing so casually with the prisoner. Quinn smiles and tells the boy he has nothing to apologize for. He reaches down and retrieves his book. He dusts it off and closes it. One piece of pie remains in the tin. He lifts the tin to Quinn and asks if she would like it. She declines and suggests he give it to the prisoner. "I hear he has an insatiable appetite," she says. The boy nods and passes the remaining piece through the bars to Porter.

"Can I help you with something, ma'am?" the boy asks.

"I understand the prisoner will hang next week," Quinn says. Stuck under her arm is a Bible. She lifts it for the boy to see. "I brought him this. I trust it may be of some comfort."

The boy smiles with bashful innocence. "I don't figure he'll get much from it," the boy says. "He is a stubborn man. I've never known anyone to dismiss God more quickly than this one."

"It is the hard of heart who need God most."

"I cannot argue that point, ma'am," the boy says. "We offered him a priest. He wasn't interested."

"A priest may hope to engage the prisoner in conversation. As I'm sure you are aware, your prisoner is a man of few words."

"I cannot dispute that, ma'am," the boy chuckles.

"A book though," Quinn says, "well, I'd guess he may welcome a book."

"If it were any other book, I'd agree, ma'am, but the holy word, I'm not so sure."

"Young man," Quinn says, smiling, "you must still be too young to appreciate the persuasive techniques of the female species."

The boy reddens and nods. "You got me there, ma'am." The boy shoots a glance at Porter and turns back to Quinn. "Your challenge awaits. I supposed this is as good a time as any to hit the outhouse. Can I trust you alone with him? I'll only be a minute."

"I will keep him under lock and key," Quinn says.

"Much appreciated," the boy says. He shuffles to the door, tipping his hat to Quinn as he does so, and then slips outside.

Quinn walks to the boy's abandoned crate and eases herself onto it. She rests her back against the wall and sighs. Porter studies her every move. Her resemblance to Rose is frightening. She looks fetching, but he would have preferred she come with the field's exertions staining her clothes rather than a proper made-up woman. Truth be told he would have preferred she did not come at all.

"So, you are set to hang," Quinn says. "For the murder of five men, according to the city charter." Quinn cocks a questioning eye at Porter. "So, you must have killed William Bath?"

Porter shakes his head.

"He's alive?" Quinn asks.

Porter shakes his head.

"The charter—"

"Rockwell killed him."

Quinn knits her brows together. Studies the name but cannot place it. "Who is Rockwell?" she asks.

"The Mormon prophet's henchman."

"Why is he in Arkansas?"

"He followed me."

"He followed you from Salt Lake?"

Porter nods.

"Why didn't he kill you?"

Porter shrugs.

"Why didn't you kill him?"

Porter shrugs again.

"So, you killed two but will hang for five?" Quinn says. "You must carry my sins and the Mormon henchman's?"

Porter looks at the pie tin he has been holding since the boy passed it to him. He takes the last piece and shoves it into his mouth. He tosses the pie tin onto the floor.

"Does the hanging scare you?" Quinn asks.

Porter swallows and wipes his mouth. Quinn knows Porter is not afraid to die. Death is nothing to fear, but the principle, exiting the world on someone else's terms, that is something Porter will resent. It is yet another example of an imposing ideology.

Quinn's hands shake. Porter noticed it when she first appeared in the jail. She stood erect and proud with a shaking hand hanging at her side. Now, as her hands sit on her lap, she sees it, too. She has been seeing it ever since the killings. She balls her hands into tight fists and then splays her fingers out wide, repeating the motion several times, releasing the tension that infiltrates her fingers. The impulse to reach through the bars and take her hands seizes Porter, but he resists the inclination. Quinn will shake for the rest of her life. All those who have killed but are not killers shake.

"I spend most nights pacing my home trying to decide what I feel towards you," Quinn says. Her voice now shudders to match her hands. "A month ago I was certain I hated you, but that determination offered no relief. I cannot fault you for falling in love with my daughter, and seeing the things you've seen, I cannot fault you for losing your faith. Hate for you will not suffice, so what should I feel for you, Porter?"

She pauses but not so Porter can interject. This is her soliloquy. She must voice her words, and Porter must hear them. So, he listens; it is what she requires of him.

"I no longer pray," she continues. "I cannot. I've tried, but silence takes me. You've got me questioning everything. Things I thought I knew for certain I now doubt. I keep revisiting that day, the day I asked you to help dig my father's grave. Why didn't I just let you stroll past and continue to California? How could such an innocent request turn into this tragedy? The curse of hindsight, isn't it? That day you walked into my yard I labeled you a godsend, and now…now all I do is question…everything." Quinn pauses. She takes in a deep breath, holds it, and releases it in measured time.

"If I cannot trust in God, Porter, then what does that mean for Rose? Am I just supposed to accept I will not see her again? That is a notion I do not want to entertain. But something deeper digs at my conscience. Something more sinister. It took me weeks to uncover it." She looks hard at Porter. "If there is a God, He expects me to repent for what I did to those men." Tears form at the corners of Quinn's eyes. She blinks, and the trapped tears escape, cutting wet paths down Quinn's cheeks. "I don't want to repent for what I did to those men because…because I…I…God help me I enjoyed it."

Quinn gasps, her unrequited admittance robs her of her breath.

"What does it say of me when I confess this? That I took pleasure in beating that man, and I enjoyed watching him and his friend die? How am I supposed to live with myself if I find comfort in hurting those who have hurt me? It is not Christian to wield the ax, Porter, but I'd rather be damned for my iniquities than praised for my forgiveness." Quinn takes in another long breath. She wipes her eyes. "What kind of God would expect forgiveness of me? To demand a mother's compassion for men who raped and murdered her daughters? I cannot fall to my knees for any creator who requires that…unfathomable level of benevolence. If that is what He requires, then to hell with Him."

Her confession voiced, now Quinn wants Porter to speak. To break the silence and bridge the gap between her diminishing faith and his lack of one. She knows, however, Porter will not speak unprovoked.

"Say something to me, Porter," Quinn commands. "What thoughts rack your heart? I must know if they are like mine."

Porter desires to reach through the cell's bars and wipe Quinn's tears with the pad of his thumb. All he sees is Rose staring back at him. He wishes Quinn had not come and he wishes she would never leave and he wonders how much longer he can live in constant paradoxes.

"I'm sorry I came into your life," Porter says, and Quinn can tell that he means this.

"I don't need an apology," Quinn whispers. "I need to know how to beat this."

"There is no beating it," Porter says.

Quinn processes his assertion. "Perhaps we do not have to beat it, son," Quinn says. "But we must endure it. We are not the only ones to lose those we love. Others have suffered similar afflictions."

"What am I to do with that knowledge?"

"Take comfort in it," Quinn says. "Some take solace knowing the same demons haunt others."

"I have no stomach for cliches," Porter scoffs.

"What cliches?"

"Misery loves company."

"Well, it does."

Porter shakes his head. "I've never been fond of company."

Quinn stands. "You must endure this with me, Porter. It is what I ask...no, it is what I demand of you. You seduced my daughter. You will not leave me alone with this suffering."

"I will be dead in less than a week."

Quinn nods a maternal understanding that eclipses Porter. *The Bible* remains tucked under her arm. She holds it out to Porter.

"Take it," she says. "I have no use for it anymore."

Porter does not want the book. He has no use for it either, and Quinn must know this, but he reads something in her demeanor that compels him to reach for the book.

"Salvation lies within, Porter," she says, nodding to the book. Her words do not reach Porter, only the intensity with which she says them.

She holds his gaze a moment, communicating something to him he does not understand. An unknown force seizes Porter, compresses him, and forces his eyes to the book. He thumbs the soft leather cover, contemplates the weight and texture of the text.

And then he opens it. Inside, like a lost emblem, lies the cell key. Quinn had hollowed out the pages and placed a key in the carved-out chasm. Porter lifts his head to inquire how Quinn came about the key, but she is already gone.

CHAPTER 39

Porter must wait for the boy to escape. If he flees on the old man's watch, he will have to kill him. The old man is foolish enough to die for a cause. Porter does not know about the boy. He has not yet seen enough of the world to know it is a place not worth fighting for. His ignorance, however, may compel him to act, to confuse prudence with bravery. Porter must explain the difference.

The boy walks into the jailhouse at his usual time. A knapsack hangs off his shoulder, and Porter suspects he has brought a new book with him. The boy must conceal his books in his bundle. He once arrived holding a book, and his father asked why he had brought it. With unabashed innocence, the boy answered: "I figured I'd give the prisoner something to read." The father derided his son and snatched the book from the boy's hands.

"He's a goddamn murderer, son. Treat him like one."

The boy did not understand what murder had to do with denying someone a book. His confusion became amplified when he considered why Porter killed. "He murdered the men who killed his lover," the boy explained, believing his rationale would inspire his father to hand over the book.

The father spat a wad of tobacco juice onto the floor. His beard trapping a line of spittle. "Leave your books at home," he ordered. "It's queer to bring them to a jailhouse anyhow."

The boy did not protest. Only nodded acquiescence and made sure to always pack his books in his bag from then on.

Today, as the boy strides through the jailhouse entrance, his father spies his bulky sack and asks what is inside. The boy shrugs and answers, "Just some food." The father does not investigate. This is the first time the boy has ever lied to his father. Porter knows he is lying. He recognizes in the boy the same demeanor Porter exercised with his own father—the necessity to lie.

The old man stands and asks his son if he finished chopping the wood and tending the chickens. The boy nods, and the old man tells his son that once Porter hangs, he will not have to come to the jail so often. He will have more time for chores soon. More time to prepare for their trek to Zion. The boy nods again and swallows the sadness that accompanies his father's proclamation. The father knows his son is soft. He sees it every time he looks at him hoping to discover someone stronger and must turn away from disappointment. The boy likes books and logic. Romance, too. A horrible combination for this world.

"I'll be by in the morning," the father says. "Make sure and dump the pot before I get here."

The boy promises he will, and the old man takes his hat from the desk and exits the jailhouse. The boy goes to the window and watches his father. His exodus is not on the path to home. There is a tavern a quarter mile in the opposite direction. The father will kill two hours drinking and then arrive home after the boy's mother is already in bed. If she wakes and asks where he has been, the father will say he had to stay late at the jailhouse. The prisoner was acting up, he will say, and his lie will go unchallenged.

Once the father has disappeared from view, the boy retrieves his crate from a nearby closet and places it next to Porter's cell. He settles himself onto it and looks at Porter.

"How are you today, Mr. Porter?" the boy asks. He asks this every day, and Porter has never offered an answer, but that does not stop the boy from inquiring. It is their routine, and the boy has grown fond of it. Porter has too.

On the adjacent wall is a small window carved out of the jailhouse brick. The boy cranes his head and looks through the window searching for something that is not there. He slumps back onto the crate, deflated. This too is part of a routine. When the boy first performed it, Porter assumed he was searching for his father, fearful the dad would make an unannounced return. But the disappointment when the boy did not discover what he was looking for proved it was not his father he was hoping to find.

"What are you always looking through that window for?" Porter asks. Porter does not ask this because he cares; he asks because tonight he must plot his escape. He must know any outside presence.

The boy blushes and answers, "Nothing," under his breath. An invading smile gives him away. Porter understands immediately.

"What's her name?" he asks.

The boy reddens even more. "I didn't say it was a girl."

"What's her name?" Porter asks again.

The boy lowers his head. "Emily," he says.

"She know you like her?" Porter asks.

"I think she may suspect it." The boy reaches for his knapsack and digs inside and retrieves a porcelain seashell. "I found this for her," the boy says. "She likes smooth things, and she wants to go to the ocean one day. Do you think she'll like it?"

The boy passes the shell toward Porter, but Porter does not take it. The boy pulls the shell back and thumbs the smooth surface.

"She usually passes by here around this time," the boy says, screwing his head up to the window again. "She takes her grandparents dinner every night. They live just past the jailhouse." The boy cocks an eyebrow to Porter hoping he will extend some wisdom in the realm of romance, but Porter offers nothing.

The boy pockets the shell and returns to his knapsack. He reaches inside and pulls a small bundle of papers from it. A fraying piece of twine holds the papers together. The boy unties the string and passes the document through the bars to Porter.

"I've been working on a novel," the boy says. "That's the first chapter. I was wondering if you would read it for me and give me some feedback."

Porter reads the title page: *An Arkansas Fall.*

"It's a story about this fall," the boy explains. "Right now. What we're livin' through. I hope you don't mind, but I based a character after you. I didn't use your name, and you're not the villain. You're…well, you're a hero of sorts."

Porter peels away the cover page and reads the first paragraph. He pauses and looks up at the boy. Porter's eyes reveal nothing.

"You don't mind, do you?" the boy asks. "They say write what you know, well, I know little, but these past few weeks have been the most exciting part of my life. Most of it is fiction, but you'll recognize your role in the story."

Porter returns to the manuscript and reads the first page. The boy watches. He shifts on the crate, nervous, not about his story but about something else. He searches for a way to say something to Porter he has not yet admitted.

"Can I tell you something, Porter?" the boy asks. Porter looks at the boy and waits. The boy glances at the window and the door. "I don't blame you for what you done," he says, his voice an octave higher than a whisper. "I don't hardly know Emily, but every time I see her or talk to her, I feel like my heart is gonna fly outta my chest. If someone hurt her the way someone hurt that woman you loved, I'm certain I would react in a similar fashion."

Porter studies the boy, wishes different circumstances had forged their relationship. Until now, Porter had forgotten the world could still produce good people.

"Don't tell my father I said as much," the boy says. "Having empathy for you would warrant a whipping from him."

Porter understands. Fathers use force when they do not know words. He reads four more pages when the boy springs to his feet.

"She just passed," he cries. "I'll be right back." He stumbles to the door, throws it open, and pauses. He returns to his knapsack and rummages through it, muttering under his breath, frustrated he cannot find what he is searching for.

"It's in your pocket," Porter says.

The boy looks at Porter and then pats his pockets. He feels something and snakes his hand into the pocket where he finds the seashell. He nods to Porter and then runs out from the jail, slamming the door behind him.

Now is the time to flee. Porter could exit his cell and slip out of the jail before the boy returns. He thumbs through the boy's writing. The first chapter is twelve pages. He has already read four. Porter guesses he can finish it before his escape. He owes the boy that much.

CHAPTER 40

Porter slides the key into the lock. An effortless turn and the door springs open. He removes the key and walks it to the desk. He turns to his vacated cell. The boy's book chapter sits on the bed. It is a good start; the writing is strong and Porter wonders what will become of it. What will become of the boy? Porter's flight will add another layer to the story. Porter believes one day he will find the boy's story in a bookstore housed beside other talented authors.

Porter takes his bundle hanging near the jail's exit. He checks for his gun and is pleased to find it inside. Outside, he hears footsteps approaching. He takes his gun and cocks it and backs against the wall behind the door. The jailhouse door opens, and the boy enters.

He stares at the empty cell, baffled by its hollowness. He spins around and finds Porter perched against the wall, his gun drawn. The boy still cannot make sense of what is happening. How Porter is not in his cell and why he is pointing his gun at the boy. He spots the key on the desk and understanding captures him. Hitched around the boy's slender waist is a gun and a string of bullets. The boy never felt comfortable wearing the firearm, but the job required it. Now he appreciates why. He makes a motion toward the gun, but Porter shakes his head, and the boy stops.

"I was good to you," the boy says.

"And that is why you will live," Porter says.

"You're gonna let me live?"

"Unless you give me a reason to kill you."

The boy looks back at the key sitting on the desk. "Was it that lady?" he asks. "The one who came a couple days ago?"

Porter does not answer.

"Who is she?"

"The mother," Porter says.

"Rose's mother?"

"Yes."

The boy cannot grasp how he did not fit these pieces together earlier. "How does this end?" he asks.

"Get in the cell," Porter says. "Your dad will be here in the morning."

The boy becomes frightened. "He'll kill me," the boy says. "I embarrass him enough already. He hates that I'm not more like him. If he were here, he would draw on you, even if it meant dying."

"There's no honor in dying."

"But there is shame in living."

"Not for you," Porter says.

The boy's face contorts into a series of emotions. "My father would disagree. He will disown me if I let you escape."

"Get in the cell," Porter says, gesturing with his gun. The boy turns to the cell, and someone knocks on the jailhouse door. Porter points his gun at the door.

"It's Emily," the boy stammers. "The girl I told you about. Please don't hurt her, Porter. It's my fault she came."

"What does she want?" Porter asks.

"She wants to meet you."

"What?"

"She read the first chapter of my book, the one I gave you." The boy spots his writing inside the cell, abandoned on Porter's mattress. A pang of disappointment punctures his heart. "I told her your story," the boy continues. "The part the papers left out. About how you killed the men because they killed your lover. Your story moved her. She asked if she could come by and meet you. I told her the jailhouse is no place for a lady, but she insisted."

Emily knocks again and calls through the door, "Billy? Billy, are you in there?"

"You can't hurt her, Porter," the boy says. Tears form at the rims of his eyes. "Please, Porter. Please don't hurt her."

Porter stares at the boy at a loss. He weighs all options. None of them end well. If the boy does not let her into the jail, she will sense something is wrong and go to the boy's parents. If Porter opens the door, then what? Force her into the cell with the boy? How long until her parents come looking for her? Porter needs the night to put enough distance between this place and the one he wishes to escape to. If he rouses suspicion, the boy's father will assemble a posse and spend the night hunting him.

"Shit," Porter mumbles.

"I'm sorry," the boy says.

Porter lowers his gun and tucks it into his shirt. He pushes past the boy and steps into the cell, and pulls the door closed, locking himself inside.

"Billy?" Emily says again. "Hello?"

Porter sits on the cell's bed. The boy does not understand. "What are you doing?" he asks.

"Let her in," Porter tells the boy.

The boy goes to the door and opens it. Porter overhears a muffled exchange between the doting lovers, before the boy moves to the side so the girl can enter. She is young, about the boy's age, and carries the same innocence. Her wide eyes take in the small jailhouse, enamored with the exciting new environment. *This is where criminals come*, she thinks. *Their final destination before their execution*. The marvels of it all consumes her. Her mouth hangs open. Porter did not think such a level of unabashed purity still existed. Not in this world. She and the boy are perfect for each other.

Her eyes settle on Porter, and she quickly turns away and hides behind the boy. Stories about a killer take a different meaning when faced with the condemned. The boy whispers reassuring words and the girl slowly steps out from behind him.

"Emily," the boy says, "this is Porter."

Emily performs a slight curtsy and mumbles, "Nice to meet you, Mr. Porter."

Porter stands and sticks his hand through the iron bars. Emily looks at the boy for assurance. He nods. Emily takes a cautious step toward Porter and accepts his hand.

"It's a pleasure to meet you, Emily," Porter says. Porter's voice is warm and inviting. He displays a newfound countenance.

The boy does not recognize the prisoner he has stood watch over for the past month. Emily stands transfixed, holding Porter's hand, hypnotized by his eyes. Porter releases her hand and flashes a storybook smile. Emily blushes and returns the smile.

"I hope you don't mind my coming," she says. "Billy has told me so much about you." Emily spots the boy's first chapter on the bed behind Porter. "Did you read Billy's book?"

"I read what he gave me."

Emily turns to Billy. "What did you give him?" she asks.

"The first chapter," he answers and then says to Porter: "You finished it?"

"Yes," Porter says. "While you were outside."

"What did you think?" Emily asks.

"I would like to read more," Porter says.

"I have seventeen more pages at home," the boy says.

"Billy let me read them last night," Emily says. "They're…riveting. I cannot wait to see how he ends it. What becomes of all this…madness."

"I'm set to hang tomorrow," Porter explains. "The ending is already written."

"Oh, that's right," Emily says and then flushes when she considers Porter's inevitable death. "I'm…I'm sorry. Billy told me, but I guess I had forgotten."

A heavy silence fills the room. Emily shifts her feet. The boy places a hand on her shoulder and whispers that it is time to leave. She nods and turns for the door but pauses.

"Can I ask you something?" she says, addressing Porter. Porter lifts his brow in anticipation. "Did those men really rape your lover and her sister?"

Porter gives a tense nod.

"And then they burned down their house?" Emily asks.

Porter nods.

"Why did they burn the house?" Emily asks.

Porter swallows and sucks in a great breath.

"It makes no sense to do that," Emily says. "Some men…they just…they only know how to destroy, don't they?"

"That's enough, Emily," the boy whispers. "Let's get you out of here."

Emily ignores the boy. She keeps all her attention on Porter. "And that's why you killed them?" she says. "You destroyed the destroyers."

Porter's eyes glisten.

Emily goes to the iron bars separating herself from the prisoner. She values Porter, views him with quiet consternation. After a moment, her lips part in a pained smile.

"I don't take you for a killer," she says. "Not unless it is necessary. I believe God will forgive you for what you've done. You were just makin' right by the woman you love."

"Thank you, Emily," Porter whispers, his voice breaking.

Emily reaches a steady hand through the bars and touches Porter's rugged cheek. Porter closes his eyes and lets the compassionate gesture arrest him. Her perfumed hand reminds him of Rose.

"You will be in my prayers," Emily says, retrieving her hand. "Goodbye, Mr. Porter."

Emily turns and holds her hand out to the boy. He clasps her hand in his and escorts her to the jailhouse door. She steals one last glance at Porter as the boy pulls the door open. Emily steps outside and the boy follows, but he does not shut the door after him. Porter can hear them speaking outside.

"He is not an evil man," Emily says to the boy.

"I know he ain't."

"That poor thing," she says.

Porter sits on his bed. He takes up the boy's written pages and begins reading them again. The young lovers continue speaking, but Porter no longer bends his ear to listen.

A minute later the boy returns. "You made an impression on her," the boy says. Porter reads. The boy scratches the back of his neck, thinks. "You still got your gun on you?" the boy asks.

Porter looks up from the pages. He had forgotten about his gun. He reaches around his waist and pulls the gun from his pants. Studies it. He could kill the boy now with it. Add another name to the tally of the dead. But Porter is past that now. He walks to the edge of the cell and holds the gun out to the boy. The boy does not take it.

"Keep it," the boy says. He goes to the desk, retrieves the cell key, and returns to the cell. He inserts the key and turns. A metal latch clicks and the door springs open. The boy moves to the side so Porter can exit. Porter does not move.

"You don't need to do this," Porter says.

"Yes, I do."

"I'm at peace with dying tomorrow."

"I'm not."

Porter considers the boy. This is the first time he has shown any suspicion of courage. He picks up the boy's book chapter and hands it to him.

"When you write about Rose," Porter says, "just think of how you love Emily. It isn't the same, but it's the closest you'll come to understanding."

The boy digests Porter's advice and nods. Porter holds out his hand. The boy takes the prisoner's hand and shakes it.

"You probably have about ten hours," the boy says. "Get to the territories. I doubt they'll keep looking if you can get that far."

Porter starts for the door.

"I need you to do something for me though," the boy says, and Porter stops. "I need you to hit me. Make it look like I put up a struggle."

Porter understands. It gives Porter no pleasure to strike the boy, but a bruised face will lessen the father's rage. Porter cocks his arm and strikes the boy in his eye. The boy staggers backward and then stands straight.

"Again," he says.

Porter strikes him again.

The boy staggers and straightens. "Again," he says, and Porter hits him a third time. He lands several more punches, and he would have landed more if Porter had not stopped the requested assault.

By the time the boy's father finds him the next day, the eye has swollen shut. Blood that flowed from the boy's nose is dried and stains his face. The father rebukes the boy for letting the prisoner escape, but though he never admits it, he respects his son and spends several nights at the tavern bragging about the fight his son put up.

They hunt Porter for more than a month. Going into various towns, making inquiries, and establishing leads that go nowhere. The boy never tells his father about Quinn's visit. Instead, he tells his father he is certain Porter headed east.

"He had family and a job waiting for him once the war ended," the boy claimed. "He said as much whenever I permitted him to talk."

Of course, these claims were lies. The boy knew Porter would never venture east. Nothing for him there except war memories and a girl he no longer loved. The boy figured Porter would head west. Territories were west. So was the ocean. Porter never revealed much, but the boy recalled one occasion when he let slip he was heading west before Quinn stopped him in Oklahoma.

Porter did trek west, but the boy never learned if he made it to the ocean. He received a letter a couple months after Porter's escape. It read: "When you finish your book, send it here." A post office address in Oklahoma was scribbled at the bottom of the letter. Porter did not sign the letter.

Eventually, the authorities gave up the search. Porter was responsible for killing five men who were also known killers. People accepted that somehow, amid all the chaos, justice was served.

EPILOGUE

Today, like all days, she waits on the porch. She cannot decide if what she is waiting for will ever arrive. If it does, if *he* does, will it be a comfort or a condemnation? She does not know. In the past she tackled so much uncertainty with prayer. Those days are long gone. She is yet to decide if this abandonment is a blessing or a curse.

She holds a hand to her eyes and squints at the horizon, searching. Heat from the barren landscape outfits the distant skyline with scorching, undulating lines. On her lap rests a copy of *Frankenstein.* She purchased it months ago in an Arkansas bookstore before returning to Oklahoma. She has read it twice and is reading it again. Each time she gets something new from it—a hidden metaphor, an epiphany, symbolism that reaffirms beliefs just recently discovered.

She admonishes herself for wasting so much time with that other book when her own daughter's room is a cache of novels. She has read—devoured—almost all of them. The novels offer comfort and discomfort in equal measure. Their lessons speak truths better than the other book ever did. Each new author, each new discovery brings her immense joy and unbearable pain. How come she could not have learned to learn while her daughter still lived? How many conversations could she have had with her daughter? What discourse could all those books have inspired had Quinn cracked them open and let the contents consume her? Now, she wonders, what is there to do with so much missed opportunity?

She takes up *Frankenstein* and begins reading. That is when the drifter appears unnoticed. He walks steady and with purpose. He always has, even if this past year has taken something from his step. His hat sits low, shielding his eyes. His knapsack hangs flung over his shoulder carrying the usual contents: food, books, and his gun.

She finishes a chapter and lifts her gaze. Sees him. Refuses to turn away, to even so much as blink, for fear that he is not real. As he comes closer, she knows she is not imagining this, imagining him. She wondered what she would feel if she ever saw him again. Now she knows, and the feeling is…satisfaction. A completed task. A confirmed ally. Perhaps even a homecoming? It is a paramount effort on her part not to smile, and it is even harder not to cry.

Next to her chair is a table. She sets her book there and stands. He arrives.

"Where you headed?" she asks.

He stops. Looks at her for a moment.

"West," he says.

"How far west?"

"California."

"What's in California?

"The ocean."

"Why do you want to go to the ocean?

"I've never seen it."

"It's vast."

"So I've heard."

"See that field?" she says, pointing her chin past him.

He looks over his shoulder to the desolate field.

"It needs tilling," she says. "You help me turn it over, and tonight you can sleep in a soft bed with a full belly."

He considers the offer. "And what about tomorrow?" he asks.

"We can figure out tomorrow tomorrow."

They stare at each other. Both understanding that each is offering the same thing—a reset. But is this the life they want? Can she find solace in the person responsible for bringing so much pain to her doorstep? And could he look at her every day and not collapse under the weight of seeing traces of his dead lover in her mother's face? What do either of them owe to those who have died? To those who live? Neither knows. Maybe they are not meant to.

He massages his neck. His back hurts. So do his feet.

"What do you say?" she asks, her impatience wearing thin.

He nods, and she bites the inside of her cheek to keep from smiling.

This will be their life. Talking around things, avoiding hard truths, saying things without saying them. He does not know how long he will stay at the ranch. Neither does she, but they both know one day he will leave. When he does, he will not tell her, and she respects him more for not doing so.

When he departs, it will be west. He does not know if he will stop in Salt Lake. He has not yet decided if Rockwell and the Mormon prophet are worth his vengeance. He does not know if his killing days are behind him. All he knows is tonight he will sleep in a warm bed with a full belly, but before that happens, he will sit on Quinn's porch and talk with her about all the things he once debated with her daughter. She will understand how her daughter came to love a man her faith forbade, and he will discover the source of Rose's unflinching determination.

They will not speak of the tragedy that binds them.

Then, separately, daily, each will visit the knotted oak to tell Rose how much they love her. And even though neither believes in a life after this one, Quinn and Porter cannot help but think somehow Rose hears every word they say.

ABOUT THE AUTHOR

Michael Wojciechowski started his mid-life crisis last week. Writing helps. He believes everyone should read Kurt Vonnegut; everyone else should read *Blood Atonement*.

NOTE FROM THE AUTHOR

Word-of-mouth is crucial for any author to succeed. If you enjoyed *Blood Atonement*, please leave a review online—anywhere you are able. Even if it's just a sentence or two. It would make all the difference and would be very much appreciated.

Thanks!
Michael Wojciechowski